P9-CEN-545

Praise for *Jumped In*:

An Indie Next List Selection

A Walden Award Finalist

A YALSA Best Fiction for Young Adults

An IRA Favorite Book of the Year

A Bank Street College Best Children's Book of the Year

A Washington State Book Award Winner

An Evergreen Teen Book Award Finalist

An ABA Indies Debut Author

A TAYSHAS Reading List Selection

An NCSS-CBC Notable Social Studies Trade Book for Young People

A Great Lakes Great Books Finalist

AMERICAN
ROAD
TRIP

Patrick Flores-Scott

Christy Ottaviano Books
Henry Holt and Company · New York

Henry Holt and Company, *Publishers since 1866*
Henry Holt® is a registered trademark of Macmillan Publishing Group, LLC
175 Fifth Avenue, New York, NY 10010
fiercereads.com

Library of Congress Cataloging-in-Publication Data
Names: Flores-Scott, Patrick, author.
Title: American road trip / Patrick Flores-Scott.
Description: First edition. | New York : Christy Ottaviano Books,
Henry Holt and Company, 2018. | Summary: Brothers Teodoro and
Manny Avila take a road trip to address Manny's PTSD following
his tour in Iraq, and to help T change his life and win the heart
of Wendy Martinez. Includes information and resources about PTSD.
Identifiers: LCCN 2018004255 | ISBN 9781627797412 (hardcover)
Subjects: | CYAC: Coming of age—Fiction. | Conduct of life—Fiction. |
Post-traumatic stress disorder—Fiction. | Brothers—Fiction. | Automobile travel—
Fiction. | Mexican Americans—Fiction.
Classification: LCC PZ7.F33435 Ame 2018 | DDC [Fic]—dc23
LC record available at https://lccn.loc.gov/2018004255

Our books may be purchased in bulk for promotional, educational, or business
use. Please contact your local bookseller or the Macmillan Corporate and
Premium Sales Department at (800) 221-7945 ext. 5442 or by e-mail at
MacmillanSpecialMarkets@macmillan.com.

First edition, 2018 / Designed by Katie Klimowicz
Printed in the United States of America
1 3 5 7 9 10 8 6 4 2

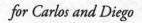

for Carlos and Diego

AMERICAN
ROAD
TRIP

THURSDAY, SEPTEMBER 4, 2008

Daylight creeps into the game cave.

I turn to Caleb. "We played all night, man. We played all night."

Caleb Ta'amu does not respond. His wide body is sucked into the sofa, long hair frizzing wild, eyes bugging on a flat screen, zombied out on too much Halo.

I toss my headset. Dig through fast-food wrappers on the coffee table. Grab my phone and shove it in Caleb's face.

He slaps my hand, pissed I'm messing with his gamer trance. "What the hell, T?"

"Check the time!"

Caleb checks it. He whips off his headset. "Do not tell me it's tomorrow."

"It's tomorrow, Caleb."

He drops his controller. Hops to his feet. "You gotta get outta here."

We sneak upstairs. Caleb opens the door. He rubs his eyes in the gray morning light. "Second day, junior year. We're off to a stellar start."

"Yeah," I say. "We're killing it."

"You gonna try and make first period?"

"I guess. You?"

"I guess. If my dad doesn't strangle me first. You better go, T."

I hike the sidewalk-less, residential streets of SeaTac, Washington. Drizzle spraying my face. Water sloshing through my shoes. A mile of dark, evergreen-tree-lined streets. Shabby houses, beige apartments, barred windows, rusted cars on blocks . . .

I arrive at my destination.

But I can't go inside.

I stand, stuck in this spot on this potholed road, soaking up rain to the rumble soundtrack of Sea-Tac Airport jumbo jets.

They come. They go. Move in and out.

I cannot move.

And I can't stop staring at the dented-up front door of a tiny, falling-down rental house—*our* tiny, falling-down rental house.

And I can't stop thinking how we got here.

How two summers ago, we rode the happy housing bubble right into a bright blue, boxy, four-bathroom house down in Des Moines. My mom and dad's marriage needed a spark. My dad hoped a big new house would do the trick.

One year later the housing bubble popped.

The whole economy popped.

Orders for Boeing planes slowed way down and Fauntleroy Fabrication in Seattle—where my dad machined airplane parts and my mom was a warehouse clerk—went belly-up.

Papi's fat union check was gone.

Mami traded her living-wage job for part-time work at Walmart.

And we went from being a family that didn't worry much about money, to one that did.

I'll never forget the night last spring. My dad drove me and my sister, Xochitl, ten minutes from Des Moines to SeaTac. And he parked right here in front of this rental. Right where I'm standing. He told us he'd done the math and decided it would be better to hang on to some savings and walk away from the new house now, than be stuck owing way more than it's worth. He'd rather tank his credit for years than put us in a deeper financial hole. He said we'd swallow our pride and move on.

Then he pointed at the dented-up metal door. And said we'd be living here for a while.

The drizzle turns to showers. I take a step toward that door.

But I can't do it.

I can't open up.

Cuz I can't stop thinking about my big brother, Manny.

And I can't stop thinking about us back when we were still living in our old house—the solid little house we all grew up in—the one where we still lived when Manny left us for Iraq. For years, every time I saw our front door, I'd have this hope he'd be inside when I opened up. My brother would be sitting there, smiling at me like he never went to war. He'd be ready to toss a baseball. Take me for a ride in his Mustang. Fishing at the Des Moines pier. Slurpies. Double-scoop cones. French fries and homework help.

I'd see that old door, and I'd feel that stupid hope.

But Manny's tours of duty kept getting extended.

So I gave up hoping for Manny.

And I settled for hoping I'd walk in and catch my parents dancing or cooking together again, teasing each other like they

5

used to. Something would click and they'd remember how good they were before my brother shocked us with his big announcement.

Spring of his senior year, Manny sits us down and tells us he's off to basic training right after graduation. He says he's been planning this ever since those towers fell a year and a half before.

My mom flips. She tells him he can't go because he's headed to college. She tells him he can't kill people for this lie of a war. That's what Mami tells him.

My dad?

He gives Manny a back-pounding hug. Tells him he's proud and gives him his blessing.

And that's the start of my parents fighting their quiet war at home.

The front doors have changed since then.

But Mami and Papi haven't changed.

Screw it. I'm soaked to the bone and freezing cold. I walk up. Turn the knob. And push in that messed-up door.

My big sister is sitting at the table. Xochitl is postshow buzzed. Scribbling in her journal. Badass in her purple-striped hair and tattooed arms. Smelling like cigarettes and beer.

She shakes her head at me back and forth, dramatic, fake-parental, wagging her finger, then pointing at the spot on her wrist where a watch would go.

I shrug my shoulders. Make a pleading face, playing like I'm in big trouble.

She chokes back a laugh.

I can't help but laugh out loud.

She shushes me, leaves the room, and returns with a towel. Throws it at me.

I sit at the table. She sits across.

It's been so long since the two of us hung out.

And so long since we played Radio Xochitl. I raise my pointer finger in the air.

My sister smirks and shakes her head no.

I bob my head. *Oh, yes.*

She looks to our parents' room. Mouths the words, *It's too late.*

I know she can't resist showing off. So I press the invisible power button and Xochitl starts singing.

She's Aretha Franklin. Powerful, even with the volume on low.

> *They say that it's a man's world.*

She keeps her eyes on me.

> *But you can't prove that by me—*

I mime spinning the dial. Xochitl babbles gibberish as stations fly by.

I stop and she belts out norteño—Los Tigres del Norte.

> *Somos más americanos que toditos los—*

I turn the dial. Xochitl busts it.

> *My method on the microphone is bangin'*

> *Wu-Tang slang'll leave your headpiece hang—*

I spin again and again and she doesn't miss a beat. Dixie Chicks, Café Tacuba, Jill Scott—then serious and intense with some Ani DiFranco . . .

What kind of paradise am I looking for?

I've got everything I want and still I want more

Even in a whisper, Xochitl can kill you with a song.
I poke that power button in the air.
Radio Xochitl fades to silence. She's smiling, loving this.
I'm smiling. Loving my crazy sister.
The doors have changed.
Thank God Xochitl hasn't.

THURSDAY,
SEPTEMBER 4, 2008

Xochitl wasn't quiet enough. My mom woke up and freaked about my all-nighter with Caleb. So today I head straight back to the rental after school.

Xochitl's here, too. She's never home for dinner. I'm guessing she either got fired from selling zit cream at the mall or she quit another band.

Mami doesn't ask questions. We're all home, so she gets to work whipping up her one comfort food specialty: green chile cheeseburgers.

Mami's uncle, our Tío Ed, got married to a New Mexican and moved down there a long time ago. He started farming New Mexican green chile, and for years he's sent us a box every fall. Mami tried out the recipes they make down there, like green chile enchiladas and green chile stew. Those were tasty as hell. But the Avila family go-to became the green chile cheeseburger.

These peppers are not jalapeños. Not poblanos. I got nothing against 'em. But New Mexican green chile was created by the Almighty Gods of Flavor for the purpose of combining heat with cream or cheese and creating ecstasy in your mouth. So Mami only pulls them out of the freezer for special occasions.

I don't think this qualifies as a special occasion. But I'm not gonna argue.

It's a quiet dinner. Nothing but the sounds of faces being stuffed till Xochitl slaps a drum roll on the table. She splashes an imaginary cymbal and says, "I bring you this announcement from Fallujah, Iraq: Manny's coming home! They promised. He's home for good in February."

"How do you know?" Mami says.

"We e-mail. It's all set up. He'll call you with the details."

Mami looks at Xochitl like she feels sorry for her for being hopeful.

We've been burned so many times. I can't stand Xochitl even talking about it.

My dad says, "Vamos a ver, mija. We'll see."

Xochitl scoots her chair back. "We can't wait, Papi." She hops to her feet. "We have to get our act together now. *For Manny.*"

Barely twenty years old, and she's taking charge. "We have to make this house feel like a home," she says. "We'll paint. Put up prints. Get our old furniture in here."

"Xochitl, stop," I say.

"I'm not stopping. And I'm reinstituting game night. Everyone plays." She points at our parents. "And you two are going out on mandatory dates."

"*Xochitl,*" Mami says.

"And counseling?"

"Déjalo, mija," Papi says.

"At least talk to Father Michael?"

What is Xochitl talking about? We haven't been to mass in forever.

Then she points at me. "What's Manny gonna think when he sees you, you big lazy clown? There's a world out there, T. Find a passion. Set a goal. And go for it, bro!"

I make a beeline for my room, pissed at my sister for turning on me. Pissed at her for jacking up the volume on our quiet dysfunction.

Before I can slam my door, she says, "He's coming home, guys. Let's see some energy. Let's see some smiles. Oh, and I quit the Art Institute."

"No, Xochitl, no." Mami drops forehead onto palm and shakes her head. "You can't do that."

"I already did."

Xochitl tells them it's great she's quitting because it's too expensive. Plus she can work full-time during the day and help with rent and bills till Papi finds union work again.

"This way I'll be home afternoons before rehearsals to help out," she says.

"We're okay," Papi says. "No te preocupes tanto, mija."

Xochitl looks at the bare walls of the rental. Looks at our parents. Shakes her head. "We have to get right. And we need to do it before Manny comes home."

I wanna tell Xochitl that's impossible. Cuz Manny being here—being with us—is the only thing that can get us right.

WEDNESDAY, SEPTEMBER 10, 2008

Breaks squeal. Rubber doors slap open. I hop a bus headed for Seattle. I do not care where.

It's been a whole week of my sister telling us stuff we already know about how bad we suck. A whole week of her taking charge in a way our parents should be taking charge.

Plus, she bought Risk. And tonight she will open that box. My mom will grumble as Xochitl explains the rules. Papi will ask a ton of questions. Xochitl will try *very* hard to explain. Mami will roll eyes at both of them. Then Xochitl will bawl them out like she's the parent.

If I'm there, I'll get pissed and walk out and my sister will throw down another lecture about my lame life. And the whole night will be a confirmation that Manny's still gone, my parents are a lost cause, and Xochitl has flipped and she's no longer my sister.

I flash the driver my pass. He nods. The breaks exhale. The engine rumbles and jerks us into traffic.

I would be over at Caleb's, but his dad got on his case after our all-nighter. Kennedy Ta'amu told Caleb it was time to get a life. *Play a sport. Volunteer at church. Get a job.* So now he's working a couple nights as a dishwasher at Vince's Pizza.

The bus winds its way north. Up Pac Highway. Past Sea-Tac Airport. Onto 405, then I-5. Into Seattle. The U District. The University of Washington campus.

I hop off at the Husky Union Building—*the HUB*—a brick, ivy-covered, dry place to kill some time.

I pull open the old wooden doors, walk past a bike shop, past a little branch of University Book Store, into a big open corridor. College kids lounge at tables and couches. They flirt. Surf the web. Read important novels. Argue about important things.

I head over to a newsstand to grab a Coke. I pay the lady and turn to go. No big deal.

But I almost bump into the girl behind me cuz she's on one knee tying her laces. She's got this shiny, dark brown hair hanging down so I can't see her face, but I got a feeling she might be cute and I want to find out.

So I fake sneeze.

The girl springs to her feet. "Do everyone a favor and cover that stuff up."

All I've got are *uh*s and *um*s because she is, in fact, kind of cute. Cute cheeks. Cute scowl as she stands there with cute brown eyes staring at me through long lashes and black dork glasses.

"Sorry about that," I say as I walk away fast.

"You wait, mister." She grabs me by the arm and examines my face.

And I'm like, "What?"

And she's like, "Your momma taught you better than that."

13

"Excuse me? My *momma*?"

"Yeah. She taught you better."

"Leave my momma outta this cuz you don't know my momma."

Then she slips a bit of a wicked smile. "I think maybe I know your mamá."

I can't help but slip some of my smile and say, "How you think you know my mamá?"

And she says—her smile growing bigger—"Summers in Florence, Oregon. My great-uncle Frank's place."

I'm frozen stupid as time and space mess with my head.

This is *Wendy Martinez*, Frank O'Brien's grandniece.

But the Wendy Martinez from way-back summers was not cute. She was a bossy little busybody who chased me around and drove me nuts and—I'll admit it—I was a tiny bit scared of the little Wendy.

"You had better manners back then," she says. She busts out a full-on smile. "Teodoro Avila! Dude! Hug it out!"

We go in for the hug. Wrap arms like people do and . . .

Oh. My God.

This hug. It's like firm? But soft and warm.

I turn to jelly in Wendy's arms as she squeezes tighter and my mind—everything fades and this is all there is. Me wrapped around Wendy. Wendy wrapped around me.

Then both of us—*at the same exact time*—inhale deep and fast and look big eyes right into each other.

Holy.

Crap.

That breath, those eyes—it's all way too much. So we let go and step back.

"My mom's at the bookstore," she says. "You have a second to talk?"

"I have lots of seconds," I say. But I'm thinking, *I got the rest of my life, Wendy Martinez.*

We find a bright spot in the atrium. We sit across a table from each other. Smile some nervous smiles. Then Wendy asks me about the family.

I tell her to go first.

Wendy says she and her mom still live a couple hours away in Vancouver, across the river from Portland. She's here at the University of Washington looking into a scholarship for women in science. She says this is the place to study health care. She's thinking about med school already. Wendy's got all the data and all her stuff one hundred percent together.

Before I know it, she asks me what I'm doing here.

I start telling Wendy about staying away from game night, but that feels way too complicated. So I sneeze again—I cover up this time—and I tell her that I am also here checking out the University of Washington, only I call it U-Dub so she knows I know people call it that.

And I say it with a straight face. As if I believed they would let me into the University of Washington. For actual college.

That's the first of my lies as I try to convince beautiful and brilliant Wendy Martinez that my parents are doing great. Xochitl's got a great music career going and she's doing awesome in art school. And I'm carefully considering my many college options before making my decision.

The thing about Wendy—besides her smile, her hair, her not-skinny curves, and those smart-girl glasses—is she is so full of caring. Like when the subject of Manny comes up and I tell her how bad I miss him. How scared I am he might never come back. Wendy looks me in the eyes as I talk. Touches my hand to make a point. Asks me if I'm okay—like *really okay*.

And when a stupid tear slips when I say I miss him, she acts like it's nothing. She just reaches over and wipes it away with a finger midsentence and says she can't imagine how stressful the waiting must be. How difficult it must be on all of us that Manny keeps getting redeployed. How much she hopes he makes it back.

When people try to make us feel better about Manny, they say, *Everything's going to be okay. God has a plan. Everything happens for a reason.*

Wendy doesn't say any of that BS. She gets that it's way more complicated. And that makes me like her even more.

In a minute, Wendy's mom walks our way. Rebecca O'Brien acts thrilled to see me. She asks how the family is and I keep my lies straight as Wendy takes off running. We watch her go and I'm about to ask, but Rebecca sighs and says, "You never know with that girl."

Rebecca tells me Uncle Frank misses us terribly. She says it'd be great if we all spent a week in Florence, like old times. I tell her I'll let Mami and Papi know.

Pretty soon, Wendy's standing there again, one hand hidden behind her back.

Rebecca edges away and it's clear they have to go.

I don't want this moment to end, so I say, "Wendy, being here, soaking this place in, I think this old U-Dub might be tops on my list."

"That's awesome," she says. "It'd be great if we both went here."

Then I totally lose it and I tell Wendy if she comes here, I'm coming here.

She smiles her wicked smile and says, "That sounds like a pact, Teodoro Avila."

"Wendy Martinez," I say, "it *sounds* like a pact because it *is* a pact." Then I fake spit on my hand and hold it out for a shake.

She pulls her hand from behind her back and she's holding a cupcake on a napkin.

"For me?" I say.

"Uh-huh," she says, smiling bigger—even though it's clear she's trying not to because of her mom.

Then she comes at me for one more hug.

One more *just us in the world* hug.

Holy.

One more same-time breath.

Crap.

"Check the napkin," she whispers. Then she looks at me like she's trying to memorize my eyes.

"*Wendy.*" Rebecca points at her watch. "Good to see you, Teodoro."

Wendy smiles at me and pulls away. She walks into the crowd streaming out the HUB doors and just before I lose track of her, she turns and jumps in the air, making a wacky face, waving both arms up high.

I hop and wave, hop and wave till she's gone.

Then I look down at the cupcake in my hand. White frosting. Still warm. I peel the wrapper and take a bite. *Red velvet.*

I devour the whole thing right there. And stuff the wrapper—red crumbs and all—and the napkin with Wendy's digits, into my front pocket.

I pull out my phone. Check the date. Grab a pen off a table. I say the numbers out loud as I write them on the palm of my hand. . . . *9/10/08.*

Then I close my eyes and make a promise. *This is the day everything changes.*

It's just past nine when I finally make it to Caleb's place. He's got his headset on, butt planted in sofa, hair poofing, smelling like garlic and dishwasher soap. He's got soda and Vince's Pizza sitting on the game cave coffee table and he's twitching his controller. Caleb Ta'amu is Halo ready. "I got two hours, man. My dad's cool with it. Let's do this."

I tell him we have to talk first.

"You breaking up?" he says. "You can't do that, T. We've built a virtual life together."

"Shut up, Caleb. And listen." I plop into the sofa and tell him the whole story. I tell him how amazing Wendy is. How beautiful she is. I tell him how she gets Manny being away like no one else does—besides him, of course. And I tell him about the cupcake.

"Red velvet," Caleb says. *"Red velvet."*

"You think it means anything?"

"It means there's one girl in this world who actually likes you. *You,* Teodoro Avila." Caleb laughs and slaps me on the back.

I do not laugh. Instead, I tell him about my lies.

And I tell him about *the pact*.

Caleb calls me an idiot and says, "This may come as a mind-blowing surprise to you, T, but women have this thing about a thing called *honesty*. So if you want a shot with Wendy, you got to make it right."

"I can't tell her the truth yet," I say. "But what I *could* do is I could . . . uh . . ."

"Spit it out, T."

"It's too stupid."

"I bet it's not your stupidest."

"What I could do is . . . I could go for it, Caleb. You know? Like I could start doing the stuff people do to get into college. And maybe . . ."

I immediately regret it because Caleb is gonna crush me. He knows I got all-but-failing grades and the idea of me doing anything but community college is stupid.

But he doesn't say anything. He just locks eyes on the flat screen and starts twitching his controller, selecting his player. But just as he's about to start shooting, he pauses the game. And he stares at the floor.

"Caleb?"

No response.

"What's going on, Caleb?"

He tosses his controller. Grabs the remote. Hits the power button. He turns to me real serious. "You go for it, T."

"Yeah?"

"Hell yeah!"

"Are you messing with me, Caleb?"

"No way. You go for it. You go!"

Then Caleb looks around the room. The sofa. The junk food. And he calls himself a loser. He says he's been a waste of space in this world. He tells me I been keeping him down. And he apologizes for keeping me down. Then he whips off his headset and says, "I'm gonna do it, too."

"For real, Caleb?"

He stands, steps over the coffee table, and walks to the Xbox. He bends down and grabs the power cord. Follows it to the wall. He turns and holds up a shaking hand for me to see. "I can't believe I'm doing this."

He reaches for the plug.

"Caleb, you don't have to—"

He yanks it hard.

"Damn, Caleb! I'm not *that* ready."

He unscrews the cable. Wraps the cords. "This box owns us. I don't wanna be owned."

I remind him of our Halo friends all over the world. Splazer3000 in Berlin. Plasma17 in Buenos Aires. DUspartan in Melbourne. "We've been through a lot of battles with those guys. Let's log on and blast some Covenant ass up for old times' sake. And then, maybe—"

Caleb grunts and shakes his head. "Are you really into her, T?" He holds up the box. "Cuz a girl like Wendy wants way more than *this*. And right now this is all you got."

"It's not that easy, Caleb."

"Doesn't mean we can't try."

I look at the box sitting in his hands. Then I look my best friend in the eyes. "Caleb Ta'amu, I'm gonna need your help."

"Teodoro Avila, I'm your brother from another mother. You just say *the word* and this is for real."

I close my eyes. Picture Wendy. See her brown eyes again. That smile. I fight to feel her hug again. Take in a deep breath. And I say it. "The word."

Caleb says "The word" right back and we do the ridiculous handshake we made up when we were ten.

I stand facing that dented door, praying I don't get trapped in the messy aftermath of game night.

I turn the knob. Take a step inside.

"Hey, T," Xochitl says. She's sitting at the table. *Smiling.*

With my parents.

Who are also smiling.

And giggling.

At each other. Like, *with* each other.

I walk slowly into the room. Because something is very wrong. And I'm concerned it's drugs. "Hello, family," I say. "May I ask what is up?"

My mom giggles more and says, "How's Caleb?"

"Fine," I say. "Are you people all right?"

"I'm not all right," she says. "I could have used your help against these brutes."

My dad walks around the table and gives her a hug. "Ay, lo siento, Rosi. I'll make it up to you later." He plants a fat kiss on her cheek.

Xochitl tells them they're gross and would they please get a room.

I'm stuck there, wondering who stole my parents and replaced them with these sick, happy clones.

Mami hugs me and wishes me good night.

Papi musses my hair—the man is *not* a musser.

I watch them walk to their room. *Together.* "Xoch," I say. "What did you slip into Mami and Papi's Diet Cokes?"

"It's the magic of game night," she says. "And it wasn't Coke. It was red wine."

"So I'm thinking there should be a lot more booze up in here?"

Xochitl smiles big. "It's Manny," she says. "He called and told them he has his ticket. And tonight, Mami and Papi were kind of like when we were kids."

Wow. "Did they play 'Con los años que me quedan'? Did they do their dance?"

"One small step at a time, T."

"It didn't look that small."

Xochitl stares up at the ceiling. Stares at the beige walls. "Help me paint."

I tell her I don't think these walls are worth it.

"We're worth it. Manny's worth it. Let's get some color in here."

"All right. I'll help you paint this dump. But you gotta promise, no more lectures."

"Deal." She shakes my hand on it. "I'll get everything ready. It's gonna look great, T."

"Worth a shot," I say.

"Cuz Manny's coming home."

"Even if it's just another false alarm."

"It's not. He's coming home."

I go to my room. Pull out my phone. And shoot off a text.

WED SEP 10 9:55 P.M.

T: Make it home ok?

Wendy: Hey you!

Wendy: Yeah, thanks. We got home

fine.

T: Great cupcake

Wendy: Oh good! Someday you can try

one of mine.

T: I'd like that

Wendy: What's your favorite

flavor?

There's a bunch more. But that's the start of it.

THURSDAY, SEPTEMBER 11, 2008

We wait outside Ms. Bradley's office door before school. When she finally walks our way, my heart is thumping. Caleb looks sick to his stomach.

"Good morning," Ms. Bradley says. She unlocks her counseling office door. Flips the light. Sits and tells us to do the same. She pumps antibacterial lotion and rubs it in good. "What's up, gentlemen?"

I turn to Caleb because he's better at talking. He juts his chin at me. *You do it.*

"Ms. Bradley," I say. "I need, uh—*we* need—to know, um, what we would hafta do"—I swallow the lump in my throat—"to get into the University of Washington."

She tilts her head. "The Seattle campus?" Her fingernails *tap-tap* her desk. "The main, biggest campus?"

"Yes, ma'am. The big one."

Ms. Bradley turns to her computer. She prints our grades and reaches for a binder with the University of Washington admissions requirements. She studies them for a minute. Then she takes a deep breath to tell us the bad news.

I stand up to leave. "You don't have to, Ms. Bradley."

"You sit," she says.

"Yes, ma'am."

"Your grades are not college material." She leans in. Studies us long and hard. "But you might be."

Caleb and I shoot looks at each other. "We might?"

"I don't know. Admissions folks are all about *What have you done for me lately?* Grades. Test scores. Activities. Overcoming adversity. You boys have spent two years creating a big mountain of adversity. So at least you've got that going for you."

Then she tells us about AVID, this program for underachievers with potential. Kids whose parents didn't get a degree. She can stick 'em in college track, honors, and AP, along with an AVID support class. They do a tutorial in there where seniors and college kids come in and help students on new concepts.

"Your grades don't meet the requirements for the program," Ms. Bradley says. "But I have some discretion. . . . If I believe in a student, I can make it happen." She looks us in the eyes. "I don't know, gentlemen. Shoud I believe in you?"

That's when Caleb starts talking fast. He says his parents are so smart but they never had the opportunity to go to college. He talks about how hard his sisters work in school and he knows he can do better. He swears to Ms. Bradley that he's gonna work his butt off and make her proud. He's gonna make his parents, his church, his aunties and uncles and cousins—the entire Polynesian community—all proud. "You got my word, Ms. B."

Ms. Bradley turns to me.

I fake sneeze.

Because I can't make any promises.

She grabs me a Kleenex.

I wipe and blow, thinking it's one thing to realize you have to change yourself. And it's a whole other thing to fight through that overwhelming mountain of adversity to make change happen.

I plant my feet hard on the ground. I lean forward to stand and walk outta that office.

But before I can . . . I feel it in the palm of my hand.

And I sneak a peek.

Yesterday's date in faded ink. I feel the pen pressing sharp into my skin back at the HUB. I see Wendy waving good-bye. I see her eyes. Feel her hand on my hand. Her finger wiping away that tear. Her body hugging my body. And in all my guts, in every part of me, I feel a massive, magnetic tug of *want*.

I know I can't say, *I'm doing this for Wendy*, so I say stuff about wanting to be the first in my family. Stuff about my mom starting college a couple times, but each time stepping away for family reasons. I tell Ms. Bradley that us kids making it became her big dream.

And because Manny was a big star at Puget High and everyone loved him—I say, "My brother, Manuel, is coming home. I want to show him I can do this." Even though I say that because I know it'll sound good—when I hear myself talk about my brother, the words hit so deep it hurts and I gotta stop another tear from coming.

Ms. Bradley prints out two AVID student contracts and says

26

all we have to do is sign on the dotted line. But before she hands over the pen, we need to look her in the eye and promise we will not waste this opportunity. Or make her look like a fool.

Caleb looks her in the eye and says the words.

Ms. Bradley hands him the pen and he signs.

She turns to me. "Mr. Avila?"

"I will not let you down, Ms. Bradley."

I take the pen. And I sign.

FRIDAY,
SEPTEMBER 19, 2008

I hop off the Metro bus and into the sunshine after a week of sitting in those classes. One whole week with a sharpened pencil and a sharpened backup pencil and a shiny new notebook with crisp dividers. One week of scholarly freaking posture and eyes on the speaker and trying so hard to make this all look perfectly normal.

Finally, the weekend is here and Ma Nature is giving us one last shot of summer.

For the old T, this would have been time to cut loose.

But instead of heading to Caleb's, I'm marching down the cracked streets of SeaTac sporting a bulbous one-ton backpack. I got the periodic table whirling in my mind and I can't drop the idea that the formula for calcium phosphate is C-3PO, when it's really Ca3-PO-something. And I'm kicking myself for the time I've lost trying to find the compound whose formula is closest to R2-D2.

I have to unlock the mysteries of linear equations for Algebra Two. They're in their second book in AP English. *Dante's Inferno*.

Eight chapters to read by Sunday night. Six chapters from the AP US History textbook, *Out of Many*, and an essay about a colonial rebellion called "Persons of Mean and Vile Condition."

And I have to be prepared to talk pros and cons of sentencing convicted kids as adults for Socratic Seminar in Ms. Hays's AVID class. *Everyone talks. That's the rule.* And I have to keep my three-ring-binder in order. That thing is checked daily by Ms. Hays until I prove I'm a wizard of organization.

Ms. Bradley said it'd be like this. Like you're trying to hop on a merry-go-round spinning a thousand miles per hour. You have to keep reaching for it, jumping up for it, keep getting smacked down. Eventually the spinning will slow and you can just step up for the ride.

Right now, I'm motion sick with all the spinning, but I'm choosing to trust Ms. Bradley.

I get to the house and onto the porch. But before I open the door, I lift the lid on the mailbox and reach in. There's a utility bill, some ads, and an envelope from Puget High School.

I sit on the step and open up the parent version of the AVID contract. All this stuff Mami and Papi are supposed to do to support me. All the promises they're supposed to make.

I turn to the second page. Pull a pen from my pack. Find the dotted lines. I've been practicing for this moment. I sign, *Daniel Avila*—long, curvy, and clear. Then *Rosario Avila*—big *R* and a big *A*, the rest a fast mess.

I'm not ready for any Avilas to know. College has always been the most important thing for my mom. She had high hopes for Manny. But he chose to join the army. Xochitl is the smartest of us all, but she thinks college will slow her down. My brother and sister disappointed Mami because they had real potential. I have never really shown any of that, so I don't want to get her hopes up and end up being another disappointment.

But maybe the real reason I'm hiding all this is cuz when I blow it, it'll be easier to quit if no one knows I tried.

I stuff the contract in my pack.

And before I head inside, I shoot off a text. Wendy answers right away.

FRI SEP 19 3:37 P.M.

T:	What's ur favorite class?
Wendy:	AP Physics. But anything math or science.
Wendy:	And I kind of love my history teacher. Your fave?
T:	DK . . . year is still young
Wendy:	Oh, and band. I play tuba.
T:	Lol you crack me up
Wendy:	I play the tuba, Teodoro.
T:	Wow that's
Wendy:	Cool? Awesome?
T:	Cool and awesome and kinda
Wendy:	?

T: Cute

Wendy: The tuba?

T: U

T: Playing the tuba

Wendy: Aww. You are sweet. I have to

run.

T: Me too gotta hit those

books

WEDNESDAY, OCTOBER 1, 2008

I collapse in my bus seat, *pissed*. I zip open my pack and yank out my chemistry notebook.

Amu.

It's not a hard concept. An *atomic mass unit* is one and a half times the mass of a carbon atom that contains six protons and six neutrons. No big deal. But the reason I didn't know that when Mr. Clegg asked is I can't possibly study everything every night. So I pick and choose and hope the things I don't study get covered during tutorial in AVID class. Two weeks in and I'm still trying to catch up. So studying is like putting out brush fires or playing Whac-A-Mole.

Last night I whacked the wrong mole. So today, when Clegg asks me the question, I tell him *I don't know*. Yeah, it hurts my pride a bit. I'll admit that. But it doesn't kill me.

What kills me is Clegg's *I told you so* headshake as he ticks a mark in his grade book.

And those kids. The ones who rolled their eyes when they saw me walking into their exclusive, smart-kid classes on my first day. I know what they're thinking. And I can't let it go.

I try, but I can't.

The bus rolls past shabby Pac Highway used-car lots and junkyards and a voice from deep inside me says, *Don't let it go, T. Do. Not. Let. It. Go. Channel it. Focus your anger and show those snobs what you can do.*

There's a chemistry quiz in two days. I'm studying with Caleb for it. I'm studying till I know the material backward, forward, and upside down.

The bus stops. I hop off and there's a buzz in my pocket.

WED OCT 01 3:13 P.M.

Wendy: How's school going?

T: Chuggin away

Wendy: What are you reading?

T: Dante's inferno

Wendy: I've never read it.

Wendy: But I've heard it's hell.

T: Wah wah nice try but

please leave the comedy to . . .

T: The divine

T: See what I did there?

Wendy: Wah, wah, right back

atcha.

Wendy: What else?

T: Chem quiz Friday

Wendy: Gonna ace it?

T: U-Dub, Wendy. U-Dub

FRIDAY,
OCTOBER 3, 2008

Mr. Clegg's quiz sits before me.

I travel toward that place in my brain where I got polyatomic ion formulas, binary compounds, metals, and nonmetals categorized and formulas memorized.

I know this stuff.

Those answers are in my head.

Someplace in my head.

I close my eyes. Breathe in. Breathe out. Searching my brain.

But all I can find in there is a pack of arms-crossed, eyes-rolling kids standing in the way of those answers.

And one of the kids . . . he looks just like me. He's got his gamer headset on, controller in hand. He's jumping up and down, shaking his head, wagging a finger, growing angry till tears and spit fly as he shouts, *Impostor! Fraud! Clown!*

The bell rings. I smack my test onto Clegg's desk.

And I run.

*   *   *

Caleb gives me a ride in his beat-up Civic.

I tell him about the quiz. I tell him I can't do this anymore. Because I'm too dumb. "Sorry, Caleb," I say. "I'm out."

Caleb pounds the steering wheel. Says my attitude sucks and my thinkin' is stinkin'.

I tell Caleb I do not care.

He explains our new plan for success. "We will study together. My place. Every weekday afternoon. I'll help you in math and science. You'll help me in history and English."

"I won't."

"*U-Dub, T. Wendy. Your future.* You can do this."

"I can't."

"I believe in you, Teodoro Avila, and that better mean something."

"It doesn't."

"Then I'm sorry I have to do this." Caleb looks at me sad, like what's coming is gonna hurt him more than it's gonna hurt me. . . .

AVID stands for Advancement Via Individual Determination. I have lost the *D*. I no longer have that. But it turns out I do have a best friend who FREEEEAKING thigh-punches like a damn cannonball.

Caleb pulls the car into his driveway and yanks the brake. "You with me?"

I'm bent over trying to breathe through the pain. "Yeah, Caleb." I grab my pack and reach for the door.

Caleb stops me. "That sucked, T. First and last time I punch you."

"Forget it, Caleb."

"Huh-uh. If you wanna give up and I can't talk you out of it with words . . ."

"What?"

"You can quit. It's all right. I won't judge."

"Damn, Caleb. Let's just study."

SATURDAY, OCTOBER 11, 2008

Xochitl shakes me awake bright and early on a Saturday. Paint day.

As rough as school has been, life in the rental is a lot better. My parents are actually talking to each other. Xochitl's around more, and that's okay because she dropped her bossy act. She's her old self even though she's working hard to get us ready for Manny.

Today that means spreading color on walls.

And that means I can take my mind off school for a while.

"Don't tell Mami and Papi," Xochitl says. "Let's just get to work and see what they say."

We cover our crappy furniture with plastic. Tape up stuff we don't want to paint. And we crack open a can of sea-foam blue.

When Mami and Papi walk in, their eyes get big but they barely say a word. They just pick up brushes and get to it.

In the afternoon, Xochitl and I take off in a borrowed truck. I fake hitting the radio power button and she busts out a spot-on Jonas Brothers. I know it's a joke, but I don't turn the dial, and

Xochitl keeps singing bubblegum love songs like she means it. I can't stop laughing. And singing right along with her.

Xochitl rolls the window down. Lights up a cigarette.

"You have to quit that," I say. "It's gonna kill your voice, Xoch . . . then kill you."

"It's not a black-and-white deal, T. There's a continuum," she says.

It turns out, on one end of the continuum there's *Dangerous levels of smoke*. And on the other end there's *No smoke*. And somewhere in the middle is *Just enough smoke to get your voice rich and cracky but not enough to do serious damage to your health*.

"I keep it in that sweet spot," she says, "and not one cigarette more."

"You know how dumb that sounds, right?"

She reaches over and pretends to turn up the radio. And she sings way dramatic in Alejandra Guzmán's smoky, cracky, power-ballad voice.

Tengo un pobre corazón

Que a veces se rompió

You can feel all the pain of a breaking heart. My sister's Alejandra is almost worth smoking for.

I reach over and turn down Radio Xochitl, cuz I gotta ask. "Why'd you nag Mami and Papi so hard? Why'd you lecture me like that?"

She stares at the road for a bit. "That night I told you Manny was coming home, I had just read his e-mail."

She makes me promise I won't say anything to Mami and Papi.

"Manny's worried about coming home," she says. "He's worried his head isn't right. He doesn't want them to know. He doesn't want you to know." Xochitl stops at a light. She drags on her cigarette and lets the idea sink in.

The light turns green. She blows smoke out the window. "I was a little messed up about it. That's why I came at you guys. Sorry."

"No worries, Xoch."

"I just figure if we're doing better—if we're more like we used to be—that'll make it easier for Manny."

The part I get stuck on is why it was okay for him to tell Xochitl but not me. I ask her.

"You know how Manny always was with you," she says.

"What do you mean? He was Manny."

"T, Mami and Papi were good before. Really good. And Manny was a great big brother. But you have this fantasy that everything was perfect. And it's because Manny spoiled you. You were his little brother, and he only wanted you to see the best of him . . . the best of us."

I watch the road go by. Office parks. Trees. Gas stations. And I think about my brother. "He might not have been perfect," I say, "but he's the most solid person I know. And when he finally gets here, he's gonna be good. And being home has to be way better than war."

"That's true," Xochitl says.

"He's going to be the same old Manny."

"I think so, too," she says. "But we should be prepared."

"He's gonna be great, Xoch."

We grab stuff from our storage up north on Pac Highway. Our

old table and chairs. The painting of the Last Supper that used to hang in our dining room. A box of family pictures.

We drive to a house in Normandy Park for a Craigslist deal. Xochitl hands over the cash and we carry out a recliner that looks like Papi's chair from way back.

We haul the load into the rental. Papi helps get the table through the door. We all know it's too big for the space, but that doesn't stop us.

Mami goes through a box of old pictures. She goes out for a while and comes back with some Dollar Store frames. Every now and then, she holds up a little-kid photo of one of us and we all say *awww* and laugh. She tacks up this black-and-white family portrait of us dressed up in cowboy stuff. It's from Disneyland. We stopped there on a trip down the coast when I was a toddler. In the photo everyone is looking old-school serious, but I've got this huge Kool-Aid smile beaming out from under my cowboy hat. It's hilarious.

Mami even hangs up a portrait of her and Papi. It's them on their wedding day. If they weren't my parents, I'd say they look kinda hot. I do not say that. What I wanna say out loud is how happy they looked back then.

Before dinner, Xochitl leaves for a gig with some new band.

I dine with Rosario and Daniel. We're at our real table. Surrounded by those photos. And Jesus supping with his disciples. There are smiles. Mami and Papi might not look hot-young-couple happy. But like they're on the road to some new kind of happy.

Mami asks me about school.

I lie and say it's going all right.

"I notice things, Teodoro."

"It's nothing, Mami."

"That's not true. You're working hard. I'm proud of you."

She's *hoping*.

"Nah, Mami. Don't," I say. Because hope hurts when it goes.

Maybe it's gone already. Maybe that chemistry quiz was it. Maybe that was the end. Maybe it should have been the end.

I get up from the table and carry some dishes to the sink.

"Ándale, mijo," Papi says. "We got the dishes tonight. You get to work."

Mami smiles at him. Then at me. "Go on," she says.

So I head to my room.

SAT OCT 11 8:23 P.M.

T:	Looks like Manny might be coming home in feb
Wendy:	I got you all in my heart.
T:	X and I painted. Wanna brighten things up for him
Wendy:	You are awesome, Teodoro.
T:	Thanks for recognizing my awesomeness. Hold on. Taking a moment to recognize urs
T:	There. I took a moment
Wendy:	A moment of silence in recognition of my awesomeness?

T:	A moment of loudness. I opened up a window and yelled WENDY MARTINEZ IS AWESOME!!! Thought the world should know
Wendy:	I just opened the window and yelled, TEODORO AVILA IS A NUT! Thought the world should know.
T:	Happy ur the one to spread the news
Wendy:	☺
Wendy:	Time to hit those books!

I toss the phone on my bed and stare at my pile of work.

All right, Wendy.

I drop and crank out a bunch of half-assed push-ups. Hop to my feet. Jump some jacks.

Then I crack open my chemistry notes.

Read chapters from *The Crucible*.

Study colonial response to the British victory in the French and Indian War.

Get messed up graphing quadratic functions.

I fight to grab the merry-go-round and slow that mother down.

TUESDAY, NOVEMBER 4, 2008

The whole day, I keep telling myself this is not going to happen. Because a dude who looks like that and has a name like his
can never, ever become president.

After school, the Avilas and I settle in for a long, nervous night
of TV news, web updates, way too many chips, and too much
popcorn.

Then, finally, it happens.

TUE NOV 04 11:01 P.M.

Wendy: You watching this????

Wendy: NBC just called it!!!!!!!

This country has turned a

corner. We've changed.

We're better. Everything

feels different.

T:	I hope so, Wendy.
T:	Maybe this means Manny will come home sooner
Wendy:	I hope so.
Wendy:	I can't stop crying.
T:	My mom and Xochitl are crying
Wendy:	I can't believe the first time I vote, I'll be voting for a sitting African-American president.
T:	That's what I said and my dad was like if he's still alive in four years. Ugh
Wendy:	For tonight, I'm going to celebrate. This country did it. Woo-hoo!!!
T:	Woo-hoo!!!!

I get in bed. Pull up my covers and close my eyes. And I can't stop thinking about this thing.

One day Ms. Bradley stopped me in the hall and said, "I believe in you, Teodoro Avila. I believe you can make it to college."

In my head I was like, *That's really nice. But I think there's a possibility that you are lying to me.*

I wonder if, when Obama was a teenager, some teacher walked up to him and said, *I believe in you, Barack Hussein Obama. I believe you can be president.*

If a teacher did say that, they were definitely, absolutely lying.

But look what happened. Barack worked his ass off and managed to turn some dreamy do-gooder's easy lie into the most outrageous, unimaginable truth ever.

I throw the covers back. Get my ass up.

I reach into my pack and pull out my textbook and get cracking.

Algebra sucks.

And I'm *this close* to quitting.

But I can't.

Not after tonight.

Thanks a lot, Obama.

FRIDAY,
NOVEMBER 28, 2008

I stand in the wet and dark, cued up at the end of a line wrapping its way around the Tukwila Best Buy. I'm about to blow my life savings because, although change has come to America, change has not come to Teodoro Avila.

I studied alone. I studied with Caleb. I was the annoying guy in tutorial, asking question after question. It got so bad I started dreaming about elements, compounds, reactions, graphs, equations, functions . . . but none of that studying did me any good.

I got a D in algebra and I failed chemistry.

Bradley let me know how she felt about it. She told me Clegg cornered her in the packed staff room and he publicly asked her why she enrolled me in his class.

She told Clegg she believes in my potential.

He told her—and everybody else—that I failed my midterm . . . and I had C-3PO, R2D2, Han Solo, and Chewbacca as answers.

I don't know how to dig myself out of that one.

I'm pretty sure I got a C on my Language Arts and US

History midterms. Cs would be good enough to keep me in AVID, but those are my strong classes, and my grades are still nowhere near good enough for U-Dub.

The Best Buy doors fling open. I get pushed from behind. There's impatient shouting. Then it's like the mob lifts me off my feet and carries me inside.

Minimobs scatter this way and that, toward cheap laptops, flat screens, and cell phones. I battle my way toward the games.

A few Xboxes lie scattered on the floor. I swoop in and bear-hug a box and the old twitch kicks in. I wanna get home. I wanna bust this thing open, plug in the cable. Get back in touch with Splazer, Spartan, Plasma . . . and blast the crap out of each other.

But before I get five steps, I see it. Halo 3 on display. I don't have to wait.

I set my box down. Squeeze it hard between my heels. Pick up the controller. Flick it to the menu. And get my thumbs shooting.

I haven't lost a thing. I've got this world inside me. In my muscles. In my blood. I'm back where I belong.

I'll call Caleb later and tell him it's over.

On Monday, I'll go into Bradley's office and let her know.

Then, eventually, I'll tell Wendy the ugly truth about me and this will all be over.

Right now, I got Covenant ground forces on my ass, so I'm blasting fast but . . .

There's a buzz in my pocket.

Might be home.

Could be Caleb.

I know it's not.

But I can't pick up because I'm fast approaching this Ark and

I gotta disable it before Halos activate and put an end to all sentient life.

Another buzz.

I'm not gonna look. Because looking means facing up to my lies. Facing up to my failure.

Buzz, buzz

Looking means facing up to where I am and what I'm doing right now.

Buzz, buzz

Aw, hell . . .

FRI NOV 28 5:18 A.M.

Wendy: Hi!

FRI NOV 28 5:20 A.M.

Wendy: Good morning!

FRI NOV 28 5:22 A.M.

Wendy: Anybody home?

FRI NOV 28 5:25 A.M.

Wendy: I missed you yesterday.

FRI NOV 28 5:30 A.M.

Wendy: Fine. Don't answer me

at 5 in the morning.

Wendy: Just wanted to let you know that

there are a few things for which

I am especially thankful this

holiday season.

Wendy: You made my list, Teodoro

Avila.

I shove my phone in my pocket.
Pick up the controller.
Fire at scores of infected aliens.
Then my fingers freeze.
The controller drops.
It bangs the display and dangles by the cord.

I rip off the headset. Grab the box. Walk over and drop it where I found it. Then I reenter the chaos and fight to push against the current. Push myself right out of that store.

I lean up against the building. Pull out my phone.

FRI NOV 28 5:36 A.M.

T: Ur on my list too Wendy

T: What is up you early riser?

Wendy: Black Friday, man! Hop to it!

T: Ha! I think I better stay away

from black fridays

Wendy: Happy Thanksgiving, Teodoro.

T: Happy thanksgiving Wendy

I flip my hand over. There's nothing on my palm.

I battle my way back into the store.

I ask a clerk for a Sharpie. She hands one over.

I make the four connected lines—down-up-down-up—and I got myself a *W* right there.

I am not giving up.

I am not giving up.

I am not giving up.

I call Caleb and tell him I need a tutor bad. And I need a job to pay for the tutor.

Caleb tells me I'm in luck. They're hiring at Vince's.

Aw hell, I'm gonna be a dishwasher.

SATURDAY, DECEMBER 6, 2008

I walk inside the SeaTac branch of the King County Library.

I scan the place, looking for my new tutor. Some guy from Highline Community College. Ms. Bradley set the whole thing up after I apologized for making her look like a fool. After I begged her on my hands and knees to keep me in AVID.

Dude sitting at a table flashes me a bright-eyed smile and waves me over. He stands and puts his hand out. "I'm the tutor. Bashir Mohamed," he says.

I shake his hand and look right at him, and I think I know this guy. "Hey, are you Dalmar's brother?"

He laughs. "Everybody knows my little brother!"

Caleb and I were buds with Dalmar in fifth grade. He had moved here from Somalia in kindergarten. He was way smart and loved soccer more than anything. Bashir used to come over after middle school let out and walk him home every day.

"How's he doing?" I ask.

"That kid is a pain in my ass." Bashir laughs. "Nah, I'm kidding." He tells me they moved to Burien a while back. His brother got a scholarship to Kennedy Catholic. For his brains. "Plus he scores a ton of goals on the soccer team."

I ask Bashir about Highline CC.

He says it's going well but he can't wait to finish up and transfer to U-Dub. He wants to study chemical engineering.

Then he says, "Hey, what's the deal with your math?"

I tell him the straight-up truth and Bashir looks at me like I'm the tutoring challenge he's been waiting for. So he launches right into a review of logarithmic and exponential functions and all that crap.

It's all hard, but asking questions is easy for once. Maybe it's something about me knowing his brother. Or maybe it's just how much Bashir loves math. He describes equations as *elegant* and *beautiful*. And he doesn't care that I suck. He treats it like a game, trying to convince me that math is as awesome as he thinks it is. He makes three hours fly by.

I thank Bashir and tell him I'm headed for my first day washing dishes at Vince's Pizza.

"Aw, man. Seriously? I wash dishes at Thirteen Coins by the airport." Bashir stares at his hands with a look of disgust. "Wear the gloves, man. I didn't want to at first. But then . . . Teodoro, you gotta wear the gloves."

"I promise you, I will wear the gloves. Thanks, Bashir."

We shake hands and make a plan to see each other same time tomorrow.

And I hop a bus to Vince's.

SATURDAY,
DECEMBER 13, 2008

Three hours of chemistry with Bashir in the morning. Then seven hours of scalding water, scraping slop, and stacking dishes.

My mom is waiting for me in the Vince's parking lot. In the morning, we made a plan to hear Xochitl sing at Vera Project at Seattle Center. She's in a new band, Ray Is a Girl. It's her first gig as their lead singer.

We stand in the tiny crowd as the opening act exits the stage. Indie folk rock plays softly on the speakers. Mami says she went to a rehearsal. She says Ray Is a Girl is the best band Xochitl's ever been in.

I tell her they can't be better than Flywheel. Flywheel combined a funk bounce with punk nastiness. And they kicked ass because Xochitl can front punk like nobody else.

The PA music fades and everything gets pitch-black. A spotlight comes up on Xochitl at the mic. She sings a capella:

I'm coming back to you for good this time

I promise it'll be real soon

I'll chip away at these walls till I'm free once again

Then run miles by the light of the moon

The way Xochitl sings, you believe she's locked up, fighting for her freedom. And you wanna know the rest of her story. And you wanna tell her everything's going to be okay.

The spotlight spreads wider as Xochitl repeats the verse, this time backed by piano. She repeats it again and the guitar joins in. Next time through, the bass thumps to life. Xochitl's voice grows more and more intense and the lights are pushed brighter and brighter. Finally, the drummer pounds his tom, kicks his bass, blasting his crash cymbal as the lights fill the stage and Xochitl's belting it out and the crowd—we're swept away in the swell, blissed-out and thrilled, amazed we're being taken along on this ride.

Ray Is a Girl gets what we've always known: My sister has a voice that plunges into your guts and mixes 'em up like a blender. Her voice is a hand wrapping its fingers around your pulsing heart. So even though Ray has a bunch of kick-ass musicians, they dial it back and let Xochitl's voice do its thing.

Mami looks at me with the biggest smile I've seen in a long time. And she dances like I haven't seen her dance since Manny left us.

I used to think she was the prettiest mom in the world.

Then she got angry at Papi and blamed him for losing Manny . . . for losing our old life.

Mami takes my hands in hers. Twirls me around. Dips me. We both laugh and dance and let Xochitl's voice take us away, to a place where we can be great again.

It feels like the show is about to end, when they drop the spot on Xochitl one more time. She's sitting at a stool. Someone brings her a guitar. She strums real quiet. "They made me do this," she says. Then her eyes drop and she watches her fingers dance on the strings.

I heard your voice, on the telephone

Brother . . . brother of mine

It's country or folk. A song about talking to Manny.

Clear as a bell, from so far away

Brother . . . brother of mine

I look at the crowd as Xochitl sings. People are swaying. Hanging on every word.

Just Xochitl's words. Just her voice. Just enough guitar.

And it hits me like crazy.

This song never existed. Then Xochitl put it into the world. And this room of people—we feel different than we did before. We feel better than we did before. And we'll walk out this door and into the world with that feeling. And who knows where it will take us?

I cannot sing.

I have no idea what I *can* do. But I wanna do something. I wanna *make* something.

I want to feel what Xochitl's feeling right now as she sings:

No more telephones, no more hopes you'll come home

Brother . . . brother of mine

I wanna feel what she's feeling when she lifts her eyes, looks out at us, slows the words down even more, and nods at us as she sings—

I wanna hold you now . . .

—knowing we're gonna finish the song. And she's right. Xochitl cups her ear with a hand as we sing it with all our hearts. . . .

Brother, brother of mine

She leans into the microphone and says, "You sang that beautiful. Thank you."

Mami and me got wide eyes and we're shaking our heads. *We* knew Xochitl was amazing. Finally, everyone else is gonna know.

We don't talk much on the drive home. Just stuff about how great Xochitl was.

Then I say it. "I wish Papi could have come."

"Me too," she says. "I'm sorry. I know it's been hard—"

"It's okay," I say. "Things are better."

"That's true. But I know what it's done to you, us being like—"

"Mami, no. You don't have to—"

"We can't change the past, but—"

"It's all right, Mami. It's all okay."

I can't sleep. So I wait up in bed. And when the front door opens, I head out to catch Xochitl.

"That was awesome, Xoch."

"The band is amazing," she says.

"You aren't up there acting like a big deal. You're up there *sounding* like a big deal."

"I can't believe it's happening, T."

"Believe it, Xoch. And as awesome as Ray is, your song was even better."

My rocker-chick sister does not turn red often. She's turning red now.

"You have any more songs, Xoch?"

She shakes her head.

I tell her she has to write more.

"I don't know if I have any more in me. And it didn't feel right being up there alone."

"Felt right from where I was standing."

"That's sweet."

"That's not why said it."

"Okay, T. I get it."

"Good."

TUESDAY, DECEMBER 16, 2008

I've had a grand total of eighteen hours of tutoring over the three weekends with Bashir. Plus, I call him whenever Caleb and I get stuck on something. It doesn't sound like much. But it's made a huge difference. The concepts feel like they're coming one at a time now, instead of hitting me like a tsunami.

Bashir says my teachers should know I'm starting to catch on. He says I should show them.

So I stay and after school and I tell Clegg and Woods I want to retake midterms. They both say they can't change my grade. I tell them that's not why I wanna do it.

When I finish, Clegg corrects my chemistry test. He writes a big fat B on top of the page. Then, in a bad British accent, he says, "You have become one with the Force, young Jedi." And he hands me the test, cracking a smart-ass smile.

"Good one," I say, sarcastic as hell. But inside I'm pumping my fists in the air. *You're damn right I've become one with the Force!*

I head up to Pac Highway to catch my bus. And pull out my phone.

TUE DEC 16 4:35 P.M.

T: We never talked midterms

I did all right. U?

Wendy: Good. Except for a stupid B+

in English.

T: Ugh that sucks. I give you an a++

for perfect spelling punctuation and

caps while texting

Wendy: I don't text-punctuate for just

anyone, Teodoro. They have to

be worth it.

T: That, Wendy, means a lot.

Wendy: ☺

WEDNESDAY, DECEMBER 24, 2008

The Avila family is picking through the last of the scraggly, cheap-ass Christmas trees at a lot on Pac Highway.

Xochitl and I put on this act like we're searching for trees in a blizzard on the side of a frozen mountain. And despite the conditions, and despite the lack of actual trees, we're extremely picky. When we find the perfect one, we mime sharpening our axes and slowly chopping the thing down.

Mami and Papi tell us to stop making a scene, but the looks on their faces tell us they don't want us to stop.

WED DEC 24 11:05 P.M.

Wendy: Call me?

I'm nervous as hell. We've texted quite a bit. But barely talked on the phone.

Half a ring and she picks up.

"Hi, Teodoro."

"Hey. It's great to hear your voice."

"I just wanted to read you something. *'Twas the night before Christmas . . .*"

Ma in her kerchief. The clatter of reindeer on the rooftop. Santa's rosy cheeks.

Wendy gets into it, real dramatic. And her voice is so full of something that makes me want this story to last forever. But eventually, in a low Santa voice, she says the words, *Merry Christmas to all, and to all a good night.*

"Wow, Wendy. Thanks for that."

"I hope you all have a good one tomorrow, Teodoro."

"You, too."

There's so much stuff I wanna say, but I can't.

"I'll be thinking about you guys," she says.

"I'll be thinking about you, too."

"Yeah, Teodoro?"

"And your mom. Wish her a Merry Christmas from us."

"I will. And if you hear from Manny, tell him he's in our thoughts."

"Thanks, Wendy."

It's quiet for a few seconds.

"Teodoro?" she says.

"Yeah?"

She doesn't say anything.

"Wendy, you there?"

"I just want to say Merry, *Merry* Christmas, Teodoro."

"Merry, *Merry* Christmas to you, Wendy."

"Okay," she says. "Good night."

"Good night, Wendy."

"Sweet dreams, Teodoro."

"Sweet, *sweet* dreams, Wendy."

FRIDAY,
JANUARY 9, 2009

I'm at my desk, reading *The Catcher in the Rye*, bummed out by Holden Caulfield. He's so damn alone. And that is the one thing I have in common with Holden Caulfield.

I pick up my phone and scroll through recent texts with Wendy.

SUN JAN 04 8:38 A.M.

Wendy: Important question.

Wendy: Milkshake or ice cream cone?

T: Definitely milkshake

Wendy: Interesting . . .

SUN JAN 04 8:50 A.M.

Wendy: Knees or elbows?

T: Elbows

Wendy: Hmm.

SUN JAN 04 9:04 A.M.

Wendy: Skittles or M&M's?

T: M&M's

Wendy: WTF!?!?

SUN JAN 04 9:08 A.M.

Wendy: All right, Avila. That was an easy one. So I'm giving you one more shot: Skittles or M&M's?

T: Still M&M's.

Wendy: You don't want to reconsider?

Wendy: I'll give you a minute.

T: Don't need it. M&M's.

Wendy: You can't just go back and change your mind later.

T: Not gonna.

Wendy: So I have it right that you are firm on your answer?

T: Yes. It's M&M's.

Wendy: Wow.

Wendy: OK.

Wendy: I know where you stand.

65

SUN JAN 04 9:45 A.M.

Wendy: Aardvarks or Anteaters?

T: Aardvarks

Wendy: Oh my God, Teodoro! I cannot

EVEN!

Wendy: I'm sitting here

trying to wrap my mind around

your answers.

Wendy: I thought I knew you!

Wendy: Aardvarks? Seriously?

Aardvarks? AND M&M's???

Wendy: YOU CAN'T HAVE IT BOTH

WAYS, MISTER!

T: I'm complicated, Wendy.

Wendy: Complicated? Teodoro, you are

a boiling cauldron of contradictions.

I look over at that red cover on my bed. I pick it up. Toss it aside. *Sorry, Holden. You are not going to cut it.* Old texts are not going to cut it. I need Wendy right now.

FRI JAN 09 10:17 P.M.

T: Loved the turtle with

antlers X-mas card. Classic.

Wendy: I thought you might like it.

T: Actually gave me nightmeers.

Great to get an Xmas card in

January though.

Wendy: Better late than never.

T: That's MY motto.

Wendy: You have a motto?

T: I have like 10 mottos. U?

Wendy: I have eleven mottos.

T: I actually have 12.

T: No . . .

T: Recounting . . .

T: 73 mottos!!!!

Wendy: Wow! How are they working

out for you?

T: Made it this far.

Wendy: You are a dork.

T: I'm a dork? Who plays the tuba?

Wendy: You still don't get it.

Wendy: And I'm afraid you never will.

T: I wanna get it. I wanna get it

so bad.

Wendy: Then come to my concert.

See me in action.

T: I think that would help.

Score me some tix?

Wendy: I have connections . . .

MONDAY,
FEBRUARY 2, 2009

On the bus and I'm shaking the whole way.

Semester grades were mailed Friday.

I think I nailed my essay in English. I compared depressed Holden Caulfield to that death-wish adventure kid from *Into the Wild*. I sailed through the history multiple-choice final—American Revolution through the Civil War. In chemistry and algebra, at the very least, Bashir had me ready to attack every problem.

You can't think like that, T. Expect the worst. Expect the worst.

I reach for the box.

Grab the envelope.

Rip it open.

Scan the page and . . .

Shut the fridge up!

I got a B in History.

B in English.

C in algebra!

And another C in chemistry!

I went from failing to Cs from midterms to now. And there's only one way that happened. I kicked ass on my finals. I kicked *honors* ass.

I wipe a stupid tear and shove the card in my pocket. *I'm on my way, Wendy.*

I head inside, pumped to study. Cuz it's time for new expectations. Time to turn Cs into Bs and Bs into As.

"You're home, mijo!" My dad's got a hammer hanging from his belt and the place smells like sawdust.

"What's going on, Papi?"

He motions to the kitchen. "Pásale, señor."

He's got everything cleared out of the pantry. "Tu cuarto," he says.

It's the answer to the question I been too afraid to ask. We're a week and a half from my brother coming home and every day I ask myself, *Where's Manny gonna sleep?* Or the inverse of that question: *Where am I gonna sleep?*

I never thought the answer would be the kitchen pantry. Yeah, the thing is huge for a house that has the washer and dryer in a hall closet and barely any other storage space. But it's way too small for a bedroom.

Inside, Papi's built a platform. Thick plywood sitting on strong legs. The thing fills the entire pantry. "That's your desk, mijo."

"What about my bed?"

He whips out a paper with detailed sketches and measurements. Another piece of plywood is going to sit right on top of the desk. A mattress will go on that. When I'm working at the desk, the bed will be hanging above from the rafters. I'll lower it so it sits right on the desk when I need to sleep.

"How long you been working on this?"

"A while, mijo." We go to the yard out back. He's got a sheet of plywood on sawhorses. He hands me the power saw. "I started. You finish."

Papi used to do this stuff with Manny. Then Manny left and he'd work alone. So I never really learned. And I'm a little scared thinking about the damage I could do with this power tool. "You sure, Papi?"

"¿Cómo no?" He acts like it's no big deal. He says the blade is sharp so I don't have to push or force it. "Let the machine do its job."

I pull the trigger. The saw screams to life. I flinch and almost lose my grip.

"Bend your knees," he says. "Lean in. Look over the blade to your line."

I cut it real slow. And pretty straight.

"Eso," Papi says, slapping me on the back.

He grabs one end of the board. I grab the other. We carry it into the house together and place it on top of the desk. Perfect fit.

Papi tells me to get on the platform. He climbs up, too, and we stand, our heads in the pantry rafters.

Papi stomps and hops. I do it, too. He says, "It's strong, no?"

He shows me how to rig these funky pulleys way up in the corners. I thread rope through, and he shows me how to tie knots onto eyebolts we screwed into the corners of the plywood.

When we're done, Papi leaves the room. He returns hauling

in a twin mattress. He lays that thing on top. He takes the sheets and carefully makes the bed. Hospital corners. No wrinkles. He tells me to climb in. "Comfy?"

"Muy comfy, Papi."

Then he says, "Prepare to study."

I get out and re-make the bed just like he did. Then I yank the pulley rope and the bed platform lifts up to the ceiling. It clicks into place and stays up there good.

Papi walks out again and comes back rolling an old office chair. He motions for me to sit. I sit and he wheels me to my desk. He hands me a shiny red toolkit. Pops it open. It's full of office supplies, including—*whoa*—the expensive graphing calculator I been needing.

"Papi, how much did all this—"

"No importa, mijo."

More measuring. More cutting. Nailing, screwing. We make cubbies to put below the table. Papi bought boxes for me to put my clothes and stuff in. I slide the boxes into the cubbies.

Soon, we're standing there, staring at the bedroom-office that used to be a pantry.

"It's cool, Papi. It's strong."

"If you build something, you make it right," he says. His smile goes. "Lo siento, mijo. This is the best we can do right now." He starts putting tools away.

I don't want this moment to end, so I ask him if he has more ideas for tricky stuff like this.

He taps his head with a finger. "All up here. For someday."

"I'll help you out again next time," I say.

He holds out a hand to shake on it. "You're good with the saw," he says.

I can't help but smile. We shake to seal the deal, then I shove my hand in my pocket. I feel that paper.

I wanna tell him.

But I'm not there yet.

And that's not what this moment is about.

"It's really cool," I say.

"You sure, mijo?"

"Yeah, I'm sure."

TUESDAY,
FEBRUARY 3, 2009

Late night. Quiz in US History tomorrow. *Sectionalism* and the causes of the Civil War. It's depressing, but I got all the vocabulary and concepts down.

I put the book in a cubby.

Lower the bed.

Crawl in my covers and close the doors.

And then . . .

TUE FEB 3 11:36 P.M.

Wendy:	You are too far.
Wendy:	I want you here.
Wendy:	Right now, Teodoro.
T:	Right now?
Wendy:	Right. Now.
T:	This late?
Wendy:	Yes.

T: On a school night?

Wendy: On a school night.

T: That would be awesome.

Wendy: Yes it would.

Wendy: Because

Wendy: I

Wendy: Want

Wendy: To

Wendy: Kiss

Wendy: You.

T: Oh man.

Wendy: Just one

Wendy: Soft and juicy

Wendy: Kiss.

Wendy: And I want it now!

T: Kiss me, woman!

Wendy: My lips on

T: Yeah?

Wendy: My lips on your

T: Yeah?

T: YEAH?

T: YOUR LIPS ON WHAT?

T: ON WHAT, WENDY?

T:	YOU STILL THERE?
Wendy:	My lips on your sweet cheek
T:	WHOA NOW, GIRL!!!!
Wendy:	Are you stuck on all caps?
T:	OOPS.
T:	There. What next?????????
Wendy:	One soft kiss on that cheek,
	that fat, rosy cheek.
T:	Clarification: Are we talking
	about my fat rosy face cheek?
Wendy:	Your fat rosy face cheek.
	Right now!!!
Wendy:	I wanna taste it!
T:	Holy crap, Martinez!!!!!!
Wendy:	RIGHT NOW!
Wendy:	My mom! Got 2 go
T:	Get back soon!
Wendy:	;-)

It's hard to sleep. Hard to wipe the stupid grin off my face.

Between Wendy and school and grades and Manny coming home. And Wendy, and Wendy and Wendy . . .

SATURDAY,
FEBRUARY 7, 2009

We're all in my old room. Manny's new room. He'll need it in four days. *Four days!*

We haul in a bigger bed with a real comforter, a TV, a radio alarm clock—all that stuff. When we're done, we just stand in Manny's space. It's like we can't wait anymore and this is the closest we can get to him.

Xochitl sits on the bed. We join her. Mami grabs Manny's pillow and holds it to her chest. Papi sits close, his arm wrapped around her. She starts telling Manny stories. Stories about how smart he was as a kid. How much of a leader. Papi talks about how hard he worked at everything.

Then Xochitl says all this stuff about Manny *transitioning to civilian life* and about him finding a job in this crappy economy. "War can change people," she says. "That might make things hard."

Heads nod. But we got nothing to say. Because Manny's coming home. And he's always been strong. And as good as we've been lately, and as great as we are in this moment, Manny's gonna make us even better.

Xochitl gets up to leave for a gig and says, "Just stuff to think about."

The front door shuts and we sit in silence for a second.

And Mami picks up right where she left off with the stories. Papi, too.

I can't get enough of those stories.

SUNDAY, FEBRUARY 8, 2009

SUN FEB 08 10:30 P.M.

Wendy: I was less than ladylike the other night.

T: I was no gentleman.

Wendy: Really? I've checked the texts.

T: In my imagination.

Wendy: Oh . . . well . . .

Wendy: What did you imagine?

T: I imagined you, uh

Wendy: Don't say it.

T: You're right. That would be bad.

Wendy: Very bad.

Wendy: Say it.

T: But you just said.

Wendy: Come on, man!

T: I wanna be a gentleman, Wendy.

Wendy: Don't be a gentleman, Teodoro!

T: Really?

Wendy: YES!

T: I imagined you kissing my

T: Other face cheek.

Wendy: You

Wendy: Are

Wendy: Naughty!

T: You wanna taste that one?

Wendy: Depends on the flavor.

T: It's berry

Wendy: Which berry?

T: Blue raspberry

Wendy: Get the flip out!

T: Huh-uh, girl.

Wendy: Blue razz is my all-time

favorite berry.

T: That makes us both lucky

then, don't It?

Wendy: Yes it does.

T: I think there's a word for

situations like this.

Wendy: Kismet!

T: Not the word I was thinking of

but that one sounds real good.

Wendy: I have to run. Good night, T.

T: Good night, Wendy.

Wendy: I'm going to dream about

blue Skittles tonight, mister.

T: Me too.

Wendy: Not M&M's?

T: No Wendy. Tonight is all

about the Skittles.

Wendy: Sigh . . .

WEDNESDAY, FEBRUARY 11, 2009

Manny's flight doesn't get in till 4:13 p.m., but we're standing at the bottom of the baggage claim escalator by three thirty. I got butterflies in my gut, and I can't stop hopping up and down. Xochitl's holding Mami and Papi close. Papi's wringing his hands. We're all looking at each other and we can't stop giggling.

Finally, Mami points and shouts, "Manuel!"

He's at the top of the escalator!

We go crazy—all of us jumping now—hooting and hollering, watching him glide down.

He puts on an act like he doesn't even know us. He turns and looks up at the people behind him, like *What celebrity is back there?* When he looks at us again, he bugs his eyes out and points at himself. Then he cracks a smile and starts laughing and jumping up and down, clapping and screaming like an idiot—just like we been doing.

He finally makes it to us and we tackle him. Everybody gets a piece of Manny. Holding his hand. His face. Wrapping arms around him. *You're home. I can't believe it's you. It's me. It's really me. You've grown, T. You, too, Papi. Xoch, what's with the purple stripe in your hair? Mami, I missed you most of all.*

In the car, Manny says, "I have one wish for my first meal home."

"You can count on your mamá," Papi says.

At the rental Manny says it's way better than what he was expecting after Papi's description. He calls my room the Captain's Quarters. Says he likes it so much he might wanna trade at some point. Manny is so positive it makes me reconsider my attitude about the rental. And that makes me remember why I love Manny so much.

We talk and laugh and devour our green chile cheeseburgers. Manny jokes and tells our old stories. He has a million questions and keeps saying, "This is so good, Mami." He seems so happy it's hard to imagine he just got back from a war.

There's a part of me that's there, with everyone, enjoying it all. But another part of me is floating above the table. I'm seeing how we look and hearing how we sound, counting us and thinking, *Finally, this is us.*

"Ay, mijo, I forgot to toast!" Papi says.

We raise glasses in the air. Papi opens his mouth to start.

But there's a sound.

A rattling sound.

We all look.

Ice cubes are dancing in Manny's glass. The tablecloth is soaked. Manny's smile is gone. He squeezes his glass till his hand turns white, but he can't stop the shakes.

Manny sets the glass down and puts his smile back on. "So, if you were watching very closely there, you may have noticed my hands now have a mind of their own."

"No importa, mijo," Papi says. "Mine been doing that for a while, too." Then he raises his glass higher and says, "To our son, and brother. Welcome home, Manuel."

To being home. To having you home. To watching Mami and Papi dance. To Manny's snoring. To brother-sister movie nights with both my brothers. To more of these burgers . . .

We finally clink glasses. Manny tries, but he can't control that trembling hand.

Then Xochitl starts shaking her glass. "Damn, Manny! It's contagious!"

What the heck, Xochitl?

Manny smirks and snorts a laugh.

So I do it, too. "Look what you've done to me, bro!"

Manny says, "I must be quarantined before it takes over the neighborhood!"

Mami and Papi have no choice.

"Oh my God!" Manny says. "It's got Mami and Papi! AAAAGH!"

We all scream and shout and turn into hideous, trembling, glass-clinking monsters. We soak that tablecloth and we laugh and keep each other laughing for a long time.

Except for the shakes, and except for looking like he's thirty-five, Manny is awesome. He's funny. He's thoughtful. He's my same old brother. Manny is home. And he's strong.

I catch Xochitl's eye and nod toward Manny like, *See? I told you.*

Xochitl nods back like she's telling me I was right. And she and Manny were wrong. And everything is gonna be good.

I give Xochitl a thumbs-up, and she knows I mean thanks for getting us ready.

She smiles and mouths the words, *No problem.*

Papi's still talking. I look and see Manny's hand on his lap. I reach and give it a squeeze.

Manny looks at our hands. He squeezes back. He looks at me. Smiles. Nods. He shakes his head, like he can't believe it, either. He squeezes hard, and he doesn't let go till he's wiping his eyes.

When Mami, Papi, and Xochitl finally go to bed, I get up and dig through my backpack. I grab the paper and head over to Manny's room. Knock on the door.

He opens up. And we're looking each other right in the eyes. Manny's wider than me, but I'm just as tall. Manny notices, too.

"You got big," he says.

"Yeah," I say. "And I grew up."

I show him my report card. I tell him I got a job to pay for a tutor. I tell him how hard I studied with Caleb the whole semester and that's why I did so well on my finals.

"After what I heard, I was worried about you," he says.

"I was worried about you," I say. "*Bad.* For a long time."

"Tell you what, T: I'll quit worrying about you and you quit worrying about me. Deal?"

We shake on it. Then I say, "I still might need some help with math. I know you got the grades and all that, so . . ."

"Of course, T," he says. "Anytime. I'm home now."

WED FEB 11 8:38 P.M.

T: He's home! And he's great.

Wendy: YAAAAAAAAAAAY!!!

T: I'm feeling . . . I don't know. It's too big, I can't describe it.

Wendy: Wow, Teodoro. Hugs to Manuel and to you and the whole family.

T: Don't know if I could have survived the waiting without you. Thanks, Wendy.

Wendy: You are welcome. And I love that comma there, Teodoro.

T: And the period.

Wendy: Yes, Teodoro. I've been loving ALL the punctuation.

TUESDAY, FEBRUARY 24, 2009

I get home from studying at Caleb's and head for Manny's room. The door is closed. Reality TV is blasting. I don't want to bug him, but he's been back a couple weeks and we've hardly spent any time together—just us. Every day, Papi takes him to check out his old favorite spots. Dick's Drive-In. Pike Place Market. Ivar's on the Seattle waterfront. When Mami's off work, she drags him to Highline Community College and U-Dub and Seattle University.

Tonight, I got my shot, so I knock. "Hey, Manny. Can I come in?"

"Hey, T. What's up?"

I walk in and close the door. And I ask him to be my adult-like parental-figure tomorrow night for these student-led conferences at Puget. I'm supposed to share my portfolio with my parents and set goals for the new semester.

Manny runs a hand through his hair. "Shouldn't Mami and Papi go?"

I remind him about my sixth-grade conference. Papi had to work overtime for a big deadline at Fauntleroy and Mami was in Yakima with our sick abuela, Abita. So seventeen-year-old Manny stepped in. He asked all the right questions and my teacher loved him. Then he took me out for ice cream.

I tell him it'd be cool if he could do it again, ice cream and all.

And I tell him I never mentioned it to Mami and Papi. "They been so stressed. Now it's last minute and I don't wanna piss them off."

"Geez, T. I don't know. Maybe you should ask Xochitl."

I laugh at that. Manny cracks a smile, then gets serious quick. "T, it's just . . . It's been a long time. You know what I mean?"

I don't know what he means, but I tell him it's all right. No worries.

He turns back to the TV.

I head to the Quarters. Crack open my chemistry notebook and try to take in some new vocab. But Manny keeps turning up the volume. It's been a thing, him staying up way late watching TV. We share a paper-thin wall, so it's annoying.

But it's a small price to pay because I finally got my brother back. And he's doing fine. Yes, there are small things. Like the TV. And Manny brushing his teeth like he's trying to sand them down to nothing. Like how he always adjusts himself so he's facing the open part of the room. He'll ask to trade chairs or, if I'm standing, he'll move toward me and I know to switch places with him. But that's pretty much it. Minor stuff.

I can't concentrate. So I clear my desk. I reach up and grab the rope and lower my bed from the rafters. I climb in and pull up covers. Close my eyes.

It's a clicking sound that wakes me. A lamp switch or something. Something loud.

Manny clicks it for a long time, then stops and slaps the wall so hard everything shakes.

I get up and knock on his door. "You okay, Man?"

Real gruff, he says, "You gotta keep it down in there."

I open up a crack so he can see me. "I was sleeping, Manny."

He hops up from his bed. "Is that you?" he says.

I walk right up to him. He looks confused. Out of breath. "It's me, Man." I put a hand on his shoulder.

"Right," he says. "I knew that. How you doing, bud?"

I tell him I'm fine. And I ask him how he's doing.

And my brother tells me he's doing real good.

WEDNESDAY, FEBRUARY 25, 2009

Manny catches me leaving for school. He says he'll do the conference.

When evening comes and it's time to head out, I tell Mami and Papi I'm stealing Manny for a brothers' night out.

He's been in his room all afternoon. I knock. No answer, but the TV's going, so I push the door open a bit.

Manny's sitting on the bed staring at the wall mirror—lapels up on a crisp white shirt—superfocused on tying a tie.

I say, "Hey, *GQ!*"

He looks up from his knot. His hair is gelled up. He's got pressed pants. Shined shoes. That nice shirt. Manny went shopping for this. He smiles and says, "You ready?"

"Heck yeah," I say.

He goes back at the tie, but those shakes. He asks if I can help.

I go over and loop the tie around his neck like I know what I'm doing. "This goes under here. Then it wraps around again. One more tug and . . ." I whip the thing off and throw it across the room. I step back, check him out, and say, "Whattaya think?"

He cranes his neck to look in the mirror. "I think you nailed it. Thanks, bro."

That's what I mean about quirks. Yes, Manny shakes. Yes, he's, like, wired and anxious and up at night. But when he's with you, he's *with* you. And he's funny like he's always been. And that's what really matters.

The conferences take place at the Puget High gymnasium. It takes a while to get in there because Manny reapplies hair gel and tweaks and re-tweaks his collar in the car mirror. Then he takes forever getting himself, like, pumped to walk through the gym door.

Inside, the teachers are at tables set up around the periphery of the basketball court. Parents and anxious students wait in chairs in the center of the court. By the time it's our turn, I'm freaking out.

Manny stands and buttons his jacket. He looks nervous but he gives me a wink and says, "Let's do this."

"If you say so, Man."

At each conference, Manny asks my teachers how I'm doing. He doesn't let them get away with *Teodoro is doing great.* He asks what *great* means. He tells them to *Stay on T's case. Let him know when his work is not college material. Improved isn't good enough. Good isn't good enough.* He gives them his number *in case you can't reach our parents.* And I know my teachers see me different because of how Manny carries himself and his expectations of me.

We start walking out and Mr. Hart—this young biology teacher who actually went to school with Manny—walks up and says, "Avila! Welcome home! You look great, buddy. You remember? You remember the play?"

"Hey, Rick," Manny says. "Of course I remember."

Manny and Rick Hart were team captains and they hooked up on a last-second shot that won a big Vikings playoff game way back when.

Mr. Hart drapes an arm over Manny's shoulders. He looks concerned for Manny and talks like he doesn't want anyone else to hear. "How are you, really? I mean, how was it over there?"

Manny looks toward the exit. "Ah, geez, Rick—"

"Did you, uh, have to . . . ya know . . . put a stop to anyone? Did you have to? Over there?"

Manny freezes. His face turns red. And for a second he's someplace else.

He snaps to when he spots some old teachers walking our way. They're waving at him and smiling, wanting to talk.

Manny brushes Mr. Hart off hard and grabs me by the arm. He doesn't say a word to Rick or the teachers. He just races for the door, dragging me behind.

We get in the car and I thank him a bunch of times, but he's got his head on the steering wheel. He breathes deep and hard. Runs trembling fingers through his hair. Then reaches both hands out and grips the dash, like he's trying to steady himself.

I put a hand on his shoulder. "Sorry, Man," I say. "I'm so sorry. I didn't realize—"

He opens the car door. Steps out. Comes to my side, opens the door, and motions for me to scoot over. He wants me to drive.

He has me stop at the 7-Eleven on Pac Highway. I wait in the car. He comes back with a twenty-four-pack of Budweiser cans.

92

We get to the rental. Before we head inside, I thank Manny again and wish him good night.

He bites a lip and takes in a breath and tries to force a smile. It's like he's telling me he failed. And he's sorry.

"You're good, Man," I say. "It's all good."

He opens the door and walks straight to his room.

I try to study. Try to sleep. But it's impossible with the TV and the lamp switch clicking and can tops popping.

And the horrible feeling I made Manny do something he couldn't handle.

THURSDAY, MARCH 26, 2009

I ace an algebra quiz and get a decent grade on a draft of a paper on the *The Crucible*, so I tell Caleb I'm taking a night off. I'm headed home right after school.

Every night for a couple weeks, after we study together, I been staying for dinner at Caleb's. Then we study more and I don't come home till real late.

See, I started going downhill grades-wise a little since Manny got home. And after the conference, he quit leaving the house. There's a lot of him watching loud TV and drinking and the clicking weirdness. And Xochitl bugging him about his job search and sometimes they really get into it. So it's hard to study. I got a couple Cs on chemistry quizzes. Not the end of the world, but I'm not a C student anymore, so . . .

Staying away from the rental worked.

And today I'm back early to check things out. If it seems like Manny's doing okay, I'll ask him if wants to take a walk or something.

I step inside and I can hear Xochitl in his room.

The door is open a crack, so I sneak to a spot where I can look in.

Manny's smoking pot and Xochitl's on his case about it. She and weed are not strangers, so I don't know where she gets off.

You are an amazing person. But you're using drugs and alcohol as a substitute for . . .

She goes on and on with a bunch of intervention BS as Manny closes his eyes and does a Zen toke-out. Slow drags. Holds his breath forever. Even slower exhales.

Xochitl throws empty beer cans and yells at him, saying she's going crazy watching him do this to himself.

She just about knocks me over, storming out of Manny's room. "You still live here?"

"You all right, Xoch?"

She glares. I immediately regret asking.

"This isn't good, T. He's getting worse."

I don't know what to say.

"We need you here," she says.

I don't want to be in this conversation.

"I need you here," she says.

I nod my head yes to end it. "Okay."

"Seriously?" she says.

"Yeah, Xoch. I'll be here more."

She lunges at me. Hugs me. "That's great, T. Another set of hands, you know? Another pair of eyes. That's all."

Papi walks in from his job search and Mami gets home from work. They barely manage to say hi to each other. Since Manny started isolating himself, they're as cold as ever.

Manny manages to join us at the table. It's a nervous, quiet dinner, uncomfortable as ever.

95

I try to do subtle stuff to get Manny's attention. Try to make eye contact when I pass him a dish. A silly elbow poke in the ribs. He doesn't bite.

At some point, Xochitl starts in. She says she's going to drag us all to this support group for families of vets. She says we need to talk. Manny needs to talk. Mami and Papi need to talk. She begs them to get counseling again. Begs Manny to get out of the house. *To AA. To the VA. To the VFW. To the YMCA!*

Finally, Manny elbows me back, real subtle. He's looking down at his lap, so I look down. He's got his napkin wrapped over his hand like a puppet. He opens and closes the napkin mouth, synced to Xochitl's voice as she goes on and on with her lecture.

I look up at Manny's face.

He winks at me.

I roll my eyes.

He rolls his.

That's the Manny I used to know. That's my brother.

Xochitl doesn't stop talking, so after stuffing his face fast, Manny silently leaves the table. Soon there's Metallica, smoke, and smell coming from his room.

Xochitl hops up and bangs on the door.

"Give it a rest," I say. "You're making it worse."

The volume gets turned way up on the TV.

Xochitl shoots me a death stare and bangs more. Then she wheels around to Mami and Papi. "Are you gonna let him do this?"

Mami takes the same tone with Papi. *"Daniel?"*

Papi shrugs his shoulders. "No sé que decir, Rosi."

"You knew what to say when he told us he was leaving. You

knew then!" And she keeps going like she's been saving up words since the day he gave Manny his blessing.

Since the day she started blaming Papi.

He pushes himself from the table. Tosses his napkin and heads into Manny's room.

The TV and music get turned down. We can hear Papi's voice. Just a few words.

Maybe Manny says something. It's hard to tell.

The volume jacks back up. The stereo blasts.

Papi comes out holding one of Manny's beers. He closes the door.

All eyes on him.

He's thinking real hard. He closes his eyes. Takes a sip from the can.

Finally, he speaks. "Necesitamos paz," he says.

We need peace? That is it? Come on, Papi!

He waits for a response from my mom and Xochitl.

Doesn't get one.

So he leaves the room.

Mami goes to the kitchen and scrubs a pan like she wants to put a hole in it.

Xochitl goes to her room. Slams the door.

I head for Caleb's. My phone buzzes on the way.

THU MAR 26 7:22 P.M.

Wendy: With my bud Megan working on

an app idea.

T: App?

Wendy: A program for an iPhone. Short

for application.

T: Fancy! Tell me about it.

Wendy: Our app measures heart rates/

body temps in teens and parents.

Wendy: It takes into account external

stressors of all parties, as well

as barometric pressure.

Wendy: Analysis of conditions indicates

whether parents and their teen

may attempt face-to-face

conversation.

T: Any particular reason you

decided to work on this app?

Wendy: My mom is a total nightmare right now.

T: Why?

Wendy: Oh, the me growing up thing. The

me being an independent

human being thing. She can't

handle that I have my own ideas

re. my own life and my own future.

So she's on my case 24/7. It's

madness.

T:	Will the app work on siblings?
Wendy:	Wish I had some right about now.
T:	Be careful what you wish for.
Wendy:	Wish I had a house full of family.
T:	Sounds better than it is. Believe me. I'd trade spots with you right now.
Wendy:	Pretty lame thing to say, Teodoro
T:	Messed up drama taking place
Wendy:	Still. U don't know what it's like being one kid/one parent
Wendy:	Stuff gets crappy and there's no one else.
T:	Talk later?
Wendy:	Maybe
T:	When?
Wendy:	Not sure. I'll text u

What the hell just happened?

SUNDAY,
APRIL 5, 2009

Caleb drops me off real late, but I'm not finished studying. I got the light on in the Captain's Quarters, trying to wrap my brain around the Roosevelt Corollary.

It's impossible to concentrate. It's been days since I've heard from Wendy. I guess it was stupid what I texted. Only it wasn't *that stupid*. Maybe she needs space. I don't know.

Whatever it is, I am spinning the text—all the texts—over and over, remaking choices, rewinding and revising, trying to make it right in my mind.

And even if everything was fine with Wendy, tonight would still be impossible. Because there is television-stereo-popping-cans-jackhammer madness on the other side of my wall.

Screw it. I put my books in a cubby, release the latch, and lower the bed down into place. I put in earplugs and flip off the lights. I squeeze my pillow over my head and lock my eyelids tight. *I'll work tomorrow. I'll hope for Manny tomorrow. Hope for Mami and Papi tomorrow. Hope for Wendy tomorrow. Just let it all go, T. Let it go. Let it go.*

The wall explodes.

I pop awake. Bolt upright. Something's on my lap.

I'm crumbling—breathless—soundless screaming as the thing pulls itself over my body and back through the wall.

When it's gone, light pours in through a hole the size of Manny's fist.

I stand up on the bed. Manny punches through one more time, just missing me.

I throw the pantry doors open and jump, running barefoot out the kitchen. Before I can reach the front door, something stops me. I turn and look.

He's standing, bent over in his doorway.

He lifts his head. Wild eyes.

He's looking at me like I'm someone else. Like we're someplace else.

"Manny!"

His eyes light up. For a split second, he sees me.

Then it's gone, washed away in tears.

Something pulls me to my brother.

Something stronger stops me.

The door shrieks as I throw it open.

An echo as it slams behind.

I run away as fast as I can. And I don't look back.

Caleb picks me up. Kennedy and Rita Ta'amu are waiting when we get to his house.

Caleb tells them I need a place to stay.

"We've known your parents a long time," Kennedy says.

"They're good people. If we're going to do this, you have to keep communication open. You have to show your face over there."

I tell him I'll call every day and head home for Friday dinners.

Kennedy looks me in the eye. Puts his hand on my shoulder. "You have a home here, son. Long as you need." Rita sets up a bed on the old game cave sofa. She tucks me in with a kiss on the forehead.

I wait till she makes it up the stairs.

Then I lose it.

There are tears. Snot. Full-body shakes.

Whatever hope I got left, after years of waiting for Manny to come home and make us right again, I try my hardest to cry it all out.

And when my eyes finally dry, I decide that I'm done hoping for us.

But I'm not done hoping for me.

MONDAY,
APRIL 6, 2009

On the phone with my mom.

"But this is your home, Teodoro."

"It's temporary. I was doing so good. I been trying for college, Mami."

She sniffles. There's a catch in her throat. It's like she's getting herself calm before she talks because she doesn't want me to know she's crying.

"Oh, mijo, I know. I'm so proud of you."

"I can study here. And I'm not afraid to go to sleep."

No response. I can hear her blow her nose.

"I know it's hard, Teodoro. But your father—"

"I don't want this, Mami. I want Manny to be okay. I want everything to be better."

"I'm sorry, mijo."

"Don't be sorry, Mami. *I'm* sorry."

TUESDAY,
APRIL 7, 2009

It's late when Xochitl's standing at the Ta'amus' door.

"God, it's good to see you, Xoch."

We head downstairs toward the sofa. I wanna tell my sister how scared I was. How hard it's been seeing Manny like he is. How hard it was to move out. How bad I want to be home.

It's only been a couple days, but I want Xochitl to say Mami and Papi made up and Manny started talking. She doesn't say any of that.

"I had asked you if you would be home more. You said yes. And now you run away?"

"You weren't there Xochitl. You should have seen him. I can't go back as long as he's—"

"He's better when you're home, T. He's always been his best for you."

"You don't know how crazy that sounds, Xoch."

"We can switch rooms," she says.

"That's not it, Xoch." I reach for my pack. I pull out the paper. My report card. I hand it to her. "Remember when you told us

Manny was coming home? Remember you called me lazy and you told me to do something good?"

She looks up from the paper with smiling eyes, like she can't believe my grades. "You did it!" She tackles me. Punches me in the arm.

"I'm going for As, Xoch. By the end of the year, I'm going for it."

"Amazing, T." She closes her eyes for a second. "But . . ."

"But what?"

"No," she says. "No buts." She smiles like she means it and hands me my report card. "Just amazing. And I'm proud of you."

"What were you going to say, Xoch?"

She takes a huge breath. Exhales. Sweeps the purple streak of hair out of her face. "I need you, T." Her voice cracks. "I need you to come home. Now."

I look down at the floor, thinking whoever made up the phrase *Do the right thing* must have had a simple life. I look at my sister. Shrug my shoulders.

"Come on, T."

"I can't."

She nods her head. Sucks in a deep breath.

She stands up.

And walks out fast.

THURSDAY, APRIL 9, 2009

I help clear the table after another great dinner. There's silly talk about people at the Ta'amus' church and ridiculous coworker stories. Big laughs when Kennedy gives Caleb and his sisters a hard time. They flip it right back and Kennedy puts on a show like he's scary angry—and the scarier-angrier he gets, the louder Caleb and his sisters laugh and Rita apologizes for her family's behavior, like she's afraid I think they're all too crazy.

The Ta'amus are crazy in the best way possible.

When Caleb and I finish for the night, he heads up to bed. I read some chapters in my book, then put my stuff away. I grab blankets and make my bed on the sofa and crawl in and turn out the lights.

And in the dark and quiet, I miss home. I can't even say why. But I do.

I pull covers up tight. Close my eyes. And just as a Manny dream kicks in . . .

BUZZZZZZZZ!

I throw off blankets, spring from the couch, and dive for that phone.

FRI APR 10 12:07 A.M.

Wendy: Sorry it's been a while.

Wendy: I was mad at you.

T: I'm sorry. I was insensitive.

I know it's hard with your mom.

Wendy: It's just us. So everything gets amplified. But, Teodoro, I'm sorry I shut you out. That was stupid. And mean.

Wendy: It wasn't you. I was oversensitive.

T: It's all right, Wendy.

Wendy: Teodoro, this is new territory. Unexpected. Not part of the master plan.

T: What isn't?

Wendy: Feeling very much like for a person. That domino isn't supposed to fall yet.

Wendy: Maybe a ton of patience is in order.

T: I have two tons of patience.

Wendy: Is there a chance you have 3?

T: I think so. Hold on. Recounting . . .

T: Whoa, I was way off. Looks like I

have 1,476 tons of patience.

Wendy: I really missed you, Teodoro.

T: I missed you too, Wendy.

SAT APR 11 12:57 A.M.

Wendy: May concert coming up . . .

T: I'm going to see ya tuba?

Wendy: Yabba Dabba Dooba!

Wendy: Whoa, that was corny.

T: I wasn't going to say anything.

THURSDAY,
MAY 7, 2009

Caleb pulls out of the Puget parking lot after school.

"I'm gonna be honest," I say. "I'm a little bit nervous."

"T, you're shaking and you look like you're gonna puke. I'd hate to see what *very nervous* looks like."

We get to Caleb's. I prep for Wendy. He double-checks my wardrobe and hair. Talks me through that first moment of seeing her. What to say. How to read her body language. Kiss or no kiss . . . how many seconds to hold the kiss if kissing happens . . . all that stuff.

I tell Caleb I'm not sure if I should go.

"That's a normal feeling," he says. "Normal *for you*, T. Because you're an idiot."

Then he pushes me out the door.

As I pull away in the Civic, I watch Caleb waving, getting smaller and smaller.

It's not that I don't wanna go see Wendy blow her tuba.

The problem is I wanna go too much. And I'm afraid I'll mess everything up again. I'll try to be funny and say something stupid or insensitive. And Wendy will catch onto me. She'll realize I'm a fraud and she'll figure out I been lying about my family.

I get halfway down to Vancouver on I-5 and I'm so messed up I take my foot off the gas. I take the Centralia exit. Pull the car to the side of the road. Take out my phone.

THU MAY 07 6:13 P.M.

T:	Dang, Wendy! Car broke down. Still an hour away. Not gonna make it.
Wendy:	Oh no. A little bit crushed here. You okay, Teodoro? You got help?
T:	Triple A says it'll be an hour and a half, so . . . Sucks. I wanna see you do tuba so bad.
Wendy:	I know. I've been waiting for that face cheek kiss, Teodoro.
T:	Me too, Wendy.
Wendy:	Now Tom's the only one getting kissed.
T:	Um . . . Tom?
Wendy:	Tom Tuba.
T:	This is awkward.
Wendy:	?

110

T:	I'm jealous of a tuba. That's messed up.
Wendy:	Don't tell him I said this, but Tom's a little jealous of you. I have to go, Teodoro. Text me when you get home. Don't forget.

I think about stalling and showing up at Caleb's way late. Telling him how great the concert was. How awesome Wendy was. How much we clicked.

But I'm in too deep. Any more lies and I'll drown.

So I drive straight back and tell Caleb I wussed out.

And before he can bust me up, I tell him I still got stuff I need to make right. "And until I do that, I can't—"

"It's okay, T," he says. "I get it. Now come here." Caleb spreads his arms wide and pulls me into a hug. He squeezes hard. Pounds my back with his palm. Lifts me off the ground.

I fully admit it, *I need this hug.*

We sit in the cave and have the same conversation about my life—and his—that we've had a bunch of times this year. Only this time, it's bigger, stronger, deeper. We've only got a few weeks left. But we can still listen better. Take notes better. Ask more questions. Study harder. We've got finals coming up. Tests and papers. We're gonna see this thing all the way to the finish line.

And if we do, dreams can come true. That sounds corny as hell. But it's the way we're talking now.

THU MAY 07 10:27 P.M.

T: Made it home safe.

Wendy: Thanks for letting me know. I'm a worrier, Teodoro.

T: Thanks for worrying about me. How'd it go?

Wendy: We were good tonight.

T: You and Tom?

Wendy: The whole band. It all came together.

T: That's really cool, Wendy.

Wendy: I think so, too.

FRIDAY,
JUNE 12, 2009

I cannot leave school.

The bell has rung. Students have fled. The halls are quiet. Summer has arrived.

But I'm still here, strutting the halls like I own the place, soaking it all in.

I'm living in multiple-A territory. One in English and one in History. *Boom and boom!* I'm up to a solid B in Algebra Two and a freaking B-minus in chem, which is the biggest victory of all.

I visit my core teachers from the year . . . check in with next year's crew. I thank Ms. Bradley and Ms. Hays. Chat them up about summer plans. It's awesome.

Then I bus it to SeaTac. To the rental.

Kennedy Ta'amu called my dad and learned I missed some dinners. *All the dinners.* So he sits me down and says stuff about taking me in. Feeding me. Treating me like family. *Because you are a member of my family, son.* And he tells me when he heard I hadn't been home, he was gonna kick me out.

Then Kennedy tells me that Jesus Christ taught him to forgive.

I say, *I'm so sorry, I'm so sorry.* All I want to do is win back that man's trust.

The bus makes its way up Nineteenth toward Pac Highway, and I send a text to break the ice with Xochitl. I tell her I'm gonna hang out a couple hours before dinner. I leave out the part that if there's drama, I'm grabbing my burger to go.

The whole bus ride I'm going over summer plans in my head. Yeah, junior year was great. But it's over. First semester senior year is going to make or break me now. And my summer prep is going to make or break that first semester. In order for my transcripts to fully reflect my complete transformation by application deadline time, I gotta turn myself into a math and science whiz ASAP. So this summer, when I'm not working at Vince's or studying with Bashir, I'll be cramming with Caleb or by myself if he's on shift.

Vince's promised me thirty hours a week. That means I can see Bashir four, maybe five times a week and still save up money for senior year crap . . . pictures, AP tests, my UW application, and prom.

Prom. I got my fingers and toes crossed.

Outside of all that, I'll go to a couple movies with Caleb, sit through Friday dinners at the rental, and make some day trips to Vancouver if I can get myself brave enough.

I hop off the bus, drop the long-term thinking, and go over my immediate strategy. After I moved in with Caleb, and after Xochitl's visit, she started texting me updates about how Manny and Mami and Papi were doing. All bad news. Those guilt trips worked for a while. Then I stopped returning her texts. And she gave up. So . . . tonight, there will be no apologies. I'm not starting that conversation. I'm gonna strike first and come right at my family with my two As, my U-Dub goals, and my plans for senior year.

And wherever the conversation goes after that, I'm gonna stay positive. I will not let myself get emotionally sucked in. I will smile. Nod my head yes. I will not let my parents and Manny get me down. I will not let Xochitl make me feel guilty. I will breathe and I will get my green chile fix and get outta there in one piece so I can concentrate on prepping for physics with Bashir in the morning.

Get in.

Remain positive.

Get out.

Easy.

That's what I'm thinking when I see Xochitl bounce out of the rental.

I put on my hardest smile, ready for anything she's got.

Xochitl sees me. She smiles back and waves big. She pulls a cigarette from her mouth and shouts, "Hey, stranger!" as she skips to the curb and onto the hood of a beat-up, ancient blue station wagon. She flips some purple hair out of her eyes. "T, meet Sally." Then she leans into the car and goes, "Sally, this is Teodoro. We try hard to love him."

Before I can get past her and that beast car, she skips around to the passenger side and opens the door. "Hop in, T. You and Manny get the first ride in the dream-mobile."

"I'll pass, Xoch. I'm gonna head in and say hi to Mami."

"Mami's still at work and Papi's at the hardware store. Manny wants to take a ride, so . . ." She runs her cigarette hand through her hair, caresses the car, and says, "Get inside Sally, T. You know you want her."

"Sick, Xoch. Why'd you get this thing?"

"Tired of the bus. Tired of bumming rides. You like her?"

"It's really old. How many miles does it—"

"She's vintage, T. A 1961 Rambler Cross Country Classic. Full engine makeover. Just outta the shop."

The rental door opens and Manny stumbles out.

"Hey, Man," Xochitl says, "Sally's ready for her close-up. Hop in."

Manny's looking beat. Squinting his bloodshot eyes against the sunlight. But he's standing upright and he's outside the house. He's in some nice jeans and that same white shirt he wore for my conference.

He arches his back, stretches tall, and flashes a Manny grin. "Hey, T. Good to see you, bud. Let's do this."

That smile about knocks me over. I haven't seen it since his first days home.

Manny hops in the back seat. Closes the door.

Xochitl nods his way. "Things are looking up, T. Get in, baby brother."

I tell myself, *It's a little joy ride. She just wants to show off the car. No big deal.*

But my gut is telling me to step away from the car. And run fast.

Manny rolls down a window. "Let's make her happy, T. Come on."

Xochitl looks at me with big, bright eyes. "Manny's better. Everything is okay. Let's . . ." She mimes holding a huge book and turning a huge page. "Get it?" she says.

"I get it, Xoch."

"We good now?" she says.

We're weird now, is what I wanna say.

She holds a hand out for me to shake and says, "I missed you, T."

I look at my sister thinking how great things used to be between us.

Then I shake her hand and it's a massive relief. "I missed you, too, Xochitl."

"Ride time!" she says.

I jump in. The seat is surprisingly springy. And there is more metal on the dash than I've ever seen in a car. I reach over my shoulder for the belt but there's just a frayed end where someone had cut it off. There's still a lap belt, so I snap that thing on and pull the strap as tight as I can. I close my eyes, take in Sally's funky spilled-milk-and-smoke smell, and prepare for what's coming. But Xochitl leans in the window and says, "Sit tight a sec."

And I'm alone in the car with Manny.

It's the closest we've been since we slept on opposite sides of the wall.

He leans into the front seat and I flinch and immediately feel like a jerk for flinching.

"It's okay," Manny says. "I'm sorry. I know I haven't been easy to live with."

I tell him it's all good and no worries and I'm sorry I haven't been around.

And Manny tells me he's doing better.

"Yeah, Man?" I say. "What happened?"

"Xoch wore me down," he says. "I figured the only way to shut her up was to do whatever she says." He pats me on the shoulder. "It's good to see you, T."

That smile . . . I tell him it's great to see him, too.

The sound of the tailgate popping open. Something heavy drops in. The tailgate slams. Xochitl gets in the driver's seat. "Here we are. *Together*. When was the last time—"

"Ándale, Xochitl."

"This is a moment, T. Respect it."

She pulls her cigarette to her lips. Breathes in a lungful. Closes her eyes and holds the smoke in her puffed cheeks for an impossibly long time. Then she blows a slow, steady stream out the window. She stares at the cigarette. Lets out a sigh. And grinds it into the ashtray. She holds the butt up in the air for all to see. "*This*, my beloved brothers, is my last smoke. Ever."

"I'm proud of you, Xoch," I say. "Now let's—"

"Good-bye, old friend!" She tosses the butt out the window and turns the key. Sally rumbles to life. Xochitl pulls down the stick to shift—*clunk-clunk*—and punches the gas pedal so hard the tires squeal and we blast off like a spring-loaded roller coaster.

Xochitl pulls the beast car from one lane to the next, weaving in and out of traffic on this airport stretch of Pacific Highway. I grip the dash and think about the day Xochitl wrecked Manny's Mustang. Manny was in Iraq when Xochitl got her license. Mami and Papi let her drive it to Eastern Washington to visit our grandma Abita. Somehow, she ended up rolling Manny's beloved car in the median on Snoqualmie Pass. She was lucky she didn't get killed.

"The car is awesome, Xoch. Now let's get back for Mami's dinner."

"No worries, T. We have all kinds of time," she says. And she lets go of the wheel, reaches back over the seat, and swats Manny in the leg. "Can you believe this car, Man?"

"Yeah, Xoch. Just like old times."

We had a station wagon like this when I was little. Papi drove it on a family trip down the coast to California, then over to our Tío Ed's farm in New Mexico. We stopped and saw friends and family along the way. I was too little to remember, but I've heard the stories a million times.

Before I know it, Xochitl says she wants to show off Sally's freeway skills and she's on the ramp for I-5 heading north.

I tell her to please make it quick.

Xochitl hits the gas hard as she darts into the fast lane.

There's an exit off I-5 coming up. She doesn't take it.

Pretty soon she taps her turn signal. And we're driving north on I-405. Another freeway taking us in the wrong direction.

"Xochitl," I say. "I love this car. Now turn around."

She pretends she doesn't hear me.

I say it louder and she says, "I can't turn around, Teodoro. There's a dear, sweet old lady in Yakima making dinner special for us."

"Aw, hell no," I say. "There's no way. Turn us around, Xoch."

"You haven't seen Abita in a whole year," Xochitl says.

"And I can't see her now. So turn us around."

119

It's worse than just my studying getting messed up. My abuela is a sour old lady. Everyone says she was fun when we were little. But to me, Abita's always been a little pissy and a little mean. Her parents named her Dolores, Spanish for *sorrow* or *pains*. Well, she's a pain and she acts like everything pains her. And the last couple times I saw her she was starting to get sick and slow from old age. So she was crankier than ever.

"I went with Mami a few weeks ago," Xochitl says. "Abita's doing a lot better."

I tell Xochitl to exit and drop me off before she gets on I-90, the freeway to eastern Washington. She says okay. Then she skips the exit and merges onto I-freaking-90.

"Damnit, Xoch. I don't have time for this."

Manny pipes up from the back. "I haven't seen Abita since I got back, T. We should see her together."

"Yeah, Man?" I say.

"She's making caldo de queso," he says.

"Serious?" I say. If there's one way to get me to go, that might be it. Mami's side of the family was from Sonora, Mexico, and Arizona until Abita's dad moved the family to the northwest. Abita's mom taught her to cook Sonoran style and it is the tastiest.

"Tortillas de harina," Manny says. "Homemade. And beans. It's been a long time."

Aw, hell.

He got himself cleaned up. He got out of the house. And he's being so nice.

I'm gonna do this for Manny.

And for some of Abita's caldo and tortillas.

120

"Sorry, T," Xochitl says. "I just knew if I told you sooner, you wouldn't have come."

"That's why you should have told me," I say. "Do Mami and Papi know?"

"Yeah. I told them the three of us were going a couple days ago. Plus, they had to work late tonight.

"Don't worry," she says, "You still had clothes in your room, so I packed for you. Toothbrush. Chonis. A T-shirt. You're set. And we'll be home before lunch tomorrow."

We blow past valley towns, Issaquah and North Bend, and quickly start gaining elevation. It's forest on all sides as we cross the Cascade Mountains, the divide separating two different worlds. When it rains on a winter day in Seattle, it's snowing in eastern Washington. When we're dying of the heat on an eighty-degree summer day in the west, it's ninety-five in Yakima. And where in metropolitan Seattle, there are a couple million walking, talking, pale reminders that you're a Mexican, in Yakima there's norteño and tejano on the radio and you're just another brown dude speaking Spanglish.

I text Caleb and tell him I won't be home tonight but I'll be back in time for Vince's tomorrow.

I text Bashir and see if we can skip tomorrow but meet for longer on Sunday.

And I tell myself it's gonna be fine. I'll put up with Abita for a night and a morning. Then I'll come home, work my shift, get a good night's sleep, and bust my butt for the whole rest of the summer. We're doing this for Manny, and I've pretty much never done anything for Manny. He's always done stuff for me.

* * *

Abita's mobile home door springs open.

"Xochitl!" It's Gladys, Abita's new caretaker lady. But she's not a lady. She's like Xochitl's age. A couple years older than me, a couple younger than Manny.

Hugs all around. She pats Manny's shoulder, smiles, and says, "It's a pleasure to meet you, Manuel."

He says hi and manages a decent smile back.

Xochitl and I walk inside. Manny doesn't. It looks like he's stuck in place. Like he's not coming in.

"Hey, Man," Xochitl says. "You coming?"

He shakes off a thought and forces a smile. "Yeah," he says. "Yes. I'm good."

Xochilt takes his hand and we enter together. I'm hit by the smells. The plastic sofa cover. The carpet. The cheesy soup simmering on the stove.

Gladys says, "Finally, I get to meet you guys. Doli talks about you nonstop. I feel like I know you already."

In the kitchen, the volume gets turned up on Juan Gabriel.

And Abita makes her entrance.

My *not-huggy* abuela throws her arms open and squeezes Xochitl tight. She's got on a sparkly blouse and her hair is cut so it comes down around her face instead of up in a tight bun, like she's always worn it. She's got some rosy cheeks put on. She looks years younger than the last time I saw her.

"¡Teodoro!" She kisses and hugs me and I'm like, *Who is this lady?* It's so weird I step back, but she pulls me in and hugs me again. "I been missing you, mijo," she says.

"I been," I say, "missing you, too."

122

Then she turns to Manny. *"Manuel."* She touches his face and kisses him all over. She wipes tears off her cheeks. Playfully slaps his cheeks. Says his name a bunch more times. She grabs him and holds on way longer than any Abita hug I've ever seen.

He laughs nervously and asks her how she's doing.

She says, "Ay, Manuel. I'm very good, mijo. Very good."

And that's a big deal, because as long as I can remember, a question like that would have been answered with a list of reasons why her life sucks, followed by a guilt trip about how you never visit.

"Where is my manners?" Abita says. And she introduces us to her amiga.

"Hi again," Gladys says. "Put your stuff down. Dinner's almost ready."

Xochitl asks Gladys how it's going with Abita.

Manny tells her she doesn't have to incriminate herself in front of *you know who.*

Abita points a bony finger. "I still got ears, Manuelito. Watch your step, soldier."

Gladys says she and Abita are doing great. "We're two peas in a pod," she says as she walks into the kitchen.

Abita points at her and says, "Esta Go-Go Gladys me tiene corriendo. She takes me dancing at the senior center. Hockey in Tri-Cities. *Hockey, mijitos!* A wine tour in Walla-Walla. I don't sit no more. No more novelas."

"You're looking good, Abita," Xochitl says.

"Ay, mija. I'm feeling good."

I can't believe it. I don't see Abita in a year and she's like a different person.

We sit for dinner. It looks as good as ever. I lean in to the bowl and breathe in that steam.

We been through so much this year. Now I'm smelling these smells again and it's like all the years of Abita's cooking add up to this thing in my brain that makes me feel like something—this one thing—is the way it's always been. She passes me a buttered-up tortilla and I feel that thing even more. My body in this old chair at this old table . . .

Gladys asks Abita what we were like as kids, and Abita tells our most humiliating stories. But it's different. She's got a sparkle in her eye as she tells about me falling into a kid's pool and just about drowning in ten inches of water. There's the story about my and Caleb's magician phase. It's funny the way she tells the stories, and everyone laughs.

Then Gladys asks how Mami and Papi met.

Xochitl and Manny start telling the story at the same time. Then they both stop and look at each other. Manny says, "You go," and Xochitl says, "No, no, you go."

"Mami worked at the perfume counter at the Nob Hill Kmart," Manny says. He looks at Gladys. Then away. He's shaking. His voice is shaking. "She was a senior in high school. Papi was picking onions out in Granger. Mami saw him walk in the Kmart door. . . . She just knew. . . ."

Manny checks in with Gladys as he tells the story. He smiles. She smiles back. He's quiet and slow. It's not easy for him. But he keeps on going.

Manny tells her Mami and Papi had a picnic at this boulder at the Yakima River. And it sounds crazy, but they started making plans right away. Then Papi told Mami he had to go soon. He had to follow the seasons. But he'd save money. They'd write letters every week. He'd come back in a few months. She'd graduate high school. They'd get married. He'd get his papers. Learn a trade. She had plans to go to college. They'd start a family. Mami waited for Papi. She made wedding plans. Plans to move away from Yakima.

"They met at that boulder a year later," he says, "and promised each other that, no matter what, they'd stay together forever."

Gladys looks at Manny all dreamy and says, "Awww. That is so sweet." She looks at Abita. "Isn't that sweet, Doli?"

"I was wrong," Abita says, superserious. "I told your mami she can't marry Daniel. I told her your papi is a maleducado nothing. Your mami says it didn't matter what I think. So I don't talk at the wedding. Ni una palabra. She and your papi move away. I still don't talk. I don't call. No letters. They try to talk. They try to call. But I don't—"

Xochitl reaches over. Grips Abita's hand. "That was a long time ago," she says.

"I almost lost your mami," Abita says. "I could have lost you."

"You came around," Xochitl says.

"I never tell your mami and papi I'm sorry."

"They know," Manny says.

"But I need to tell them, mijito. They need to hear it."

When Abita's second husband died, Mami and Papi came back and took care of the funeral arrangements and took care of her. They never mentioned how cruel Abita had been to them. And

Abita treated them like that grudge phase had never happened. And that was the start of them—then all of us—visiting Abita in Yakima every month.

It's unbelievable she opened up like that. Unbelievable she admitted she was wrong.

When Xochitl said *Abita's doing better*, I thought that meant she wasn't going to die. I didn't have any idea it meant Abita would be *nice*.

Abita isn't the only shocker.

I been watching Manny the whole night. His hands are shaking bad as ever. His eyelids look like they're stuck open wider than normal. He might look even older than he did the day he came home. But there was no craziness on the ride over. No craziness now. He looks like he's listening and like he's thinking about what people are saying. He's joking with Abita. He's sweet with Gladys. And the way he told the Mami and Papi story . . .

Maybe it's getting him out of the house. Getting him back to a place where our family spent so much time, and where—even with Abita being Abita—he always managed to have a good time.

When it's time for bed, Gladys takes off to a friend's place so we can have her room. There are two twin beds in there. I tell Xochitl I'll take the living room sofa and she and Manny can have the beds.

She says why don't we all cram in the room.

I look at her, trying to tell her there's no way I'm sleeping so close to Manny.

She says, "You take a bed, T. I'll get cozy on the floor. Right in between my bros."

I get tucked into one bed. Manny gets tucked into the other.

Then Xochitl sneaks in, holding a wooden box. She looks at Manny. "Are you thinking what I'm thinking?"

She empties the contents of Abita's ridiculous figurine collection onto Manny's bed and they proceed to use the figurines to re-create most of the first Pirates of the Caribbean movie. Xochitl does her Johnny Depp as Captain Jack impersonation and Manny is hilarious as just about every other character. Xochitl pokes Manny and reminds him how he used to say the wench lines and pushes him to say the silly stuff even sillier. I go in and out of sleep through the big showdown sword fight, a giggle fest that they try to stop over and over, and the shattering of a gnome figurine, followed by a bunch more giggling through attempts to repair said gnome and a ridiculous argument about how best to dispose of the evidence.

SATURDAY, JUNE 13, 2009

I wake up alive.

I'm exhausted after the late-night silliness. But that's fine because there was no slapping or punching of walls in the night. No clicking. No loud TV. No booze or weed. Nothing close to scary.

And Manny's still sleeping like a log.

Xochitl wasn't exaggerating. He's doing a lot better.

Gladys helps Abita make chilaquiles. Abita throws in some green chile—Tío Ed in New Mexico is her much younger brother, so she's got the chile hookup. It's a tasty consolation after missing out on my mom's burgers last night.

We pack up and say our good-byes. Abita kisses us all. Hugs Manny extra hard. Xochitl promises her we'll come back in a month.

Gladys gives Manny a hug. She tells him she'd like to keep in touch. They exchange numbers. Another hug. It's not awkward. Manny just goes with it.

And we're on our way.

I'm shocked I'm even thinking it, but I'll come back in a month. I'll come back for sure.

It's a quiet drive out to Butterfield Road. Then west on Terrace Heights Drive. Over the Yakima River, where Mami and Papi made their promises. Out to I-82 north toward I-90, where we'll head west, back home to south King County.

But Xochitl takes the ramp onto I-82 *south*.

I tell her she's going the wrong way.

"Oops," she says. "That's weird."

We've done this trip so many times there's no way that was an accident.

Xochitl says she'll turn around, then she misses every chance to do it.

"What the hell, Xoch? Turn around *now*."

She takes her eyes off the road and says, "You know what, T? I think we should pay ol' Florence Frank a visit."

Florence, Oregon, is seven hours away. "No way, Xoch. I'm not going there."

She clenches her jaw, eyes back on the road.

"I'm on shift today," I say. "I'll miss Bashir tomorrow. I gotta pay him either way. Take me home now."

Xochitl shushes me and points back at a sleeping Manny. "Things are looking up, T," she says. "But Manny's still got a long way to go. This trip to Abita's and to Frank's . . . We can connect him to good memories. Old friends. Ocean air. Help clear his head."

"That's great, Xochitl. Very supportive and sweet and cool. But I got stuff to get done this summer. And I can't do it if I lose my job."

"The timing sucks. But I need you here."

129

I tell her to let me out in Sunnyside. Maybe Caleb can get me.

"I can't do that," she says.

"Fine," I say. "Next time you stop, I'll just hop out and figure out how to get home."

"This is a family trip," she says. "So you're staying with us."

"When did a drive around the block become a family trip? And if it's a family trip, why aren't Mami and Papi here?"

"They have stuff they need to work on alone. And we have stuff *we* have to work on without them, so—"

"Xochitl, there is zero I need to work on with you or Florence Frank. And if you wanted me to come so badly—"

"You would have said—"

"I would have said there is no way in hell I'm going with you, Xochitl!"

There's no use. I've got enough in my account. I'll just bus it home from wherever.

Xochitl's phone rings. "Hello," she says. And she flashes me a creepy smirk. "I was expecting this call so much sooner. Really? Seriously? That is great!" she says. Her smirk turns into an evil smile. "We'll see you in a few hours, then, *Rebecca O'Brien, Wendy Martinez's mom.*"

Wendy.

Wendy.

Wendy in Florence.

I swallow but I can't, like, normal swallow cuz I'm trying to breathe and I can't get enough air and my hands are tingling and they're, like, numb, so I start hitting my legs to get feeling back while I choke in air, and I do that real loud.

"You all right?" Xochitl asks.

I'm gonna hug Wendy.

"It's hot," I say.

I'm gonna hug Wendy.

I'm boiling over, so I stick my head out the window and let the wind blow my face like a damn dog.

Xochitl pinches and tickles me as she sings, "Wendy Martinez—Gonna be in Flo-rence!" She yells into the back seat, "Hey, Man, Wendy's gonna be there!"

I scoot back in my seat and give a big *who cares?* shrug.

"Come on, T!" Xochitl shouts. "*Wendy Martinez!*"

It's been so long since we've been to Florence. And these two have no idea about me and Wendy. So I'm like, "Who is that? Who are you talking about? I don't think I know any Wendell Martinez."

Xochitl explodes a laugh right in my face. "Nice try, T!" She turns back and slaps Manny to life. "Did you hear that, Manny? Did you hear what T just said?"

No response.

"Manny, T's being a sonso. You're missing a great opportunity here."

He wipes his eyes and mumbles, "Don't be a sonso, T," and goes back to sleep.

"You're no fun, Man." Xochitl turns to me. "It's totally cool. If you don't want to go to Florence, we'll whip Sally around. Go home immediately. No stops."

"That's okay, Xoch," I say. "I guess this one quick stop in Florence is all right."

Xochitl slows the car, puts on her turn signal, teasing like she's pulling over. "You sure, bro? Cuz we don't have to."

131

"It's fine, Xoch," I tell her. "We'll go to Florence. For Manny."

"*For Manny.* You're the bestest brother in the whole wide world, Teodoro Avila."

I text Caleb and ask him to cover my Sunday shift at Vince's. He says he'll try. I call Bashir and tell him we can't meet till Monday.

I start imagining a weekend with Wendy. I try hard to imagine myself saying all the right things. But I can't imagine what those things are.

We make our way south, down I-82. At Toppenish, we switch to US 97 and drive through the brown rolling hills of the Yakama Nation, then past sleepy Goldendale.

The Sam Hill Memorial Bridge reaches way out over the Columbia River, into the desert of eastern Oregon. Over that bridge and we'll start west. We'll leave the brown and enter forest again. Then it's not far to the coast. *Not far to Wendy.*

We're driving up the span and in a minute Xochitl's pumping the gas, pounding the steering wheel. "I got no power, Manny!"

Manny leans himself into the front seat and calmly says, "It's gonna make it to the high spot. Just keep your foot away from the brake."

"It's not going to make it, Manny."

"Do not touch that brake, Xoch."

I look behind. A truck is right on our tail. The driver lays on the horn.

Xochitl's gonna have to brake, or we'll start coasting backward.

She says, "What now, Manny?"

And the second she says it, some sort of magic intervenes and we loop over and start heading downhill. We pick up speed rolling over the Columbia, into Oregon, then slow again as we coast under the I-84 overpass. Xochitl pulls to the side of the road. She lets out a long sigh and turns to Manny. "Do your thing, bro."

I have to get air, so I follow Manny out of the car. He grabs a toolbox from the back—Papi's old kit.

I take in a lungful of truck exhaust and dust as I watch Manny fiddle under the hood. He wrenches stuff. Yanks stuff. Hums. Pours in water. Eventually, he makes a hop toward the front door.

I remember that hop from Manny's Mustang days. He's gonna turn the key.

He pulls the door open, steps his right foot inside.

I cross *all* my fingers because if the spark lights and the crank catches and that engine revs to life, I'm on my way to Wendy.

Sally fires right up. Manny sticks out his tongue and holds up his shaking hand, flashing us the international headbanger's symbol for *Rock 'n' roll!*

Xochitl apologizes to me for the delay. Then she makes a crack about getting us to Florence so Wendy can chase me around like old times.

I tell Xochitl she's hilarious, and I think the conversation is over, but she says, "You know, T, after Florence—"

"We're gonna drive straight home and thanks for that, Xochitl."

She ignores me and asks if I remember Mami's cousin Elena.

"Elena? Isn't she, like, Mami's eighth cousin or something?"

"They're second cousins," she says. "Elena's son, Rudi, was killed in Afghanistan. There's a funeral. And Manny wants to go."

"You never said a word about this."

"Mami told Elena the three of us would be there."

"When were you planning on telling me?"

"Mami called last night. After you fell asleep."

"That sounds like a lie, Xochitl. And there's no way I'm going."

"He needs to do this, T. So I'm taking him. And I need you in the car."

We watch him toss the toolkit in back and slam the tailgate. He looks our way. Shoots us a classic Manny smile and a thumbs-up.

He is trying so hard.

I ask Xochitl where the funeral is.

"It's just outside of Florence a bit," she says. "In this town called Delano. A couple hours to get there. Tops."

She says we'll just be in Florence for tonight and tomorrow. Then it's Delano and we'll head back Monday after the funeral.

"No stops?" I say.

"We're headed back as fast as we possibly can." Xochitl extends her hand for a shake. "We'll be home middle of the night Monday, early Tuesday morning, at the latest."

My next shift isn't until Tuesday afternoon. I can meet up with Bashir on Wednesday. Then we've got the whole summer.

I do not wanna go to the funeral of a distant cousin I never knew.

I do not want to be so far from home.

I do not want to keep postponing everything I need to get done.

I close my eyes. Breathe in as deep as I can.

I let it go.

I tell myself this is for Manny. And Mami. And it's the right thing to do.

Xochitl knocks on Frank O'Brien's door.

I'm sweating buckets, clutching a tiny box in my pocket. We did a little shopping on the way through Old Town. Xochitl, for saltwater taffy and talk of great memories with Manny. Me, for the secret purchase of a little shells-and-beads bracelet for Wendy. I had set aside a tiny bit of my tutor cash for a possible dinner out with Wendy, the night of her concert. That didn't happen, so . . .

Frank opens up and hollers, "Where you been all my life, Avilas?" He bear-hugs each of us. Tells us how grown-up we all look. And he gives Manny some extra man pats on the back. "Welcome home, soldier." He turns and walks. "Come on, y'all."

As we follow Frank, my stomach jumps into my throat and I'm boiling over cuz I'm finally gonna see her.

But before we can drop our stuff in our rooms and go find Wendy, Xochitl stops and grabs me by the arm. She points back toward the front door.

Manny didn't walk in with us.

I follow Xochitl. The door is still open and he's stuck standing out there, breathing hard.

"Hey, Manuel," Xochitl says.

"Hi," he says.

She gets on one side of him and holds his arm. It seems like it makes him feel better, so I go hold his other arm—whatever I can do to get him inside so Wendy doesn't see this.

"It's Frank's place," Xochitl says. "Same as always."

"Right," he says. He forces another smile. "I don't know what I'm doing out here." He laughs. "So it's safe in there, right?"

"Yeah, Man. It's safe."

"So let's get in there," he says. "Right?"

"I think that's a great idea."

We walk in all together, shoulder to shoulder. Real slow. And I'm wondering what happened. He seemed fine up until now. We drop our stuff off and Xochitl takes Manny's hand again. He's hesitant but we manage to walk through the living room, toward the deck. Windows and doors are open. Bright sun and cool breeze and sounds and smells of salmon burgers sizzling on the grill.

Frank's wife, Tabitha, is so happy she's practically crying. It's weird, because when I think of Frank's wife, I picture Raquel, who died four or five years ago. Tabitha's emotion is too much for Manny to take, so he nods and walks right past her.

I smile at her and make a beeline for the deck.

And sitting in the Adirondack chair in the shadow of Frank's big old cedar tree is Wendy Martinez.

Those tingles hit me again. Full-body this time. And sharp.

I can't do anything about it because I freeze. Seriously, I . . .

Cannot.

Move.

Wendy chomps into a massive salmon burger at the same time as her eyes catch mine. The bite is way too big. She's got squirrel cheeks full of burger and a fat dollop of tartar sauce clinging to her chin. She starts giggling at me and tiny salmon chunks shoot out and she plays horrified over the whole thing.

And I'm fighting to bend up the corners of my lips and make a smile.

She runs inside to take care of the situation, popping me one in the shoulder as she goes.

Xochitl leans into me and reminds me to breathe.

It's a good idea, so I try it.

Rebecca O'Brien gives me a hug. "Teodoro, it's great to see you again." She hugs Manny and Xochitl and asks about our trip down. And she asks about Mami and Papi.

In a sec, Wendy's back, saying, "Heckuva big old awkward burger, Frank."

She says hi to Manny and Xochitl, then yanks me inside. "How's it going, Teodoro?"

Aw, man. The way she says my name. I breathe deep and manage to say, "It's good. I'm here. Good. And you?"

She says, "I was stoked when Xochitl called and told us you guys were going to be here."

"Xochitl called you?"

As I say it, Wendy Martinez wraps me up in a squeeze.

I wrap my arms all the way around her and squeeze right back.

Oh.

My.

God. I can feel her pulling away, but I can't let go.

"All right," Wendy says. "Hug and release."

I release.

"And breathe," she says. "There ya go, buddy." She gives me another slug in the arm. "Let's get back out there. I know Frank's been waiting to see you guys."

I waited so long.

So long.

Then I screw it all up with a creepy, clingy hug.

I end up in a chair across the flames from Wendy. And her mom.

And I stare out at the ocean, wondering how I became such a dope.

She shouts, "Look alive, Avila!" and pegs me with a pinecone. And laughs right at me.

I shake a fist in the air. "I will get my revenge!"

She goes, "Ha! We'll see about that, mister."

All is not lost!

Tabitha tells Manny she's relieved he got home safe. "Frank and I got sick worrying about you over there. The *news* . . . Oh my God . . . it was unbearable."

Manny scrunches his eyebrows all serious and nods a bunch of times while she goes on about how horrible it was to watch war coverage on TV. He finally cuts her off and goes, "That sounds like a nightmare, Tabitha. I can't even imagine it."

Frank holds out a frosty beer bottle for Manny.

Manny takes it and Xochitl says, "Seriously, Frank?" She says it like she's playing, but it's obvious she's not.

"Xoch." Manny glares at her.

"We talked about this, Frank," she says.

"Cooler's near empty," he says. "We'll be cut off pretty quick."

Xochitl tells him "pretty quick" better be pretty quick.

"Enough, Xochitl." Manny says it like he's about to boil over.

I roll my cyes all goofy at Wendy, trying to distract her from this awkward moment. She grins and shakes her head like she's telling me not to worry about it.

"We had a deal, Man," Xochitl tells him.

"That's fine," he says. And he walks over to the cooler and thrusts both hands in the ice and pulls them back out, gripping a shaking bottle in each one. "Thanks for the beers, Frank."

Frank holds out a bottle for Xochitl and says, "Trust me kid; we won't go overboard on the booze tonight. We good here?"

Xochitl throws Manny a worried look.

Manny throws the look right back. Then he smiles like he's promising everything is going to be okay.

Xochitl sighs. She takes the bottle. "We're always good, Frank." And she gives him an exaggerated kiss on the cheek and takes a seat.

"Attagirl," Frank says.

In a minute, Xochitl's got Frank going on his old stories about Papi and the characters they used to work with at Fauntleroy Fabrication.

It's not long before Manny clears his throat and says, "How about the thumb story, Frank?"

Frank raises his left hand. Shows off his half thumb. "You mean this old nub?"

Tabitha says, "We're eating, Frank. I don't think—"

"Aw, who's it going to hurt, babe?"

Xochitl starts chanting, *"Nub! Nub! Nub!"*

Manny smiles big. *"Nub! Nub! Nub!"*

Wendy and I join in. Even her mom can't help but laugh.

"The people have spoken," Frank says to thunderous applause and hooting.

He tells about working at Fauntleroy during a rush to get out parts for the Boeing 727. He comes into work and fires up the band saw to train an apprentice on safety procedures. But for some reason, he loses focus, takes his eyes off his job, and . . .

Frank gives a bloodcurdling holler as he reenacts the moment.

Groans of disgust all around. Manny lifts a shaking hand to wipe a tear, he's laughing so hard. And he keeps laughing uncontrollably way after everyone else has stopped. It's funny at first. Then it's just awkward.

Frank doesn't see it that way, so "The Tale of the Tiny Thumb" is just the first in a series of gruesome, bloody shop stories.

Before we know it the sun has set and the moon and stars are doing their thing. Wendy looks my way over the dancing flames. Then she stands up in a way that says, *You're coming with me.*

She kisses her mom on the cheek and turns to walk, but Rebecca grabs her arm and pulls her in. She looks a lecture right into Wendy, then looks at me like, *Have fun. But don't you dare have too much fun.*

I follow Wendy into the house. She pulls a sweater off a hook by the front door. "We'll get a better view of the stars away from the fire. Sound good?"

Uh-huh.

We walk the streets of Florence. Wendy talks about school and her future. Then she apologizes for doing that again and says, "You ever think about the day we ran into each other?"

I tell her I think about it all the time. I tell her I think that day was meant to happen. "It was like running into you was part of a big cosmic plan."

Wendy knocks her shoulder into mine.

I knock shoulders back. "And us coming to Florence? And this walk under these stars? It's all part of the plan."

It'd be a perfect time to stop talking. Because this night is amazing enough. The moon lighting up the sandbar on the bay. Its reflection flickering in the tide. Families licking cones at Al's Ice Cream. An old couple holding hands just ahead of us. Me and Wendy following, walking at their slow pace. Wendy, smiling, saying there's no place she'd rather be.

I can't help myself.

I tell Wendy that her eyes are beautiful. Serious and fun at the same time. I tell her I love hearing her talk. About life plans and the majestic tuba. All the goofy random ideas she comes up with. I tell her I know she liked me when we were kids. But I never imagined we'd get to a moment like this.

Wendy takes my hand in hers—*Oh, man, it's warm.* "Teodoro, I've imagined it."

Jazz saxophone floats out of a bar, and the old man of that old couple . . . he stops walking. And he wraps his arm around the old lady's waist.

She turns to him with a way-serious face.

Wendy and I look at each other like, *What's going on?* And we watch.

Then the old lady thrusts a hand high in the air.

The man clasps it. Holds it up there. He looks into her eyes, his nose touching hers, and then—I don't know who starts it— but they do like eight intense steps of a tango, or something. And at the end of the steps, the old man freaking *dips her*! And he holds her in the dip, so she could be looking up at the stars, but she's not. She's got her eyes locked on his eyes. And all the old lady says is,

141

"*Oh, my.*" And she giggles. The man pulls her up and they walk the streets of Old Town Florence, Oregon, like it never happened.

We start walking quiet, and I can't help but think that dip happened for a reason. It's like that old couple is a future Mami and Papi—like from another dimension. From a place where they've been allowed to go on, living happy lives together, growing old without wars or bad economies getting in the way of their romance.

And they've traveled back through space and time to Florence, Oregon, to deliver a message about love.

I reach in my pocket and pull out the little cardboard box.

"It's not much," I say.

Wendy opens it slow. Pulls out the bracelet. She lifts her smiling eyes as she hands it over and holds out her wrist.

I slide the bracelet over her fingers and hand. I fumble with the clasp till I finally get it.

"Looks good," she says.

"You think so? I was choosing between this one and one with these shiny—"

Wendy reaches for the back of my head and pulls it down toward hers, and I go with it, and we don't stop till our lips are squishing.

I am kissing Wendy Martinez.

Or she's kissing me and I'm kissing her back—the technicalities are not important.

What's important is my whole body is zapped alive like I been struck by a bolt of lightning. The good kind.

We separate lips and I say, "I didn't expect—"

"Stop words," she says. And we go back at it.

We share an Al's chocolate cone, kissing. We kiss on a rusted bus bench. On the warm hood of a parked limo. We leave Old Town and head up residential streets as we stumble back toward Frank's and kiss on, like, five residences' dewy lawns. We kiss at the end of Frank's driveway, feeling that Florence breeze. Smelling ocean salt and grill smoke as we kiss. Kissing up against Frank's garage. Smelling hair and sweat. Feeling warm breath on faces. Fingers in hair. Hands squeezing hips. Palms on cheeks, palms squeezing cheeks, not letting 'em go as we kiss at Frank's front door.

"Oh, my," she finally says.

"Got that right," I say. It's stupid, but what else do you say when your wildest dream comes true?

We head inside and back to the deck, walking the way people who've just been kissing walk. Hoping no one notices. Hoping a little bit that everyone notices.

Rebecca stands and says she can't stay awake another minute. She flashes the two of us another *Watch your step* look, then wishes everyone a good night.

Manny's got a clown smile pasted on his red face as he finishes off a beer. Frank's cooler didn't cut them off as fast as he'd promised.

Frank points at me. "Your daddy . . ." he shouts so loud they can probably hear him in Old Town. "That son of a bitch still owes me fifty bucks." He tosses me a beer and motions for us to take a seat. He looks up at the stars and says, "Big Dipper tonight. Beautiful. That's Raquel smiling down on us."

Xochitl looks over at Tabitha and real quick asks Frank why Papi owes him fifty bucks.

"If memory serves me right . . . I could tell ya," he says. "But it don't."

Frank looks sad about not remembering. Then he points his bottle at each of us and says, "Avilas, when you get back home, I want you to tell that bastard father of yours this: Daniel, you don't owe Florence Frank nothin'."

Then Frank explains that back in the days when he drank real heavy, it got so bad that Raquel kicked him out of the house. Papi and Mami took him in while he sobered up and Papi managed things at Fauntleroy till Frank was ready to get back to work.

Manny starts talking now. He says he remembers that time. He remembers Frank and Mami taking him for a walk at Angle Lake, Mami waddling because Xochitl was about to be born. He remembers Frank taking him for ice cream and trying to teach him checkers.

I love that picture of Mami, and I love it that Manny has held on to those memories and that he's telling stories. Under these stars. Around this fire.

"Your parents . . ." Frank says. "They loved each other so much it created a bunch of new love. They used some of it to take care of me and to save my marriage. And they used it to raise you kids."

It sounds so cheesy. But that's what beer does to Florence Frank. Beer and love.

Wendy gives my hand a squeeze and nods for us to leave.

We walk in the house. Head up toward her room. Outside the door, we hug tight and long, then pull in a same-time breath—again, just like at the HUB—but this time it's not too much for us and we don't let go.

Wendy looks up. She holds her wrist and the bracelet for me to see. "I love it, Teodoro."

"It's nothing, really. I mean—"

"You mean it's a present that says we're more than friends?"

"Uh-huh."

"And do you mean it says we'll try to be more than friends for . . . for as long as we can try?"

"Uh-huh."

"Then it's not nothing, really. It's actually something."

Wendy reaches up and gives me a soft one on the lips. "Sweet dreams, Teodoro."

"Sweet dreams, Wendy."

SUNDAY,
JUNE 14, 2009

Early morning, Wendy sneaks in and wakes me up. We tiptoe out the house and head downhill toward the water, toward Old Town and Rosebud Bakery.

We hold hands, that bracelet dangling between our wrists. There's some kissing but mostly fast walking, then skipping and giggling, then running and squealing, because we're both starving like mad and Rosebud has the best cinnamon rolls in the whole world.

We sit across a table, smiles pasted on our faces, just looking at each other and looking out at the street and the same sidewalk we strolled last night.

I tell Wendy how amazing it all is. How beautiful her face is. Her ears. Her cheeks. How lucky I feel.

Those cheeks turn red on cue. She looks down at her bracelet. Then up at me, like she's got news.

"What, Wendy?"

"Teodoro, remember when I texted you that I was fighting with my mom?"

I tell her I do.

"It was because I was considering going to San Francisco. In a couple weeks. From now. For the rest of summer. But maybe for the school year."

"The whole year?"

"My dad is an adjunct art instructor at this private high school and he got me in. So I might, like, you know, maybe, probably do senior year there."

That sucks the wind right out of me.

I lay my head on the table.

She stands and reaches over and lifts my chin. I sit up and she plants her lips on my cheek. "We'll text and talk. I'll visit you. And maybe you can come down? I'm going to San Francisco, Teodoro . . . but I'm not going anywhere."

"You're killing me Wendy. Vancouver isn't that far. We could have been kissing next year. Like a lot."

"Oh, Teodoro, I know."

"Then why?"

"It feels like, with college coming up, it's my last chance to get to know him. Like, really know him."

Wendy says she sees Mike Martinez once or twice a year, but only for a couple days at a time. He's a semifamous sculptor. He repurposes trashed cars, buses, planes . . . and he turns them into masterpieces. "Totally inspiring," she says. "But I spend too much time wishing I had a regular ol' dad in Vancouver instead of an inspiring artist in San Francisco."

"I get it," I say. But it comes out sounding like I don't.

"I have to do this," she says. "For me and my dad. And I need to break out of my Vancouver life. To break out of the grind . . . *my mom* . . . I can't wait till college."

"Is she okay with this?"

"We have a complicated relationship, Teodoro. Lots of drama around this dad stuff, the me-becoming-an-independent-human-being stuff."

I ask Wendy what happened between her parents.

She says they were once in love with each other. Her dad was this passionate young artist. But after Wendy came along, her mom needed stability. Someone to take care of the family. Her dad and his friends drank and partied a lot. Her mom hated that part of his life. So they fought a ton. Wendy thinks he even hit her mom a couple times. At some point he tried hard to settle down— to make being a husband and dad work. He got a job. Wore a suit. Mowed the lawn.

"But that wasn't the life he wanted," Wendy says. "He had a dream. And he thought we were in the way of it." She takes a big breath and blows it out from puffed cheeks. "So he left." She looks in my face and sees her story has me twisted up a bit. So she puts her hands on my hands and says, "You all right?"

I tell her I'm good.

I don't tell her I wanna punch her dad in the mouth. I don't tell her I think he's just going to disappoint her again, so she should stay home.

And I don't tell her I think I understand her dad just a tiny bit. Not the hitting part. Not the leaving-his-family-for-good part. But the dreams part.

"What, Teodoro? What is all that thinking?"

"I don't know, Wendy. You still have hopes for him?"

"I'm pretty sure there's a piece of my mom that's never given up on my dad."

148

"What about you?"

"It's embarrassing, but the truth is, I can't stop hoping he'll remember my birthday, or call for no reason, or pay a little support. Not because of the money, but—"

"I get it, Wendy."

"It's like my mom and I can't get over the idea that he might start doing that stuff, because we don't want to feel *left*. He walked out, but something in my little-kid heart wants to believe that can be undone. It's stupid."

"It's not stupid."

"Okay, not stupid. But it messes with me sometimes. Like when you texted that stuff about your brother and sister. And I shut you out a little bit. I'm sorry I did that. I know you didn't mean anything. I know you were trying to support me. But I have this habit of measuring people I might care about against this ideal."

"What's the ideal?"

"The opposite of my dad."

"I get that."

"And it's your parents. The memory of them from when we were little. Is that weird?"

"It's not, Wendy." I look at her looking at me, smiling with those eyes.

The idea of her thinking about Mami and Papi that way is a little weird. I get it, though. Cuz when she knew them they were happy. And she has no idea how much they've changed.

Our rolls arrive and Wendy's face lights up. There's steam and cinnamon smell and Wendy swipes a finger in the glaze and freaking puts it up to my mouth.

Okay.

I go in for the lick, but she pulls her finger, then wipes my nose with it. She falls back in her chair, laughing. "Got you!"

I grab a napkin. "Yeah, you got me, Wendy."

We dig in and it turns out there's something about someone you really, really like, eating something that tastes so damn good and letting you see just how good it makes them feel.

That is a new thing.

Wendy puts down her roll and points a finger in the air as she finishes chewing and swallowing, then wiping her face.

"Yes, Ms. Martinez?"

"I think maybe I drove you nuts when we were kids."

"You didn't."

"Liar! I drove you nuts!"

"You drove me up the wall!"

"I know! And the more I bugged you, the more you made it clear you weren't going anywhere. You were going to stay put and let me be my nutty self."

"Wow, Wendy."

"I never forgot that. Then after we didn't see you for so long, I started feeling like an idiot for the way I treated you. And I convinced myself I never wanted to see you again."

She leans in and kisses my cheek. "Then U-Dub happened. And we just clicked."

"Yeah," I say. "A lot of stuff clicked."

She smiles and scoots closer for a kiss.

I accept that kiss.

Then I stop. Because I have to quit pretending.

I take a huge breath and say, "Um . . ."

"Yeah, Teodoro?"

"I was not checking out U-Dub that day. It was not on my list of colleges because I didn't have a list. I was a C-and-D student with no path to college."

No response.

"But now I have a report card with As and Bs in honors. And I fully intend to do everything in my power to keep our pact."

"Teodoro," she says real slow. "I wouldn't have judged if you had told me the truth."

"Wendy, seeing you. Hearing about what you were doing . . . You made me want to take charge of my life. So I did. Now I don't wanna assume everything is gonna work itself out anymore. I want to make it happen. I want to learn stuff. I want to learn everything. I want to take myself as far as I possibly can."

"You could have told me."

"I know. I'm sorry. I shouldn't have lied. And I had plenty of chances to tell you later, but I was happier with the person I was trying to be than the one I'd been before, so . . ."

"Wow, Teodoro." And the *wow* is not like, *Wow, that sunset is amazing.* It's more like the kind of *wow* you say after someone hands you a very large slice of fruitcake at a Christmas party. And it feels like Wendy's gonna bust me up for being a liar. And I think life would have gone on just fine if I had never told Wendy the truth. "I think I understand," she says. "But I need you to know you don't ever have to impress me. And I don't believe you made that change because of me. It's sweet to say. But you made the change because you wanted to and because you were ready."

"That might be true," I say. "But maybe I needed someone to light a fire."

"I can buy that," she says. And her face breaks into a big smile and she looks at me like she's proud. "That is a serious turnaround, Teodoro."

"It hasn't been easy, Wendy. But I set my goals, you know?"

"You really did."

"And I'm going for it." I hug her again. And something about coming clean like that. The hug feels even deeper. Like we know each other even better. Then the hug ends and I say, "These cinnamon rolls as good as you remember?"

"Yeah, Teodoro. Maybe better."

She digs into her roll and asks me about our trip.

"What trip?" I say.

"The trip you're on. For Manny."

"Oh, right. *This* trip," I say. I tell her how good Abita's was and how unbelievable Florence has been. I tell her I'm a little weirded out about the funeral for our distant cousin, but I get why we have to do it.

"And the rest of the trip?"

"That's it. That's the whole trip."

"Really?"

Wendy's phone buzzes.

"Yeah, that's it."

She looks at her phone. "My mom. Time to go."

It's a slow walk to Frank's. More kissing. More talking. About the rest of the summer. About the year ahead. How we're going to keep in touch. We decide to try and write old-fashioned letters and postcards to each other.

Wendy says that since our trip is coming to an end, and we're going home, we should meet up before she takes off. "Can you come down Thursday? Real early?"

"For sure, Wendy."

"Pick me up in Vancouver and we can spend a day in Portland?"

"That would be awesome."

Wendy makes a list of all the places where we just *have to kiss*. Multnomah Falls, Council Crest Park, Powell's Books—the mystery section—the rose gardens, the Chinese gardens . . . We'll try to pack a year's worth of experiences . . . a year's worth of kissing into one day.

Something about that plan, that one day together, makes the idea of Wendy going away for the summer—and maybe for the whole year—just a little tiny bit less horrible.

It's late afternoon when I slide into the driver's seat. Xochitl's up front. Manny's in the back.

Wendy is standing at the driveway by her mom, Uncle Frank, and Tabitha. She's waving, sending me love with those eyes.

I'm wired, thinking Thursday morning cannot come fast enough.

And sick that Thursday night is coming way too fast.

I turn the key and shift into reverse.

Xochitl tells me to wait. She opens the door and walks up to Wendy. She pulls her to the side. Xochitl tells her a bunch of stuff and Wendy's smiling but scrunching her shoulders, like trying to say she doesn't know.

Finally, Xochitl gives Wendy a hug and turns back toward the car.

"Do you know what that's about, Man?"

No response, so I check out the back seat.

Manny is crashed out. Just like that.

Xochitl gets in the car.

"What were you two talking about, Xoch?"

My sister gives me a blank stare for a second. Then she says, "I just thought . . . we should do this again. Like later in the summer. But Wendy said she's headed for San Fran. Right?"

"Yeah, Xoch."

"After her date with you . . . on Thursday, right?"

"Yeah."

"So when we come back, Wendy won't be here. That's all."

She gives me directions and says she's gonna nap.

It's a quiet drive south on US 101. Then Highway 138 and over to I-5 South. A couple hours of highway driving. A couple hours of me replaying every second with Wendy. Trying to lock it in my memory forever.

At some point, we leave the valley and farmland and start uphill toward the mountains. We make a gas stop in Ashland. Xochitl yawns and stretches. Says she'll drive.

I tell her I'm fine, but she insists. "I got this last little leg to Delano, T."

We pull back on the freeway and I tell her I haven't seen any signs for Delano.

"You won't," she says. "It's a really small town." And she says I might wanna catch a quick nap before we get there.

I close my eyes and try to sleep.

But I can't.

Cuz Wendy.

154

And Manny. I tell Xochitl he seems like he's doing way better.

"Yeah," she says. But it comes out sounding more like a *maybe.*

So I ask what's going on.

Xochitl starts talking about the VA. She and Papi took Manny there. Xochitl says he liked his doctor a lot. She was positive and concerned for Manny. Then she started asking questions and talking paperwork.

Xochitl says Manny stormed out of the VA saying stuff about how the questions got too personal and the paperwork was ridiculous and he just seemed overwhelmed.

"So," Xochitl says, "Manny won't go back to the VA."

"Then where'd he get the meds I saw him popping at Abita's?"

"From his weed connection, Lucas. Manny told him his back and head were hurting. So loser started adding Oxycontin to Manny's regular delivery. Seroquel, too. The good part is there are *ups* now. And Manny acts like a hypermanic version of his old self."

"And the bad part?"

"When he comes down he crashes hard. And when he's not sleeping, he can get superdepressed . . . or ugly and mean. And you're not supposed to mix any of those drugs with alcohol."

"Damn, Xochitl!" I unhook my belt. Swivel back and over the seat. I shake Manny till he finally comes to and mumbles a bunch of stuff I can't understand.

He's alive.

I drop into my seat. Elbows on my knees. Head in my hands. "What do we do?"

"Let him sleep it off."

I tell her we have to get rid of his drugs.

"I've tried," she says. "It's bad."

"Then why the hell did you let him drink?"

"He told me he'd stay off the pills in Florence."

"Oh my God—and you believed him?"

"I'm doing my best, T."

"That's the problem, Xochitl."

She shoots me a look, then turns to the road, straightening her arms, pushing against the steering wheel. She exhales through pressed lips and nods her head up and down.

"I didn't mean it like that, Xochitl."

"What did you mean, then?"

"I meant . . . Manny needs *real* help. And we are not it."

"You're right. But all we can do is keep trying till we figure it out."

She says it like driving our knocked-out, PTSD brother all over the country in a falling-apart, ancient car is a perfectly reasonable approach.

And *that* is why I do not live at home anymore.

And why I need to get out of this car.

And why I need to get back to Caleb's place.

We're thick into evergreens and gaining elevation fast. I need to take my mind off everything, so I switch the knob on the radio. Nothing but fuzz. I collapse back in my seat.

"It's never worked," Xochitl says. "If you want, I can—"

"Yeah, Xoch."

She starts quiet.

How can I go home

Aw, hell. It's Ani DiFranco.

with nothing to say?

I reach for the dial and spin.

Take me out tonight

Where there's music and there's people

Morrissey—the way Xochitl sings Morrissey makes me miss Wendy more than I can stand. I press the power button.

Xochitl keeps her eyes on the road and says, "Hot date with Wendy, huh?"

"Yeah. If you want to call it that."

"Come on, T. It's obvious you two lovebirds *están enamorados*." She exaggerates the pronunciation, like she's an actress in a novela. Then she goes in for the cheek pinch.

I knock her hand away.

"That girl is something, T. I don't know how you made it happen. But I'm impressed."

I tell Xochitl I can't wait to see Wendy again. And I can't believe she's going away so soon. And she might be gone for a whole year. And how do you spend so much time so far apart? And then come together again? How does that work?"

"It sucks. But Mami and Papi did it."

It's true. Mami and Papi were apart that year. Then they came together. They got married. They had kids. And we were the happiest little family. And that's where everyone puts "The End" when they tell the story.

But that story didn't end. And I don't want to think about me and Wendy like that.

157

I turn to Xochitl and ask her for a Ray Is a Girl song.

"Nah, T."

"Come on, Xoch."

"Those songs aren't mine anymore."

"What does that mean?"

"It means I quit Ray."

"No, you did not."

"Yes, I did."

My gut tightens. Everything tightens. I pound the door with my fist. "That is the most insane—those guys were once in a life-time, Xoch!"

"I don't believe that."

"Come on!" I slap the dash. "I've seen enough bands—seen you quit enough bands—to know that even once is lucky."

"Ray was great. And I was great with them. So?"

"*So?* You had a dream. And you dumped it in the trash. And it makes me sick."

"What was I supposed to do?"

"Not quit! That's the easiest solution to a problem that didn't exist!"

"Are you serious, T?"

"What are you talking about, Xoch?"

She tells me to shake Manny.

I shake him. More mumbles. Then he's back out hard.

"Manny?" Xochitl says. "You hear me, Man?"

Nothing.

Xochitl talks quiet. "I was at rehearsal the night Manny punched through your wall. I wasn't there and he could have hurt you. And you ran. And now you don't live with us."

I look away. Roll down the window.

"I am it, T. You hear me?"

I breathe deep in the blast of air.

"Papi's too busy treating Manny like he's a grown-up who can make his own decisions—which is irrelevant because Manny's fighting PTSD, not a damn midlife crisis. Mami is too busy blaming Papi and they're too angry at each other to do anything. I cannot handle them and take care of Manny by myself *and* be in a band. Even if it is the best band in the history of the world."

"I'm sorry, Xoch."

"I'm not blaming you."

"You are a little."

"It's great what you're doing, T. I'm proud of you. You have every right to go for it—"

"My God! You do, too, Xochitl!"

"Fine! But you do not get to judge me for making this choice."

I look out at the road. Headlights approaching slowly. Then shooting past in a blur. I think about all the years Manny was gone. Mami and Papi were going downhill. And I was lost. Xochitl's singing was the one thing we had. The one thing that made us special.

Now who are we?

Who is she?

She's the person fighting to hold everything together at home. And failing.

I close my eyes and try to sleep.

Xochitl starts again.

Tengo un pobre corazón

Que a veces se rompió

It's Alejandra Guzmán, her heart breaking, but never surrendering. Xochitl doesn't sing it like a power ballad this time. She sings it like a lullaby. She sings that song over and over until I'm out.

MONDAY, JUNE 15, 2009

A honking eighteen-wheeler shakes me awake.

I check on Manny again. Jostle him till he makes sounds.

I turn to Xochitl. "It feels late. What time is it?"

"Two thirty."

"Are you lost? You said Delano was close."

She just stares at the road.

"How far is it, Xochitl?"

"We have a ways to go."

"How far?"

"A few hundred miles."

"We've driven a few hundred already."

"It's a few hundred more."

I gasp for a breath. I try to talk but nothing comes out.

"You wouldn't have come, T."

Then it comes out loud. "Is Delano in Texas? Mexico?"

"Your geography sucks!" she says.

"Liars suck worse, Xochitl! And you're a liar."

She tells me Delano is in Southern California.

My head starts throbbing as my mind is flooded with images:

My manager yelling at me at Vince's.

Bashir waiting for me at the library, checking his watch.

Me bussing Caleb's table at Vince's. He's wearing a U-Dub sweat-shirt, stuffing his face with pizza, going on and on about how great college is.

Wendy alone in the Powell's mystery section.

Wendy graduating from the University of Washington with-out me.

Dr. Wendy Martinez at the altar, kissing some tool surgeon named Brad.

Manny's fist popping through the wall. Grabbing me by the shirt, pulling me into his room through the hole.

I fire off f-bombs. Coil back into the seat. Explode a kick into the glove box. "Stop the car, Xoch!"

"We're in the middle of nowhere!"

I kick that box over and over. "I gotta get home! Stop the car!"

"Manny's sleeping," she says. "Don't make me do this."

I keep kicking. Keep yelling at her to stop, stop, stop!

Xochitl stomps the brake and throws us into a fishtail skid.

We slide in the gravel till the brakes catch and Sally stops cold.

My belt grabs me at the waist.

My torso shoots forward.

My head pops the dash.

Manny's body slams my seat.

Then the ricochet and my head smashes back into the headrest.

Boom-boom. Boom-boom.

I touch my face.

Boom-boom. Boom-boom.

There's blood.

And a hammer tapping my skull.

I look up and see so many pairs of lights for the one car coming our way.

Manny's in the well between the front and back seats.

Xochitl asks him if he's okay.

"I'm awesome, Xoch. We stopping?"

He felt nothing. He felt nothing.

"T has to pee," she says. "Go back to sleep."

She jumps out the car. Flings my door open. Yanks me by the arm. Pulls me out and stands me up against the fender. Grips my shirt with a fist to keep me from falling.

"I need you, T."

"My head's busted, Xochitl."

"You're fine," she says.

"You keep lying to me," I say.

She yanks my arm again. Walks me away from the car. I stumble because the ground keeps moving. "I've got you," she says.

"Where we going?" I say.

"Away from Manny."

The crunch of gravel and dry grass. Crickets so damn loud. A semitruck rumbles past. A hurricane blast of heat and dust.

Xochitl pulls a yellow wad of paper out of her jeans pocket. Unfolds it. Shoves it in my face. "Read fast," she says. "Before Manny gets up. *Read it!*"

I fight the throbs and blur till the writing slips into focus.

Dear Mami and Papi,

I want you to know that this is no one's fault. Nobody could have done anything any different. I saw too much over there. I did too much. I learned how to be a way that I can't stop being. I know it doesn't look like it, but I been trying SO HARD. I've been fighting to get me back, but it's impossible because the old Manny died in Iraq and nothing is going to change that. I'm so tired I can't fight anymore. This is relief. I'm free now. I'm with Grandpa Tito, playing poker and drinking tequila. I'm not fighting the noise every second I'm awake and every second I'm asleep. The noise is gone. I'm all right now. I'm not going to hurt anyone. This is peace. I want you to be at peace, too. Mami and Papi, please be all right with this. Give my love to T and Xoch. Tell them they've got their brother back. Tell them to be good to each other.

With all my love forever,
Manuel

Xochitl checks the car. Makes sure he's not coming.

She grips my shoulder. "He was quiet in his room. For a long time," she says. "I got freaked and I barged in there. He was at his desk. He tried to slide the paper under something. It flew off and he dove for it, so I dove for it."

I bend at the waist. Press the paper onto my leg, trying to iron out the wrinkles and creases with my hand, like it's some important document. I stop and shove it back at Xochitl.

"He tried to wrestle it away from me, but—"

"That's enough," I say.

"You need to hear this, T."

She says Manny figured out she wasn't giving the note up, so he ran for the door. And she tackled him. Hauled him to the ground. He tried to get away, but she wouldn't let go. And she swore to him she wouldn't ever let him out of her sight. And she was never gonna let him do it.

"He finally let loose and he sobbed, 'Don't tell Mami or Papi. Don't tell T.' I promised him. I promised I wouldn't tell you."

Another honking semi. We're lit up and blinded. More dust as it goes.

"Now you know, T. But Mami and Papi don't. You cannot say a word."

I look back and try to pull the car into focus. The pain pulses in my head. I close my eyes to stop the spinning, but an image pops up. It's Manny on the basketball court at Puget. He's standing still in the middle of a raucous postgame celebration. He's got a pistol. His eyes search the crowd. He finds me. Looks right at me. Points the gun to his head.

I wanna run to him, but I'm stuck in place.

I can't save Manny.

More pictures. We're in the car after teacher conferences. Manny's got the gun again. He trembles and says, "That was too much, T."

I'm screaming, *I'm sorry, Manny! I'm sorry!* And I lunge at him, but it's too late.

Xochitl shakes my shoulders. "Look at me, T."

I look at my sister.

"I was losing hope. But a few days after, Manny thanked me

for getting in the way. And he tried to get himself right. He's doing it the Lucas way. But he's trying. *He's trying, T.* Manny is fighting again."

She grabs my face with both her hands. "We cannot leave him alone, T. You understand? He can't do it if we're with him. He won't do it."

My head bobs yes because I don't know and I got nothing else.

Back in the car, Xochitl pulls an alcohol pad from a tiny first-aid kit. Wipes the blood off my face. Presses some gauze on my forehead. "Hold that there."

She hangs over the seat and wrestles a belt around Manny. Then she sits herself in place, takes a big breath, and turns the key. The engine rumbles to life. She slams the stick into drive and pegs the gas to the floor.

I close my eyes and go to a place in my head where I can be with my brother. And I repeat it over and over. *I'm with you, Manny. I'm with you, Manny. I'm with you. . . .*

MONDAY,
JUNE 15, 2009

Xochitl wakes me in a Delano convenience store parking lot. My head *throbs*. I check my phone for the date and time because I don't have a clue. I pop whatever pill from the first-aid kit.

I call Caleb and tell him about the funeral. He says he's sorry about our cousin and he'll try to get my shift covered for tomorrow. "Be safe, brother," he says.

We get Manny upright and out of the car. He stalls at the convenience store door. Tries to keep us from going inside. It takes a lot of prodding and encouragement, but we manage to get him in there. We clean up in the restroom and change into our least smelly clothes. Then we drive out of town on a farm highway. We pass massive trucks and tractors. Fields scattered with bent-over workers, bandanas protecting their mouths from poison dust as they pick weeds and thin vegetables in the scorching sun. Just like Papi used to do before he met Mami. Before a friend of her friend introduced her to Frank O'Brien.

We turn into a dirt lot. The church is a huge, converted metal shed.

Manny's all right getting out of the car.

But again, it's a long time at the door. He does his breathing. He bends over, hands on knees. Says he's getting back in the car.

Xochitl tells him he's going to be okay and she takes her place on one side of him.

I take my place on the other.

Xochitl rubs his back and says, "We're going to walk in real slow."

"It's like my head . . ." he says.

"Yeah, Man?" Xochitl says.

"My head knows I can go in. But my body is screaming at me, telling me not to."

"I know, Manny," she says. "That's why we're going to do this together. See, by my count we got three heads and two bodies telling us we can do this. All together that's five to one. Your body loses. I'm sorry."

It takes a lot more convincing, but eventually, we walk in like that, me and Xochitl each holding an arm, the three of us connected.

We take our seats with Rudi's friends and family.

The preacher talks about how great Rudi was and how long he's known the family. About watching Rudi run around the church when he was a little kid. How Rudi took a leadership role in the youth group as a teenager. How he left to defend the country he loved.

Then the preacher says, "No one knows why God called Rudi so young. Nadie sabe. Nunca vamos a saber. La única cosa que sabemos—the only thing we *do* know—is that Rudi lived his life with Jesus Christ in his heart. If we all do the same, we'll see Rudi one day."

I'm still holding Manny's arm. He's shaking all over. His face is white ash. Skin wrinkled. It's the first time I notice how thin his hair is. And his eyes. Manny is someplace else.

Looking at him, that God talk gets to me bad.

Because God did not do this. God did not *call* Rudi. God did not kill Rudi. The God I would like to believe in doesn't start wars or kill or mess up people's brains or make them lose their jobs and lose their homes. God doesn't tear families apart.

I wanna jump up and scream at the top of my lungs: *Don't blame God! People did this to Rudi! People did this to my brother!*

I do not jump.

I do not scream.

I just squeeze Manny's arm tight.

He looks at me. And for a second, he's all there with me—I swear he is—and he's saying, *Me too, brother. Me too.*

We're at the front of the church in the receiving line of dread.

Elena's first. She's short. A round, wide face. Black hair in a long braid down her back. Xochitl steps right up and says she's offering condolences from Rosario and Daniel Avila in Washington State. "Lo siento tanto, Elena," she says. "No hay palabras."

Elena cups her hands to her mouth. "*Xochitl Avila.*" She hugs my sister and looks over at me. "*Teodoro.*" My turn for the hug. Elena looks her eyes into mine. Says she can't believe we're here. She says how much I look like Papi the first time she met him.

She turns to Manny. Takes his face in her hands. "*Manuelito.*"

She tells him she and Mami have been keeping in touch. "Se que estás pasando un tiempo muy duro, bebe."

It's crazy, but that's the first time I've heard anyone say the obvious to Manny's face. *I know you're having a rough time.* Elena says it like it's nothing. Not *nothing.* She says it like it's important, but like it's not a scary thing to say to Manny.

She tells him they've been praying for him. Then she wipes the corners of her eyes with a tissue and thanks him for coming. "Gracias, mijito. Gracias por venir. Todo será mejor." Then she grabs Manny and buries her crying face in his chest. The crying turns to sobbing and it's impossible to look away.

Manny holds Elena as tight as she's holding him. He mumbles. Tells her that Rudi died fighting for something. Elena cries harder when he says it. Manny can't handle it, and he lets loose, too.

I look at Elena's hand sticking out from a black sleeve. White tissue stretched tight around her fingers. Fingers clamped on to Manny. Tissue between her thumb and Manny's skin. Her nails digging into his arms. Not letting him go. Manny's arms around her. Holding her up. His eyes closed. His chin on her head. Not letting her go.

And all I can think is, *This it it.*

This is the reason we came all this way.

Despite Xochitl's promise, we do not go straight home after the funeral. Elena talks us into going to her place for the reception and says we should spend the night there.

I call Caleb again. I tell him there's no way I'm gonna be able to cover my shift. He tells me not to worry. I tell him I owe him forever.

I tell Bashir I'll pay him even though we can't meet.

"Don't worry about it," he says. "You all right, man?"

"Yeah. Fine. We're all good."

He can hear the lie in my voice. "You be safe out there, Teodoro. Okay? And all the best to your family."

"All the best to you guys, too. I'll call when we get back."

Outside Elena's front door, we go through the routine again, trying to get Manny to walk inside. It takes forever but we finally make it, Xochitl and I holding him up until he gets as comfortable as possible.

There's a bunch of people at the house. Some of them are our distant aunts and uncles and cousins. They trickle out of there till it's real late.

Elena sits on the sofa for hours. Her husband, Leo, on one side of her. Manny on the other. She clutches Manny's hand. Not letting him leave her side.

She and Leo are exhausted. But they won't go to bed. They have to stay up talking. It's like if they go to bed, something will end. And they don't want the new thing to start.

Elena talks about Mami. She's got all kinds of stories about the time she spent living with Mami's family in Yakima. Elena's mom and dad worked farms all over the country. She and her brother worked right alongside them. Her parents wanted her to have a stable senior year of high school, so they sent her to live with Abita and Papá Tito and Mami.

Elena goes on about all the "trouble" she and Mami got into at school and working at the Kmart. And she tells her version of the Mami-meets-Papi story. Elena tells it like Mami swept her up in the excitement of the whole thing. Made her a part of it. She

171

tells the story like she and Mami needed each other. Mami needed someone to help her get through the waiting. And Elena needed to see someone—to see Mami—believe in something so hard it came true. Elena looks in Leo's eyes and squeezes his hand. He squeezes hers right back.

Looking at them makes me think about *Wendy's ideal.*

And that makes me think about *us.*

We're not so different from Mami and Papi when they first started loving each other. We're not so different from Elena and Leo when they were young.

Elena grabs a framed photo of the three of them—Rudi in his uniform, and she and Leo looking so proud. She wipes dust off the glass with that same tissue she's been gripping the whole night. And she and Leo stare at the photo hard, like wishing they could crawl inside it.

I can't stop thinking this thing. I can't stop thinking that if you try to be more than friends with someone, and if you try for as long as you possibly can, it's scary as hell where that can take you.

Elena and Leo start in with Rudi stories. They talk about silly stuff he did as a baby and as a little kid. Even stuff about how Manny and Rudi were two peas in a pod when we stayed with them on that road trip down the coast way back when.

The stories trail off after Rudi leaves for Iraq.

Soon, Elena falls asleep, leaning against Manny. And Manny falls asleep leaning against her. Leo says we should leave them like that because Elena hasn't slept in days.

He shows me and Xochitl to Rudi's old room. Xochitl takes the bed. Leo brings me an inflatable mattress.

It's creepy being in his room, and the mattress keeps hissing, slowly deflating.

TUE JUN 16 1:38 A.M.

T:	Can't sleep.
T:	The funeral was today.
T:	So sad. And infuriating.
T:	Remember U-Dub? You said all that nice stuff about Manny? I can't tell you how much that meant to me.

I blow up the mattress and try to sleep.

It's not happening.

I tiptoe through the living room, past Manny and Elena, out the front door. And I walk.

Soon there's a buzz. I pick up.

Wendy tells me she's out on the patio in Florence.

I tell her I'm walking in Delano, California.

Wendy says she's looking up at a clear night sky.

I tell her it's clear here, too.

She helps me find the Big Dipper. "We're under the same stars, Teodoro."

I tell her about watching Manny with Elena. How good it is we came here. Then I tell her about the stuff the preacher said and how angry I got.

I can't tell Wendy it's Manny's letter—and what made him want to end his life—that got me so pissed off at that preacher. But Wendy still understands me. And she gets angry right along with me. And we spend a long time looking up at that Dipper and asking big questions about God and war, life and death, and we wonder why some people just seem to be placed where they can take advantage of all the good stuff, and why some people aren't so lucky.

After a while we run out of questions and run out of anger and we start making a list of all the amazing things and people in the world. Everything we can think of.

I tell Wendy I'm so lucky she's on my list.

She tells me she's lucky I'm on hers.

Then I tell her about Leo and Elena. The way they are together. The way they look at each other. The way they talk to each other without words. After everything they been through.

Wendy knows why I'm telling her that stuff.

She doesn't say so.

But she knows.

TUESDAY,
JUNE 16, 2009

Xochitl tells me to come out to the car after breakfast.

She's all bright eyes and smiles. She reaches out. Puts a hand on my shoulder. "What do you think?" she says.

"It's good Manny's here. For Elena."

"And it's good he's here for him," she says. "I think he's gonna make it."

"Like you think he's gonna not . . . do that?"

"Yeah, T. And I think he's going to make it to Tío Ed's farm in New Mexico, where he and I have jobs for the summer, which is what I been totally wanting to tell you since we left home."

My muscles clench.

My jaw locks. *You did not. You did not. You did not just say that.* Then it's like a missile launching from my gut. I wanna scream. I wanna kick that glove box door right through, blast it into the engine.

Xochitl sees it coming. She puts her hand on my chest and says, "I didn't know what else to do, T. I found Manny's note. I promised I wouldn't tell Mami and Papi. I was alone with it, T. Completely alone. I needed help. So I called Tío Ed. He came back from Vietnam as sick as Manny came back from Iraq. Then he got better. He told me he could help. He said we could work on his farm and he knows what to do for Manny."

"If you'd just told me all that stuff!"

"You wouldn't have come, not in a million years. But that doesn't matter anymore. I needed you and you helped get us this far. LA is a couple hours away. I have money for your bus ticket home. You got a hot date to make. You have a job to get back to. We gotta keep you college-bound, right? Manny and me, we'll be fine. We'll drop you off and then drive to New Mexico."

I wonder how fine they'll be.

Then I stop wondering and say, "Yeah, Xoch. Drop me off in LA."

Xochitl tells me there was a point where she knew she had to take off with Manny. But she didn't think she could do it alone. She needed me. So she went searching for my Kryptonite. She called Caleb, and because he's always had a gross crush on her, he spilled everything about me and Wendy.

"I call her up," Xochitl says. "I ask her how she's doing. She tells me she's taking college-level math and science. So I get this idea that maybe she'd be into a summer working on a farm in New Mexico and maybe she could be your tutor. And if she would do that, maybe you would do the drive down with me and Manny. I talked to Ed and he said he'd have enough paid work for everybody. All of us. For the summer."

I tell Xochitl how pissed I am she did that behind my back.

But I can't believe she tried to get me a whole summer with Wendy.

"I thought she was gonna do it. But I begged her not to say anything till she knew for sure. I was gonna tell you everything. Then stuff with her dad came up. Stuff with her mom. She waffled on me. We had to get the trip started fast. I was hoping I could convince her in Florence, but she's set on seeing her dad."

Xochitl tells me she's sorry her plan sucked. And she's sorry she lied. But she'll take me to the bus station and I can be home in a day.

Then she says, "T, there's this alternate plan."

All that talking was my sister working her way to the thing I really do not wanna hear.

"And that plan is we all drive to Tío Ed's together." Her voice gets shaky and full of hope. "It's about nineteen hours. Then I'll get you a plane ticket home."

Yes. Of course. I'll get you to New Mexico, Xochitl. No problem.

That's what I want to say. Because I want to help Xochitl. I want to help get Manny to Tío Ed. And I want them to be safe. I want all that.

But even more, I need to leave this car. I need to leave Xochitl and her lies and Manny and his craziness. I need to see Wendy. And for us to do our date. I need to hold her and stare in her eyes and kiss her all over Portland before we say our gut-wrenching good-byes.

After that, all I have is this summer to get ready. For senior year. For my SATs. For my application. For U-Dub and this life I been working so hard for.

I need to get back to Caleb's. And I need to do it now.

* * *

It's almost noon when Manny finally hauls his ass out of bed. So we stay for lunch.

We say some emotional good-byes and pile in the car.

Elena pokes her head in and tells us to wait. Then she runs in the house. Comes out a minute later with an old photo of her and Mami from way back.

We do the emotional good-byes all over again.

Finally, Xochitl turns the key and Sally starts steaming like crazy.

So . . . we pile out.

It takes Manny and Leo a couple hours and a can of radiator sealant to get Sally running.

So we stay for dinner.

Then it's our third and final round of way-too-long, way-too-emotional good-byes. It's nine thirty when we finally head down Highway 99 toward I-5 and Los Angeles.

And my bus ride home.

I wake up to a loud thump. The car jolts. My head blasts the dash again. *Boom-boom.*

Xochitl's at the wheel, screaming. The car speeds on.

Boom-boom. Boom-boom.

A scraping sound as we haul down the freeway.

Boom-boom. Boom-boom. Boom-boom.

"Stop, Xochitl!" I shout. "Stop the car!"

Suddenly, Manny's hands float out of the back seat and grab the wheel. "Take your foot off the gas, Xochitl." He's loud enough to be heard over the screeching, but somehow, calm and in control.

He steers the car to the shoulder.

"Good, Xoch. Brake now."

Xochitl steps on the brake.

And Manny collapses into his seat.

Boom-boom. Boom-boom. My head. My head. *Boom-boom.*

Xochitl whimpers. She holds her hands in the air like she doesn't want them near her. She turns to me. "Go see what it is."

I squeeze my head to keep it from splitting.

"Something's out there," she says. "Something messed up Sally."

I'm trying to put words together when the back door creaks open.

Manny.

Xochitl tries to call him back.

He tells her he has to pee. He says it desperate. The door slams and he's gone.

"He can't be alone, T. Follow him."

My head is killing me. I don't wanna go. And I'm afraid of what's out there.

"Go, T. Go!"

I get out. I can't see anything. But I hear steps crunch gravel as Manny walks slowly to the front of the car.

I follow him.

There's enough moon and starlight to see Manny standing perfectly still, eyes wide.

The right headlight is smashed. The corner of the hood is bent toward the sky. There's blood all over and a fleshy strip of something sticking to the corner of the hood.

The smell hits me and I'm gonna be sick.

Manny walks to the back of the car. The sound of his footsteps stop. He wails. "Awwww, God, awwww."

I scramble back there. And I see it.

A big buck head. Massive antlers on the ground. Frozen eyes staring at me sideways.

"Let's go, Man. Let's get in the car."

He drops to his knees.

"No, Man. Don't do that."

He yanks at the antlers and scoots himself under.

"Oh, God, come on, Man."

He holds the head in his lap and rocks and moans, rocks and moans.

We're lit up by headlights as an SUV glides to a stop behind us. The door opens. The driver steps toward us. He looks big with the lights shining behind him. He takes off his baseball cap. "*Jesus*," he says, running a hand through his hair. "Y'all okay?"

"We're good," I say.

Manny moans. He gasps for air.

The guy takes a step toward Manny. "Hang in there, brother." He steps closer. Says he'll call for help.

"I already did," I say.

The guy keeps coming. Bends down. Reaches a hand to help Manny.

Manny pushes the deer off.

He grips the guy's hand. Yanks him to the ground. He punches him in the face, shouting, "Why'd you do it? Why'd you do it?"

The guy rolls, fighting to get to his feet.

Manny doesn't let him.

I yell at Manny to stop. I stumble over and try to pull him off the guy. Then Manny turns and punches me in the gut. I drop to the ground, fighting to get my breath back.

Manny hits the guy more. "Why'd you do it? Why'd you do it?"

Xochitl rushes up to Manny. "Stop it, Manuel!" She tugs his arm, trying to pull him off.

Manny springs to his feet and runs.

"Follow him, T!" Xochitl says.

We race along fields of corn or whatever, chasing the sounds of him.

Xochitl's yells at me to run faster.

Plants rustle. I plow in. Stalks scrape my arms and face. I can't see him. I can't hear him.

The scrapes stop and I'm on a dirt road—irrigation ditches on either side.

"He's over there!" Xochitl shouts, pointing farther down the dirt road.

Manny's hopping, pulling off his pants. He whips off his shirt and jumps, screaming, into the ditch.

I freeze at the edge of it, watching Manny as he lands with a muddy splash.

Xochitl flies past me, another splash in the ditch.

She grabs his arm. Holds on for dear life as he thrashes.

I'm stuck there, watching them.

"Come on, T!" she shouts.

I jump. The water's slimy and cold. I grab Manny's other arm and hold him tight. Xochitl wraps her arm around his back. "It's okay," she says. "It's okay."

His body slowly starts to calm.

"We got you, Manny." She takes his hand in hers. *It's okay. It's okay. Shhh. It's okay.*

Then she gets quiet.

The sounds of our breathing. The trickle of the stream. The rustling corn in the breeze. The sound of Xochitl running her hand through Manny's wet hair.

"This checkpoint," Manny says.

Xochitl flashes me a look. "What, Manny?"

"It happened at this checkpoint," Manny says. "He took them out right over there." Manny points into the darkness.

"Who was over there?" Xochitl says.

He pulls in a desperate breath. "Aw, God." He shakes and shudders his body. Water splashes.

Xochitl wraps her hands around his arm. Squeezes tight. Nods for me to hold on. "What are you talking about?"

"The parents got out of the truck and ran. The boy, too. We did the hand signals. We shouted them down. They didn't stop. They ran into the desert. He raised his—the corporal—he raised his rifle. His buddies tried to stop him. We tried to stop him. But we didn't try hard enough." Manny closes his eyes. He shudders. Slowly opens them again. "We watched the boy scream for his parents. Then watched him run away, leaving them behind. We all watched the boy run. We let him run. Alone. Into the desert."

"Why did he shoot?" she says.

"That's enough, Xoch," I say.

"What happened to the boy?" she says. "Why didn't anyone help him?"

Manny looks at Xochitl like he's asking her. Pleading with her to explain it to him.

She puts a muddy hand on his cheek. "Oh, Manuel." She touches her forehead to his. "I don't know. I don't know."

He stands.

We stand with him. The sound of mud and water slopping off our bodies, into the ditch.

We walk our naked brother back through the stalks.

"I got him," Xochitl says. "See if you can find his clothes."

By the light of the moon and stars, I see a shoe up ahead. A sock. I follow the trail, holding Manny's clothes as tight as I can. Holding them with all I got.

A baseball cap sits in the gravel on the side of the road. The guy and his truck are gone.

Xochitl gives me a towel and tells me to dry off. Passes me the duffel. I peel off wet stuff and put on whatever.

She tells me to stay in the car with Manny while she uses rags to pick deer off the grill.

In a minute, Manny's sleeping.

I tilt my head back. Close my eyes. Try to get as far from this car and from this place as I can. But my head aches so bad, and I can feel Manny's punch with every breath.

Manny is not better.

He is so far from better.

We're all too far and it's all too much. I feel this burning and tightening. It takes over my guts. Then it takes over my muscles until my body can't contain it and it blows up out of me and that glove box doesn't stand a chance.

Xochitl gets in the car. She sits and watches me kick and scream.

She doesn't say anything. Just waits for me to finish.

Waits for me to collapse. Waits till I'm sucking air.

The glove box door hangs by one hinge. Xochitl yanks it off. Tosses it out the window. Reaches in and digs out the alcohol and gauze. Cleans my head again. No words. She cleans my face.

I lay myself down. My head on her lap.

She runs a hand through my hair.

And starts humming.

I look up at her face.

"Shhhh." She rocks forward and back. "Shhhhhh. It's okay."

It's okay. It's okay. Shhh. It's okay.

She hums more.

No sounds but her voice.

And all I can think is there's no way.

I'm not gonna let Xochitl do this alone.

I sit up. "Where are we?"

"Outside of Bakersfield somewhere."

"Xochitl, I'll go to New Mexico with you. Then I'm catching that plane."

She grabs me with both arms. Pulls me in. Squeezes tight. "You okay to drive?" she says.

I'm not okay to drive.

Doesn't matter. We switch seats. I grip the key. *Please, God, let it start.*

Somehow, everything fires right and Sally rumbles to life.

I stay on the shoulder, picking up speed. Kicking up gravel.

There's a pulsing squeal coming from the engine now.

"Try to sleep, Xoch."

"I'll try, T."

I pull onto the freeway. Eyes on the road.

But all I see is that deer head. Those eyes. I can't shake the smell.

Can't shake the image of Manny running naked.

Manny drenched and shaking at my side.

I hear him telling that story.

I picture the little boy, running into the desert. Into the void.

I picture a soldier shooting the parents.

I picture Manny running to stop the shooting.

I picture Manny . . . doing nothing . . . just standing there . . . just watching . . .

I tell myself that war can mess with you so bad it doesn't matter what Manny did.

But that's not true. It matters. *It matters. It matters.*

"Xochitl?"

"Yeah?"

"You heard that story before?"

"No."

Tears are rolling down her face.

Xochitl's been sleeping for a while. I can't keep upright. Can't keep my eyes open.

I stop the car and step out into the cool night air. I pull out my phone.

WED JUN 17 4:17 A.M.

T: Hi Wendy.

T: I heard you considered it.

Thank you.

T: Now I know why you asked

about the rest of the trip.

T: I'm thinking about forgiving you

for keeping secrets.

T: I'm going to New Mexico now.

T: I'm not going to make it

back by Thursday.

T: I'm so sorry. I have to do this.

T: Call me when you can.

WED JUN 17 6:05 A.M.

T: I need to hear your voice.

T: Please call me.

WEDNESDAY, JUNE 17, 2009

Xochitl took over the wheel sometime in the night.

I stayed awake as long as I could, waiting for Wendy to call back.

Now Xochitl's shaking my shoulder, freaking out. "What's happening, T?"

I open my eyes to an Arizona sunrise. And Sally steaming. Or smoking. Xochitl doesn't know which. Whatever it is, it's coming out bigger and faster than anything we've seen.

"Pull over, Xoch."

She exits the freeway onto a frontage road and just keeps driving. "What do I do, T?"

"Stop the car, Xoch. Stop the car!"

She doesn't stop until there's a Mount St. Helens plume coming from Sally's front end.

Xochitl looks at Manny.

Then at me.

I tell her I don't know what to do.

So she shakes him. "Manny?" She slaps his face a little. "Manny, *the car.*"

He comes to.

"I need you to check it, Manny."

He shakes his head. Stumbles out. Looks up. Squints. Scratches his head as he watches billowing smoke darken the Sonoran Desert sky. He scratches his belly. Yawns.

There is no fix for Sally.

We call Tío Ed. He asks Xochitl where we are. He tells us to stay put. He'll call us right back.

We pass around our last swigs of water. Haul our stuff out. Make a pile down the road from the car.

Tío Ed calls and says he contacted the Tres Estrellas de Oro bus company. The driver will be watching for us to flag him down out on the freeway. That bus goes across I-10 to El Paso, Texas. Tío Ed will pick us up at a stop in Las Cruces, New Mexico.

We've got an hour till the bus, and the hike to the freeway will only take a few minutes.

There's time to kill.

Manny walks up to me. He's holding Sally's tire iron. He points to the car. "You're going to need this." He says it like last night never happened. Like he never punched me. Like he never talked like we were all in Iraq.

He hands me the tire iron and I know exactly what he's thinking. "Seriously, Man?"

There are horrible grinding sounds as Manny twists the tailpipe till it pops off the muffler. He offers that to Xochitl.

"Nah, Manny," she says. "It's *Sally.*"

He bends down. Picks up a football-size rock. "You're gonna feel better," he says.

He walks to Sally. Nods at us to follow.

We surround that old car.

Manny lifts the rock to the sky, real slow, stretching his body, high as he can.

We do the same.

Heels off the ground, rock even higher, he says, "One . . . two . . . all together . . . *three*!"

A current screams through hands into bodies as we shatter glass, blast dents into doors. Meet metal with metal.

We dance and howl, swinging, pounding, exploding a storm of thunder and hail, the saguaro cactuses our only witnesses, we burn in that Arizona sun, putting an end to the life of one worthless car, the whole time wishing we could put an end to so much crap we got no way of fixing.

When we've finished our business, my brother and sister laugh as they struggle, bent over, to catch their breath.

"See?" Manny says.

"Yeah," she says. "I needed that."

I watch them pick up bags and start the walk to the freeway. Sun-drunk. Starving. Laughing. After everything we've been through.

WEDNESDAY, JUNE 17, 2009

Brakes screech. I open crusty eyelids and peel my cheek off
the bus seat.

We file off into a church parking lot. And there, stepping out
of a silver minivan, is Tío Ed. He's sporting a John Deere cap and
sunglasses. A button-down denim shirt. Work boots. He's a thick-
looking, strong guy. Way younger than Abita, but still really
old. He doesn't look it.

"Woo-ee!" Tío Ed squeals. "I would hug you people, but you
smell fuchi." He stands in the scorching heat, pinching his nose
with the fingers of one hand, holding open the sliding door with
the other.

Xochitl hops in. I'm next in line, but Tío Ed stops me and says,
"That's a serious forehead shiner, Teodoro. What the hell
happened?"

I tell him it's a couple long stories.

He says it might be better if he doesn't hear 'em. And he asks
Xochitl to grab me some Tylenol from the glove box.

Then he squeezes Manny's shoulders. Looks in his eyes.

Manny forces a smile, like he wants to show how positive and together he is.

Tío Ed says, "Manuel, it might not feel like it, but all the fighting you're doing? Just to be standing here? It's worth it."

"I know." Manny punches his smile a notch brighter.

Tío Ed bear-hugs him. "You're lying to me now, mijo. But you'll see."

We drive through Las Cruces on our way to the farm. The craggy Organ Mountains overlook the city to our right. To our left, it's Chihuahuan desert plains, isolated mountain peaks, and mesas all the way to the horizon. Shiny strip malls, big-box stores, hospitals, and the New Mexico State campus share the town with dusty streets and old abandoned storefronts.

Tío Ed points out water bottles and a towel in the back of the van. He tells us to get cleaned up as good as possible before we get to Dr. Fuentes's office.

Then he says, "Manuel, you got three things on your summer to-do list. Number one: Work hard on the farm. Every day. Two: Attend my support group for dinged-up vets. And three: Pop your pills and do your counseling as directed by Doc Fuentes. Those are the keys to staying alive and getting yourself healthy. Worked for me. They'll work for you. Got it?"

Manny nods his head more. Smiles more.

Xochitl tells Tío Ed she's not sure how we'll pay for the doctor because Manny only has VA insurance.

"Don't worry," Tío says, "Manny ain't stepping foot in no VA." He turns to Manny. "Me and Doc known each other a long time. We got it all worked out. He takes care of my visits and pharmaceuticals, and I take care of his green chile needs to the tune of half an acre each season. That's a lot of chile, Manuel."

In a few minutes we're parked in the clinic lot. But Tío Ed isn't finished with Manny. "You can trust my doc. But you got to let him do his job. That means showing him everything you been taking, mijo. *Everything.*"

Our tío watches like a hawk as Manny digs through his bags and empties all his pockets. He's got a scowl on his face and he's shaking as bad as ever.

"Trust me, Manuel. I know."

He hands the van keys to Xochitl. "I got him. You two go get something to eat."

We watch Tío Ed walk Manny to the door. He reaches out for it. Opens up. But Manny stops. He can't go inside.

Tío Ed lets the door swing shut.

He's calm. He tilts his cap back. Puts his hands in his pocket as he talks to Manny like he's shooting the breeze.

When Manny finally talks, Ed listens close.

After a lot of back and forth, Manny nods at our tío.

Tío Ed nods back and they disappear into the clinic.

We devour Circle K hot dogs and watch our clothes slosh round in a Las Cruces laundromat.

Xochitl looks over at me. "We are *here.* And he is not here. And that is okay."

"I can't believe it, Xoch."

"If we didn't make this trip . . . if we didn't have Tío Ed . . ."

"No *ifs,*" I say. "Manny's gonna be all right."

"I can sleep tonight. My God, I can sleep."

"You deserve it, Xochitl."

"Does that mean you're not mad at me?"

"I'm too tired. But don't worry, after I get some rest, I'll be pissed off at you again."

"That's good." She puts a hand on my cheek. "It's not good. It's just—"

"You should get some Zs, Xoch." I pat my shoulder.

Xochitl rests her head. Yawns big. "I don't know if I can sleep here."

In a minute, she's out. I pull the hot dog foil from her fingers. And watch our clothes go round and round.

Manny is safe, and I'm finally heading home.

We take the scenic route along the Rio Grande.

Crops stretch to the edge of Valley Drive. Tío Ed points out pecan trees, rows of cotton, and acres of knee-high chile plants. The river is a ribbon of green oasis squeezed in by towering mountains, their jagged rocks glowing purple and pink in the sunlight.

He points out the farm as he drives past it. In minutes we're in the tiny town of Hatch. It's easy to imagine cowboys and saloons—all that Wild West stuff. Seems like half the stores are boarded up. Barely anyone walking outside. Some tourist shops with clay pots and dried red chile ristras hanging from beams.

We get to this cross street and see a bunch of colorful cartoon statues wrapped around a corner building. Ronald McDonald, Colonel Sanders, and a twenty-foot-tall chicken.

Tío Ed says, "That, my friends, is Sparky's. Best green chile cheeseburger in the state. And that makes it the best burger in the world. They have live music going all the time. Sparky's is the heartbeat of Hatch these days."

We leave the town and backtrack along the river, toward the farm. I wanna ask Tío Ed about plans for my trip home, but he won't stop with the farm talk.

He says he's always grown ten acres of chile with his old farm-hand, Hector. But he just bought ten new acres from his neighbor, and it's become clear that they can't handle it on their own. He needs Manny and Xochitl to help him work the fields.

Tío Ed cranes his neck and says, "Teodoro, I got you and your tutor gal signed up for chile stand duty. Truth is, it's just a crumbling old outbuilding. I'm leaving it up to you kids to turn it into the best roadside stand in Hatch."

I turn to Xochitl and whisper, "Tell him it's not happening."

She says, "Tío, Wendy decided not to come. T's heading back home."

"Mija," he says, "your tía Lucía is on her way back from El Paso. She just picked Wendy up from the airport. We good here?"

OH MY GOD.

Xochitl's got the wild eyes now as she looks at me and says, "That's some good news, Tío. Right, bro?"

Sharp tingling again. Shaking again. I cannot control my body or make words with my mouth. They just fly around inside my head. *She's choosing me. Florence was real. She's choosing me. Florence. It was not a dream. This is not a dream. Wendy. Is choosing. Me! Not San Fran! And I . . . I've got a job here for the summer. I've got a tutor for the summer. I've got Wendy for the summer. I've got everything.*

Xochitl shakes my shoulder. "T?"

194

I hold out a fist. And I pop my thumb up.

"You sure?"

I nod my head yes.

Xochitl whoops. "Good to go, Tío Ed! T is staying for the summer."

I don't know how good to go I am because my heart's trying to punch a hole through my chest. I try to hold my breath, but that makes my forehead pulse and ache even worse.

"I need to hear it from you," Tío says. "You my farm stand guy for the summer?" He looks in the rearview mirror.

The words shoot out my body, way too loud. "I'm your farm stand guy, Tío! For the summer! Uh-huh!"

Xochitl pokes me. "What possibly could have changed your mind?"

"Xoch, I couldn't handle the thought of being away from you for even one minute."

"Ha! That's what I thought."

I pull out my phone. I have to tell Caleb.

WED JUN 17 1:43 P.M.

T:	Working on my uncle's farm in N.M. Be back for school in fall
Caleb:	Ha!
T:	No joke. Tell ur folks thanks for everything. And I'll see em in September

Caleb:	Ur leaving me hanging
T:	I gotta do this. Family thing
T:	And Wendy's gonna be down here
T:	She's gonna be my tutor. X hooked it up thanks to your big mouth
Caleb:	NOT a family thing then it's a Wendy thing
T:	Come on C
Caleb:	You can't let kissing mess up your goals
Caleb:	How am I gonna keep tabs on u? Make sure u don't screw up
T:	I still need you C
Caleb:	COME HOME NOW

We make a left turn toward the river, onto Tío Ed's property. There's a pole with a US flag and a yellow-and-red New Mexico flag. And a black one that says, POW-MIA.

We pass an ancient wood shack. "It's got good bones," Tío Ed says. "Put a picture in your head of a sweet little farm stand. Then make it happen."

All I got in my head is a picture of me and Wendy lighting that shack with a match and watching it burn. Then a picture of us hiring someone to build a new one.

196

An amazing house comes into view. "Casa de Lucía," Tío Ed says. "She pretty much designed the whole thing. Even did a little of the construction when our first contractor skipped town. Yeah, she's a lawyer lady who defends all manner of travieso punks. But she can also hang drywall and run a power saw."

The house has a flat roof. Two stories surrounded by tall desert shade plants. Huge windows in the front and back so you can see clear through it. The cream-colored paint is peeling. The weathered look makes it feel like it belongs in the desert—like it's been here for a long time—but it's totally modern.

I can't believe that house is here. I can't believe my tíos own it. And I can't believe the sight of a house has my guts, like, churning. I've seen millions of houses in my life—what's so different about this one?

Maybe it's just the road trip getting to me. Maybe it's the thought of seeing Wendy.

Maybe it's comparing Ed and Luci's amazing place to the depressing rental we been forced to squeeze into. Or comparing it to the soulless box we had to walk away from. I don't know. It just feels like that house belongs here and Ed and Luci belong in that house. And that's the way it should be.

Ed parks the van in the carport. Pulls the brake.

We unload and I have to remind myself to breathe again. The bass drum is back, pounding my head. I reach up and check for blood and puss. It's crusted over. I washed my face and I'm wearing clean clothes, but underneath I'm still covered in Arizona grime. And my pits . . . not my freshest for Wendy.

Wendy, who is walking my way, smiling huge at me. Wendy, who is looking kinda goofy and kinda hot in cowboy boots and a cowboy hat. Wendy, who is still wearing the shells-and-beads bracelet. Wendy, who is sandwiched between Tía Luci and her mom.

Rebecca O'Brien does not let Wendy out of her sight. Except for an awkward hug moment, we don't get a minute to ourselves. No time to establish what the heck we're both doing here.

Tío Ed tells us to clean up before dinner.

I take a steaming shower and watch miles' worth of sand, sweat, and blood flow down the drain. I look up to the heavens through the bathroom skylight, and send thanks for the miracle of us making it here in one piece.

As the sun sets, Tío Ed give us the grand tour. Turns out he's going for organic certification, so no pesticides.

"I'm small-time," he says. "I needed a niche, so I figured I'd try organic. Plus, it makes me feel all warm and fuzzy inside."

Wendy and I lock eyes and smile when he says it.

Ed points out chile varieties. *6-4s, Sandias. Slim Jims.* He shows how the drip irrigation system works. It's just a bunch of connected hoses with tiny holes in them, but they need to be checked and adjusted constantly.

At one point he reaches down and picks up a bug. Holds it for all to see. "That, my friends, is a thrip. Keep your eyes peeled for damn thrips," he says, pinching it till we hear a tiny cracking sound.

He tosses it aside and pulls a baby plant out of the ground and says, "I got two words for you: weed control. Look close."

We gather around him.

"This is mustard weed. It is the enemy. He yanks another. "Russian knapweed. Be vigilant. Cold war ain't over out here."

We walk the fields and Tío Ed looks right at Manny as he talks about the healing powers of growing and eating large quantities of New Mexican chile.

Manny nods, eyes-wide and manic. It's like he's trying to convince everyone he's listening and taking it all in.

We poke our heads in the shack where Wendy and I will be working.

It's full of ancient farm equipment, spiderwebs, and dirt.

I ask him when he's gonna get the junk hauled out.

He looks at me and says, "When are *you* going to get the junk hauled out?"

"That is right," I say. "Very soon."

"I don't need it to look like no Walmart," he says. "Just a festive little place people will trust they can buy some untainted chile."

I have no idea how we're gonna pull that off, but Wendy assures Tío Ed we got this and she nods at me with a smile and eyes that are totally convincing.

Inside the house, Wendy and I squeeze another quick hug in front of her mom and say good night. Then Wendy and Xochitl head up to the room they'll be sharing.

I'll be sleeping with Manny.

Not even a wall between us.

I pull Tío Ed aside and tell him I'm not sure about the arrangements. Tío Ed says Dr. Fuentes gave Manny a few nights' worth of something to knock him out. He wants Manny to sleep hard. And soon the heavyweight antidepressants and antianxiety meds will kick in. Tío Ed says Manny should be all right at night. But we'll monitor and adjust as we go.

I choose to trust Tío Ed and the doctor.

I head into the room and Manny's taking his time figuring out which bed to sleep in. His brows are scrunched. Jaw locked. He looks from one bed to the other. Hops in one, then the other. It is a difficult and almost overwhelming decision. But when he finally picks his bed, my big brother is out hard and fast.

I don't know if I've ever felt this tired.

But I can't stop thinking about Wendy. I mean, I'm going to see her every day. I'm gonna see that smile. I'm gonna hug her every day. Feel her hand in mine.

And she's going to be my tutor.

And I'm going to be exposed as dumb. Because I'm not going to *get* pre-calculus.

And I'm going to say stupid, unfunny stuff because I can't craft and then send her texts because we're going to be in the same places, like face-to-face, so texting would be extrememly awkward—*Breathe, T. Imagine yourself being not an idiot. Breathe. Imagine yourself being the kind of person who deserves Wendy Martinez.*

The self talk isn't working.

I get out of bed and walk outside, into the cool night air.

I pull out my phone and dial.

My dad picks up. "Mijo!"

"Papi, can you put Mami on speaker?"

I tell them I miss them. I lie and tell them our trip was great.

I tell Mami her tío is doing well and he's getting Manny on a solid program.

A deep sigh of relief. "That's good."

"Gracias a Dios," Papi says.

"Yeah," I say, "And Xochitl's good."

Mami says she's still mad at Xochitl for taking me away before she and Papi could say good-bye. They were both on their way home.

So everyone knew but me.

Mami says she knows I had my job and my studies and she thanks me for taking time out to help Manny for the summer.

"I'm sorry I moved out," I say.

"We know it was hard," she says.

I tell her I'd been scared to let them know exactly how hard I was trying and how well I was doing, because I was convinced I'd eventually fail. I tell them I almost did fail and then everything got better and I got two As and, if I can keep up the improvement, I'm applying for U-Dub next year.

I have to hold the phone away from my ear because Mami's screaming, "Ay, Teodoro, that's the way!" Then she tells me how much she and Papi are going to miss us this summer. Turns out Xochitl already called and gave them the update.

"You're doing a good thing for Manuel," Papi says.

"Thanks, Papi."

"You listen to your tío. And be good."

"Love you, Mami."

"We love you, Teodoro. Say hi to Wendy for us."

"I will."

"You respect her, mijo."

"Geez, Papi."

"She was always so cute," Mami says.

"All right, you two. I gotta go."

THURSDAY, JUNE 18, 2009

Rebecca O'Brien sits between me and her daughter at the breakfast table. She doesn't look at me one time. She just talks at Wendy about trust and phone calls home and *being smart*.

A last gulp of coffee and she taps my shoulder. "Let's step outside, Teodoro."

Rebecca tells me she's got a flight to catch. She has to work. She says she wishes she could stay longer.

"I think that would be nice," I say.

"I bet you do," she says.

Then she tells me she's grateful that—because of me—Wendy's not going to San Francisco. She won't be attending her father's art parties with his alcoholic art friends and she won't be checking out art schools, "And whatever other art plans he has for her."

Rebecca calls Wendy's dad a boy who never grew up and never took responsibility for anything. She says she's positive he's undiagnosed bipolar, *like most successful artists.*

"And whenever Wendy comes back from visiting him, she's absolutely *incorrigible.*"

"That sounds really bad."

Rebecca goes on about her own ancient history with Wendy's dad and says, "So you understand how I'm feeling about this situation with Wendy."

I'm thinking, *What situation?* Then it hits me. This conversation has been less about Wendy and her dad, and more about Wendy and me.

"So if things between you and my daughter get serious—and you know what I mean, Teodoro—for God's sake, pay a visit to the drugstore." She hands me a twenty-dollar bill. "And that's all I'm going to say about that."

I tell her she doesn't have to worry, and I try to give her the cash back.

"Keep it," she says. "You're a nice boy. But I don't want Wendy to make the same mistake I made with her father."

Whoa, that was the tiniest compliment followed by a powerful kick in the nuts.

I breathe deep. Then let it go. "Rebecca, you did a great job raising Wendy. So you can trust her to make good decisions."

"Oh, Teodoro." She gives me a cold, quick hug. "Just be good."

"You, too, Rebecca. Bon voyage."

Wendy plops a stack of math materials on an old workbench. "So, mister . . ."

"So, mizz . . ."

She looks around the dusty shack, swipes a spiderweb, and says, "Here we are!"

"Here we are," I say.

Then the hug happens.

The kissing happens.

It's fast and wild for a second. Then it slows way the hell down. And it's personal. That sounds dumb, but, like, the slowness deepens everything. Like we're talking with kisses. And we're telling each other important stuff. Like kissing to tell each other Florence was real. Kissing to tell each other all those months of texting were real. U-Dub was real. Everything about this crazy situation is real.

When we've said everything we can with kisses, we're just standing there, arms wrapped, belly to belly, eyes on eyes.

"My mom give you a hard time?"

"Your mom was . . . awesome."

"Please don't tell me how awesome she was."

"I will not."

Wendy steps back and laughs. "I can't believe any of this, dude. I mean, here we are, right? You and me? In a farm shack? In New Mexico? And I'm your tutor?"

"What happened with your dad, Wendy? Your year in San Francisco?"

"Um . . . okay. Going down there seemed like the right thing. And then it didn't."

"If you'd like, you could be more specific."

"Once when I was little, I drew a duck. My dad thought it was brilliant. Ever since then, our relationship has been about drawing and hunks of clay and museums."

"Are you an artist, Wendy?"

"Oh, Teodoro." She kisses me on the cheek. "He's never even asked me that! And he set up all these tours of art colleges this summer. It's so stupid because I am so *not* an artist."

She takes my hand in hers and we lock fingers. "When you left Florence, I asked myself what I was trying to accomplish going to San Francisco. And I realized I was going down there to change him. And that's stupid. I mean, he can't change me."

"I hope not, Wendy."

"I can't change him. And it's not even worth trying."

I tell Wendy it makes sense. And she looks into me so serious and kisses my cheek so soft and says, "Teodoro, I can't make him love me the way I should be loved."

That feels heavy as hell.

"So here you are!" I say.

"Here I am, Teodoro." She reaches out and touches my forehead. "How's that little volcano? You all right?"

"It was a crazy trip, Wendy."

"Tell me about it. On the plane, this old guy falls asleep with his head on my shoulder, slobbering on me, snoring in one ear. And in the other ear, my mom's going, 'I hope you know what you're doing, young lady'—the whole flight! Oh, and our connection from Phoenix was delayed for, like, two hours."

I tell Wendy I think our trips were crazy in different ways.

"I'm kidding, Teodoro."

"Ha ha, you spoiled airplane flyer."

"*Spoiled?* It was a nightmare! The peanuts and the Southwest flight attendant comedy were totally stale."

"Oh . . . okay. You win. That does sound like a nightmare."

We laugh till it's quiet. I thank Wendy for the conversation the night of the funeral. "I was losing it. You helped me see the good stuff."

"You're the good stuff," she says.

"You're the better stuff," I say.

"I have an almost uncontrollable desire to kiss you more. However . . ." Wendy grabs a pen and a notebook. She dusts off an old wooden bench and takes a seat. Motions for me to do the same. "We are here to prepare you for pre-calculus and physics this fall. And we have a shack to build. So it's time for ground rules."

"You're right. We need rules."

We talk over the situation real mature. We decide that each morning we'll set teaching and learning goals. If we both agree that the goals have been met in a professional manner, studying may be followed by a period of kissing. After lunch each day, we will set shack-building goals. Once again, if and when we are successful, a period of kissing may follow.

Then Wendy brings up the *slippery slope*. Like how—if you're not intentional about it—kissing can be a gateway drug to more awesome forms of kissing . . . and potentially, more devastatingly problematic forms of kissing.

"To be clear on this," she says, "we have a long way to go— like a *looooong* way—before we *go there* or anything approximating *there*. Teodoro, if we do go there someday, it will be a decision we make together after a lot of conversations. It won't just be a dumb, thoughtless slide down a stupid slope. We'll both know exactly what's going on and when it's going down. Deal?"

We shake on it. And I act supercool about it. Like the deal is a good deal but not a *huge* deal. But the truth is, that deal is the biggest relief ever.

Don't get me wrong, I have fully daydreamed and night dreamed of sliding up and down that slippery slope with Wendy.

But dreaming is one thing.

See, I have all kinds of dreams. Like this recurring one where I'm jumping a motorcycle over the Grand Canyon. In my deepest REM sleep, I soar on my Kawasaki for an impossibly long time, flying over that beautiful, unbelievably wide canyon. And I stick the landing every single time. I stick it and there's a huge roar from the crowd followed by mad applause. Then a hot, smiling lady hangs a flowery lei around my neck. She kisses my cheek as I take off my helmet and thrust a fist in the air, cuz I'm a freaking moto badass.

Then morning happens. And in the light of day, I know that no matter how real it seemed, it was just a dream. And the obvious truth is I have as much knowledge, experience, and confidence about long-distance motorcycle jumping as I do about having actual sex with an actual other person. So, yeah, I'm a dude with the natural dude urge to jump motorcycles. But for now, when that urge hits, I'm more than happy to take a deep breath and a cold shower and stay away from motorcycles until Wendy and I are both good and ready to jump.

In the meantime, it does not hurt to dream.

Because of the catching up and the ground rules and the not-going-there talk, we decide it will be enough progress just to set up a good tutoring spot and figure out our work schedule. We decide to study in the mornings, break for lunch, and work on the stand in the afternoons.

We walk into the dry, midday New Mexican sun and into the house. Wendy says she's going to power nap before she eats. Tío Ed took Manny to see Doc Fuentes again and then to meet his support group. Tía Luci is at work. Xochitl's alone eating at the kitchen table.

She sees me and points at the fridge. "Tortilla. Cheese. Green Chile."

I heat my tortilla over the flame on the gas stove. Pinch it and flip it. I tuck in the chile and cheese and join Xochitl. Turns out we both got cross-examined by Wendy's mom. "Tío Ed did, too," she says. "So you better not mess this up, T."

I tell her not to worry. Wendy and I have it all figured out.

I ask about her morning in the fields.

"We're pulling weeds. Adjusting drip lines. Spotting bad bugs. Just like Tío Ed said."

"Sounds like the worst kind of hell."

"It's exactly what we need."

"And Manny's good with it?"

"Yeah. He's working hard. You should see him."

I bite into my tortilla. The chile stings so sweet I jump out of my seat. "*Damn!*" And I point at my plate. "That is perfect food, Xochitl!"

"I know, T!"

"Chile tastes good at home, but this is . . ." I take another bite. "*Damn.*"

"Close your mouth, T."

"I can't chew this and not say *damn.*"

"Please don't do that in front of Wendy."

Xochitl says she has some news. Turns out Tío Ed told Manny he could stay down here after summer's over, after the harvest, for as long as he needs. He even said that in a few years he'll be too old to farm. And when that time comes, Luci wants to move to a city.

"So," Xochitl says, "if Manny likes it here, and he likes farming, Ed says he can take the farm over."

"Whoa. What does Manny think about that?"

"I think he's actually considering it." She takes in a deep breath. Exhales. "Tío Ed has Manny thinking about a future."

"That's great, Xoch."

"It's everything, T."

Afternoon comes. Wendy and I pick through rusting old equipment, beat-up leather saddles, sand-caked window frames, and piles of garbage.

"Can you see it?" I say.

"Can you?" Wendy says.

I hesitate and she goes, "*Come on*, Teodoro." She points at a wall. "We'll put a counter there. A little cash register. Hang ristras. Shelves over here. Old pictures of the farm."

"That sounds cool. What else?"

"*You* what else?"

All I can think about is Tío Ed and Luci's house. It's not that big. But high ceilings and all those windows and light make it feel like it's got space. And you wanna be in that space.

So I say, "How 'bout we bust out all the siding on this front wall and we replace it with some of those old windows over there. We'll leave a big opening in the middle for an entrance."

She points out some canvas tarps lying in a corner. "We could use one to cover up the entrance at night."

We pull a tarp off the pile, unfold and stretch it. It reaches the length of the shack. We decide we'll frame it and attach that frame to the shack on hinges. The framed canvas can cover the entrance and protect the windows at night. And during the day we can prop it up as an awning for shade.

And since we'll have shade, we can get a couple tables and chairs. Serve limeade and horchata, Cokes or whatever. Chips and homegrown salsa. We'll make it a spot where people wanna hang out and spend some cash.

We talk until the words stop and we're standing real close, pumped on our ideas—looking at each other, smiling—not saying a thing. Just the sound of the breeze between us.

And pretty soon we're not saying a thing for so long it's obvious we're both saying the same exact thing.

"Um . . . Wendy? We haven't met our goal yet. Have we?"

Wendy looks deep in my eyes, smiles wicked, and says, "That is so professional of you, Teodoro." She hops off the bench. Slips on work gloves. "You ready to bust this wall up?"

"I think so, Wendy."

She grabs a big ol' sledgehammer and drags it across the dirt floor by its wooden handle. "I believe this is the correct tool for the job, sir."

"You could smash the crap outta stuff with that, ma'am."

"I'm going to need you to take a step back for safety." Wendy pulls the handle off the ground, swings the hammerhead forward, then back, gut-shouting as she loops it up and over her head in a windmill arch before it falls and explodes through the wall with a thundering *CRUNCH!*

It's silent for a second.

Then Wendy starts giggling, still holding the hammer handle in a cloud of dust.

"That felt fantastic," she says.

"Do it again," I say.

"I'm doing it again," she says, readjusting her gloves.

She picks up the handle and throws the head out and up to loop it over her shoulder. But this time she stops midloop. "Come here!" she says, grimacing, full-body shaking, holding that hammer head in the air. "Fast! Feel my muscle!"

I run over and squeeze it. "You are strong, lady!"

"YEAH!" She lets the hammerhead swing down and around, then up and over again. A crash. Splinter sound. Flying dust. "BOOM, BABY!"

We decide right then to take out the opposite wall, too. Double awnings. Double entrances. And double destruction.

We sledgehammer the hell outta those shingles. There are karate kicks. Whoops and high fives. We yank and twist 'em off and toss them in a pile as we bust up two walls and a whole barrelful of teenage sexual tension.

When we're done, we hammer the tarps up where the walls used to be—at some point we'll take them down and frame them for real.

"Did we meet our goals, Wendy?"

"I believe we did, Teodoro."

"Well, then, may I?"

"Uh-huh." She makes a fist. Pulls it back and flexes. "Put the first one right there."

"On your muscle?"

"Yup."

"That thing is pure steel, Wendy. I'm worried it might break my lips."

"I'm willing to risk your lips, Teodoro. Kiss it."

I kiss it and cover my mouth with my hand, wailing in agony. "They're broken! Your muscle broke my lips!"

"Oh my God! I'm a monster!" She puts a finger to my lips. "A monster with beautiful biceps I never knew I had."

I wince.

"You poor thing. I promise to always love you, even if—"

"You promise to *what* me?"

Her face turns red. "I mean, Teodoro, I promise to like, adore and like, *like* you even if your lips can never heal back to their full kissing strength."

"Serious, Wendy? You'll like, *like* me, even with these hideous, unkissable lips?"

"Yes, Teodoro. It will be very, very, extremely difficult. But I will."

"That's some pretty serious *like*."

"I guess it is . . . that sort of *like*."

In bed after a long day. It's time to turn out the lights, but I got this need to talk to Manny.

"Sweet beds, huh, Man?"

"Pretty good."

"I know, right?"

"Yeah, T." Manny pats his pillow and burrows his head in.

"What about these summer plans, Man?"

"I don't know," he says.

I ask him what he doesn't know.

He stares at the ceiling. Breathes out hard. "The doctor thing . . . the *group* thing."

I tell him Dr. Fuentes sounds pretty good. "And those sleeping pills . . . not bad, huh?"

"Yeah," he says. "But the other stuff makes me feel *off*. I have to see Doc every couple days. He wants to make sure I'm reacting right."

He closes his eyes, like he's gonna sleep.

I'm not ready for that, so I say, "What's Tío Ed's group like?"

"It's a bunch of old guys who been through what I been through," he says.

"What do they talk about?"

"Their war experiences. And they say I have to talk about mine. Oh, and I have to see that counselor, Dr. Chapman, in a couple days. . . . That'll be more of the same."

I ask him what he thinks of all that.

"Not my thing," he says. "Talking about stuff with people I don't know."

"Or people you do know," I say.

No response.

I'm not ready for quiet, so I ask him about the farming.

"I been sitting on my ass for so long. The work feels good."

The conversation seems over.

Then Manny really surprises me and asks how I'm doing.

"New Mexico?" I say. "For the whole summer? It's a shock. And Wendy? She's great, and it's good when I'm with her. But when I'm not with her, I spend a lot of time wondering how I'm going to mess it up. And studying with her? One of us is smart, and the other one is me. I'm gonna be exposed and Wendy will—"

"T," he says. "Just study hard. Work hard and get that stand ready. Then let the chips fall."

"You're right, Manny. You're right."

In a minute, the sleeping pills take hold and he's out like a log.

I can't sleep.

Because that was the most Manny's talked to me since he got home.

And that has to mean something.

FRIDAY,
JUNE 19, 2009

We're in the shack at seven thirty for our first study session.

We've got books out. Pencils at the ready. We're on that bench, sitting so damn close I can feel vibes, like, shooting off her body. And there are so many vibes it's impossible to dodge them. And the vibes are so powerful, it's taking all the self-control we have to not hurl ourselves at each other because it's freaking electromagnetic up in here.

Wendy leans my way, so I lean her way, and she starts moving her lips—*my God, her lips*—all I see is lips! And when words come out of those lips, they say . . .

"I need you to dial it *way the hell down*, Teodoro. *Way down*. Right now."

"Awesome, Wendy!" I take a gulp from my water bottle. "I am dialing it down." I take a bunch more gulps.

"And scoot." She points to her side of the bench. "This is my bubble of teaching." She points to my side. "That is your bubble of learning. And between those bubbles . . . is space. A space bubble."

"I am hearing you. And I am dialed down so low."

"*Lower.* Teodoro."

More gulps. Then I wipe my face with the back of my hand and say, "I am ready to be professional for you."

"Good. First question: What is calculus?"

I got this one. "Calculus, Wendy, is often referred to as the mathematics of *change.*"

"Yes, dork. But what does that mean?"

"*I* know what it means. But since you'd like to land the job of tutoring me in calculus, I need to be sure that *you* know what it means."

Wendy rolls her eyes and smirks. "I'll take a stab at it. You measure straight-line, same-speed kinda stuff with regular math— algebra and geometry. You use calculus to measure changes in slope and speed and force and that kind of thing. Like figuring out the amount of materials needed to build the roof of a domed stadium. Or the amount of energy it takes to pull a trailer over a mountain highway. Or how much cable you need to hold up a suspension bridge."

"Very interesting, Ms. Martinez."

"Did I get it right, Mr. Avila?"

"Close enough. You may tutor me now."

"You're not just a dork. You're the biggest dork."

Wendy says the best thing we could do to ensure I ace precalculus is to review algebra. Cuz when you're dealing with those curves and slopes in calculus, you're actually just zooming in so superclose that you get little tiny straight lines. You do the algebra on each of those tiny straight lines, and you add 'em all up? That's calculus. But you have to understand the algebra first. If you do, then calculus will be a lot easier.

Caleb and Bashir helped drag me to that B. But I'm not sure how much I've forgotten and how much I really *know*. Wendy's right. I better review.

For a couple hours, Wendy kicks my ass on everything you can do with a fraction. Then we get into absolute value and powers.

Each thing we do in algebra, she gives a quick explanation of what it will look like in calculus. We're reviewing, but she makes it feel like we're always looking ahead.

"Don't forget any of this, Teodoro. Lock it in there. I want to move on to roots and simplification of roots tomorrow. If you're really good, we'll get to factoring, which you totally need for calc."

"Let's get there," I say.

Wendy points at me. "That's the attitude, Teodoro!"

"Yeah?"

"Yeah! You can do it!"

"Yeah!" I pop off the bench and hop onto a dusty crate and thrust my arms in the air. "I think I can do it!"

"You *think* you can do it?"

"I *know* I think I'm almost pretty sure I can maybe do it!"

Wendy laughs and says we'll be working on my math confidence throughout the summer.

Then hugs. And kisses. And talk of how we earned them. By being so professional.

I have to admit, I don't think the first study session could have gone any better.

* * *

We break for lunch. Wendy keeps with the power nap routine.

I throw down a cup of coffee with my burrito. And flip through some bad daytime TV.

Wendy gets up and I prep her burrito.

She takes one bite and freaks about the green chile. She says *damn* way more times than I did! And each time she says *damn* I can see chewed burrito in her mouth. And she doesn't even care.

Sometimes I think it's impossible to fall for Wendy any harder than I already have. Then she lets herself get disgusting eating green chile. Right in front of me. It's a wild thing to watch. And I think maybe my love for her knows no bounds.

We head outside for an afternoon of dividing junk. Some goes into the adds-character-to-chile-stand pile and some goes into the haul-it-to-the-dump pile.

The afternoon feels as productive and fun as the morning.

Afterward, Wendy goes upstairs to clean up.

Manny and Xoch are still out.

I want to call Caleb. I want to hear his voice and tell him how great everything is going. But I don't want him to get on my case for leaving him. And I don't want to hear him tell me to come home.

So I call Mami and Papi again.

I tell them about my schedule with Wendy. I tell them Xochitl and Manny are working the fields in the morning and afternoon, except for when Manny takes a break to see his doctor. I tell them about the group and about his counselor.

"I got some news, too," Papi says. "I took a job at Home Depot. And I'm trying to get Mami one there, too."

"That's great. Right?"

Papi says he'll be making a third of what he did at Fauntleroy Fabrication. "But it's something, mijo." He says it feels good to be working after so long but the best part is the employee discount. It turns out Papi's gonna need it because Mami told a teacher friend about the Captain's Quarters and the friend says she wants Papi to build her this room-divider/shelf thing for her classroom. Papi's busy with the designs. Says it's gonna be very Swiss Army Knife–y.

Mami says he's real excited about it. She sounds excited, too.

About Papi.

And that is amazing.

The hard thing about talking to them is hanging up. You can hear in their voices how bad they miss us. But it's not about missing us. I think a big reason for the emotional good-byes is how bad they feel that Manny had to leave home—*leave them*—to get better.

SUNDAY,
JUNE 21, 2009

"It's time for your first quiz, Teodoro."

"What are you talking about?"

"Linear functions, man! You've been doing great. We're moving fast. But are you retaining stuff?" She hands me a page. "You ace this and we'll move on to factoring." She walks over to some splintered old shelves. "Don't mind me. I'll just be over here polishing these jars."

"Don't mind me," I say. "I'll just be over here killing this quiz."

Wendy has me learning this stuff for real. Some secret night-time studying has me retaining it. I'm done with her quiz in minutes.

Wendy checks it. She scrunches her eyebrows. "Hmm. Uh-huh. Mmm-hmm." She squeals with delight. "I thought I'd be a good tutor, but I didn't know I'd be *this* good."

"Hey, I'm the one who took the quiz. Give me a little credit."

"I'm prepared to do that. I'm offering you . . ." She winks at me, sexy. "A prize."

"Whoa. What's the prize, lady?"

She reaches behind our stack of books and whips out a red folder. She slides a page out of the folder, hands it to me, and says, "Pick one."

It's a sheet of wild animal stickers.

"You get one each time you ace a quiz," she says.

"Stickers, Wendy? Seriously?"

"You deserve them, Teodoro! Take one."

I hesitate and she pops me on the shoulder.

"Ow! All right, all right." I choose a grizzly bear and stick it on my shiny red folder.

"Doesn't look like much now," Wendy says, "but soon, your folder will be covered with stickers. And when that day comes you'll say, *Wow, that's a lot of stickers.* And you'll know you're ready to conquer pre-calculus this fall."

I know it's stupid, but I want to fill that red space up. I want my folder to be the Point Defiance Zoo of folders.

"You've earned one more thing," Wendy says, grabbing a small white sack from behind a wooden box. She holds it out to me.

I reach in and pull out a frosted cupcake. It's got writing on it: *Nice work, kid!*

"Wow. You bake this?"

"I get up a lot earlier than you. And I have the single-serving recipe memorized."

"That's cool. Split it?"

We're all quiet and smiles as we eat our cake.

"I like this, Wendy."

"I like this, too, Teodoro."

* * *

At lunch, it's just me and Tía Luci in the kitchen.

She offers me some reheated pizza.

I can't turn down the offer, or the opportunity to finally grill her about the house. "So you designed this place?"

"I did. What do you think?"

I tell her I like how open the house is—the way the kitchen and dining and living rooms make up one big room. It makes the house feel bigger than it really is. The skylights, the patios off the bedrooms, the windows and glass doors running the whole length of the room, the cactuses and trees straddling the windows inside and out, the way the exposed beams jut out the wall into the sky. All that stuff makes the house feel connected to the outside.

Luci smiles big, "Where did all that come from?"

"I don't know, Tía. The second I saw this house . . . it was like . . ."

"Yeah, Teodoro?"

"I want to know how you did it."

She leaves the table and says, "Follow me."

Upstairs, in her office, Luci pulls out blueprints. She boots up her computer and opens a design program. She walks me through her project page. She explains why the house faces the way it does. Why she placed the rooms where she did.

I ask her if I can start a new design.

She opens a fresh project window. Shows me how to get going. I plot out a quick footprint and name the file *Lopez Farm Stand*.

I start tinkering around with door and window placement. It's fun. And the more I work on it, the more fun it is. I click and drag and pretty soon I'm thinking about Papi's design for the

Captain's Quarters—how seriously he took it. And I think about us building it together.

I wanna tell him about this program.

And I don't just want to make Tío Ed's farm stand. I wanna make it great.

I'm awake in bed again, thinking about how well things are going. With Wendy and the work we're doing. And my conversation with Luci.

I can't sleep because Manny's on his way back from group. I wanna talk to him and I wanna hear that things are going good for him, too.

When the door finally opens, I act like he wakes me up. And I ask him how it went.

He says it was fine.

"That's better than bad," I say.

"Yeah," he says.

"Hey, you think you might take Tío Ed up on his offer someday?"

He slaps his pillow a couple times. "I dunno, T." He climbs in and tries to get comfy.

"Here's a scenario, Man. Say you take over the farm. And say I don't get into college, and I got zero job prospects . . . do you think I could work for you?"

"T," he says, "if there are no other workers around, and I get a debilitating disease so I can't do the work myself, and farm robots still aren't functional and selling the place isn't an option, then I'd consider hiring you. After a lengthy application and interview process and thorough reference and background checks, followed by a couple years' probationary period."

"That means the world to me, Manny."

A pillow flies in the dark. Nails me in the gut.

"So that's how it's gonna be, Man?"

"That's how it's gonna be."

"Then you better check yourself, bro."

He laughs at that. I laugh right back.

"What's so funny, *bro*?" he says.

"You are," I say. "Funny looking.*"

I get slammed by the pillow one more time. It hurts, but I can't stop laughing.

Manny can't stop laughing. But it's not like in Florence. This laughing sounds silly and normal. Not manic. It sounds like my brother.

MONDAY,
JUNE 22, 2009

I'm sitting in the kitchen, alone at lunch, when I hear something coming from down the hall.

I get up and follow the sound. It's coming from Tío Ed's office door.

It's Xochitl. She's singing and playing guitar.

I knock.

"Yeah?" she says.

"You should have heard Manny last night. He's back, Xoch. He's—"

The door opens. She pokes her head out. "You gotta drop it, T." Her smile is so big it looks like it's gonna pop off her face.

"He was hilarious. He was joking and laughing and—"

"I know, T. You should hear him talk when we're working. But it's too new, so you can't go around saying stuff like—"

"He's a human being again. He's really—"

"T, I need you to do two things. One: Shut up. And two: Find some wood, and knock on it. *Now.*"

I knock on wood.

"When stuff is good," she says, "enjoy the hell out of it. But don't ever *say it*, dumb-ass."

"Okay. I'm not ever gonna say, *Thank you for making this all turn out great.*"

"Good. Now get outta here." She closes the door.

I wait till she starts strumming again.

I poke my head back in. "This what you been doing at lunchtime?"

"Good-bye, T."

"That song sounds great. Whose is it?"

"Love you, T. Get out."

It's before dinner. The coast is clear, so I sneak back into the office.

See, when I was in there earlier, I noticed two things that made me real curious: a GarageBand window on the laptop screen. And a microphone and headphones sitting on the desk.

The headphones are still there. I put them on. I run my finger across the track pad. The window pops right up.

Xochitl would kick my ass for this, but . . . I press play.

The song starts with slow finger-picked, folk-country guitar. Then her voice.

Thank you, Sal, you got us this far

We needed you, you were a good old car

I'm singing this song 'cause I got to say

I'm so damn sorry we treated you that way . . .

I'm shaking by the end. My guts are churning. Because her voice. And those lyrics that put me right back in the desert. Back on the road.

I click and drag the track window outta the way. There's a folder called *Road Trip Songs*. I click on that. There are more music files. I wanna open them all. I need to hear these songs.

Footsteps tap on the tile hallway.

I click out of the files and reposition the track window in the center of the screen and set the headphones back on the desk.

And I get the hell out, thinking people have to hear that song. Somebody's gotta hear my sister sing that song.

FRIDAY,
JUNE 26, 2009

I'm at the wheel of Tío Ed's red Dodge pickup. Wendy's riding shotgun on a hot date to the county dump.

We take a right off Ed's property onto Valley Drive. The green of the farms and the pink mountains and popcorn clouds . . . It's like we're in a painting. And somehow, after only a week down here, it's starting to feel normal. So is Wendy sitting real close.

So is this feeling that I can tell her just about anything.

"Wendy," I say, "I been thinking about my essay for U-Dub."

"That's great. Lay it on me."

"First, though, I want to be an architect."

"Wow," she says. "Really?" And she asks me when I figured that out.

"It's been a few days," I say. "Luci showed me the program she used to design the house. I been messing around with it, plotting out the stand. I think I finally got our hinged frame units worked out."

"Okay," she says. "That's cool."

But she doesn't sound so excited. So I try again. "I wanna

design houses. Like Luci and Ed's house. I wanna make people feel like their house makes me feel."

The look on her face. It's like she's not understanding.

So I tell her about our house from when we were kids. Something about it made you feel like it was there to protect you. Like, embrace you. And I tell her about the big box house. It was huge. But it made you feel the opposite of embraced. I talk about how dark and demeaning the rental is. And I tell her about Papi designing the Captain's Quarters. I think that's what got me started. And seeing Luci's house . . . and fixing up the stand . . .

"That's good," she says. "But some of that stuff has me confused. Like how did you go from a big, shiny house into a horrible little rental? I'm guessing there's a story there, Teodoro. Like a big story."

"I know, Wendy, but—"

"And you're working on a design for the stand? Aren't we supposed to be doing that together?"

"I'll show you as soon as we get back. You'll love it."

"No, it's fine. It's just you could have told me."

It's quiet in the truck as we leave the green of Valley Drive and head into dusty Hatch.

I try to explain all our moving. I tell her Papi thought we needed more space. So we got the big house. Then Fauntleroy shut down and he and Mami lost their jobs. So we ended up in the rental.

She listens real quiet.

I try to tell her how I got sucked into that design program.

What I don't say is doing that program was like discovering something I was really good at. *My thing.* I don't know why, but

I had to protect it. Keep it for myself. I don't know why. And I can't explain it.

She asks if there's anything else she needs to know about me.

I tell her there isn't.

"You sure?"

"I'm sure."

"Positive?"

"Yeah."

We get to the dump and slide the junk off the back end of the Dodge.

It's a quiet ride back to the farm. We're done for the day.

Wendy spends the afternoon reading.

I spend it worrying I might be too much of an idiot to pull this off.

I'm on the floor, stewing, bouncing a ball against the wall when Manny walks in. He's home from another group meeting.

He watches me bounce and catch and bounce. He can tell I'm messed up. He asks me what's going on.

I tell him what happened with Wendy. Just enough so he gets it.

He says all I can do is move on and show Wendy my best self.

"I'm not sure what that is, Manny. So it's not gonna be easy."

Manny takes off his pants and climbs into bed. He reaches over and picks a pill bottle up off his nightstand. Makes like he's gonna pop the top. But he doesn't. He just sets it back down.

I think I should say something.

But I don't wanna bug him.

We lay there in silence.

230

And not bugging him feels lame. "None of my business, but I've watched you take one of those every night. What's going on?"

He looks at me like it's none of my business.

Then he tells me I'm right. He says he had been taking them three times a day. But now Doc Fuentes says if he's feeling good at night, he can skip his third dose.

"Sounds good, Man."

I don't know why I say that. Because it doesn't sound good at all.

Manny turns out the light. He closes his eyes and sleeps.

I cannot sleep.

Something wakes me.

It's pitch-black in the room.

"Manny?"

He doesn't answer.

I hop up. Shake his bed. He's not there.

I look out the door, down the hallway.

He's not there.

I check the bathroom.

No Manny.

I slip on shoes and run downstairs.

I bust through the front door, into the cool desert night.

And I fly right by Manny sitting on a porch step. I try to put on my brakes, but I'm going so fast I almost fall over.

Manny drops a notebook and pen to his side and looks at me like he didn't just do that.

"Hey, Man."

"Where you running, T?"

I tell him I needed some fresh air.

He says it looks like I needed it in a hurry.

I ask if he minds if I take a seat.

He doesn't say no.

We sit awhile.

Then I tell him I got worried when he wasn't in bed.

"Just sitting here, T." He looks out into the dark.

I point to the notebook on the ground and ask him what he's writing.

He grunts. "Group stuff."

"I'll let you write, then," I say.

"I'm not writing," he says.

I ask him why not.

He doesn't look back at me or say anything.

Feels like my cue to leave. But I don't. I stay right next to my brother. "Besides the writing, how's group been?"

"They won't stop talking war. I get it, already. I get it. I get it."

I try to tell him it sounds miserable, but he stands and says, "Maybe that works for them. But I'm done." He bends the notebook in half and launches it into the dark.

We hear it hit dirt, far out in the fields.

"All right, then," I say.

He sits back down on the step, his arms wrapped around his head, his head wedged between his knees.

"Manny?"

He doesn't respond so I go back up to the room and poke my head out the window.

I watch my brother sit for a long time. Until he falls asleep. Right there on the porch.

I take a blanket down and cover him up.

Then I walk back upstairs.

Back to the window.

Back to watching.

SATURDAY,
JUNE 27, 2009

I'm in the shack. I got my notebook out. Calculator ready. But first I have to talk to Wendy. Like *really* talk.

She walks in.

"Hi, Wendy."

"Hi." She gets her tutor materials and sits on the bench.

"Wendy, I'm sorry I never told you about our housing situation. Ask me anything you want."

"I already asked you."

"What did you ask me?"

"I asked you if there's anything else you need to tell me. And you said no."

Oh, hell. She knows something.

"Teodoro, you never told me how sick Manny was when he came back. You never told me how bad he got. You never told me what happened that night in the rental house. Xochitl told me. And she told me the real reason she needed to bring Manny here."

"Of course she did."

"She wasn't squealing on you, Teodoro. She told me because she's worried about Manny. And she's worried about you."

"What else did she say?"

"She told me you left home. You moved out and you're not living with your family."

"I'm sorry, Wendy."

"I like you *so much,* Teodoro."

"I like you so much, too, Wendy."

"So much that in my mind I figured out a way to understand why you wouldn't tell me what was going on. And why you lied to me at U-Dub."

"I wanted you to like me, Wendy. And it wouldn't have worked if I came out with a bunch of negative drama I wasn't handling very well. It would've been too much information. Too much emotion."

"I understand. It makes sense."

"It does?"

"It makes sense if it's just some abstract people hiding stuff from each other. But it's *us,* Teodoro." Tears start rolling down her face. She looks like somebody just died.

She reaches one hand to her other wrist and slips off the bracelet.

She holds it out for me.

I don't take it because this is not happening.

"I bought it for you, Wendy. Keep it."

"I can't, Teodoro."

"Please, Wendy."

"Take it."

"No."

"Take and hold on to it. Because maybe someday . . ."

"Maybe someday *what*?"

"I don't know, but I'll feel better if I know you still have it."

I take the bracelet. And shove it in my pocket.

I look down at my math notebook. "What now?"

"I'm not sure," she says.

I can't take the thought of us broken up and trying to keep this tutoring thing going.

But I can't take the thought of her going back to Vancouver, either. "Wendy," I say. "Are you gonna leave?"

She shakes her head like she can't believe I asked her that. "Teodoro," she says, looking at me hard and deep, "are *you* going to leave?"

At night, I'm deep in this dream where I'm working at Home Depot with Papi. He's, like, seventy-five years old. I'm pushing fifty. And we're arguing about what part a customer should buy to fix his leaky toilet. I lift a pipe to show them and wrapped around my wrist is a raggedy old shells-and-beads bracelet.

So the dream sucks already. Then Papi looks at me and starts shouting, "Show me your identification!"

That wakes me right up.

Turns out the shouting is real. But it's Manny doing it. He's standing on my bed in his underwear, pointing an imaginary rifle at my face. "Show me your ID. Now!" Every muscle in his body is flexed to the breaking point.

I look up at my brother. "It's *me*, Manny."

"Down!" he shouts. "Get on the ground!"

236

I don't know what else to do, so I get down.

He looks ready to kill. "On the ground, now!"

"I'm on the ground!"

He yells something in, like, Arabic?

"I don't understand!"

He tells me to get down, over and over.

"I can't get any more down, Manny!"

He goes to crack me with the butt of the invisible rifle when Xochitl flies in the room and tackles him. They slam onto the mattress.

"Wake up!" she says, still gripping Manny.

He keeps shouting military stuff.

She slaps his cheek. "Wake up!"

Manny shakes his head. Looks around the dark room.

I turn on the light.

He looks scared. Doesn't know where he is.

He looks at me.

He looks at Xochitl.

I move slowly to my bed.

She guides Manny back to his. "We're at Tío Ed's," Xochitl says.

He starts shivering and he looks around the room, like he's still trying to figure it out.

Xochitl helps him slip into a sweatshirt. "You had a bad dream. That's all."

She tucks him in. Kisses his forehead. "Sleep, Manuel. Then I'm taking you to see Dr. Fuentes in the morning."

Xochitl walks over and puts a hand on my shoulder. "You okay?"

"Yeah. I'm fine."

She leaves us.

I pretend I'm asleep. But I got my eye on Manny.

He sits up. Presses his back against the wall. Watches the door. The window. The door again. At some point he slips all the way under the covers and it looks like he's going to sleep.

I watch Manny till he's snoring hard. And I tell myself it's okay to shut my eyes.

Then the tapping starts.

I don't know what he's got in his hand. But he's tapping it against the wall.

Click-click, click-click, click-click . . .

SUNDAY,
JUNE 28, 2009

I walk into the kitchen and Wendy is sitting there. "Cereal, Teodoro?"

She doesn't wait for an answer. She just starts pouring.

We sit and slurp.

Sounds of spoons clinking bowls.

"You look tired," she says.

"I didn't sleep much," I say.

"That makes two of us."

Wendy pours coffee.

"You heard all that?" I say.

"Yeah," she says. "Can we talk, please?"

"About what?"

I snap at her with that.

"About what we're going to do next."

"Nope." I'm too tired and too messed up to deal. I push myself away from the table. "I can't do this."

*　　*　　*

I drive the Dodge fast down I-10.

I pull out my phone.

Caleb picks up and asks me who it is.

"You know it's me."

He says my voice sounds familiar, but he can't quite place it.

"Sorry I haven't been in touch."

"I don't like it."

"I need to talk to you, Caleb."

I tell him I'm coming home.

I talk as I drive past Las Cruces. I tell him all about our road trip. I try to tell him everything. Past tiny Anthony, New Mexico, and tiny Anthony, Texas.

Past cattle ranches and dirt-mound dairy farms. I tell Caleb how great everything was with Wendy. In Florence and here on the farm. I tell him everything about Manny.

Past the outskirt sprawl of El Paso housing tracts and the brown Franklin Mountains. I tell him how positive things seemed. But really Manny's as bad as ever. Wendy will never trust me again. It's all too much. And I want to come home.

"Are you done talking?"

"I guess so."

I exit the freeway onto busy Mesa Street and pull into a movie theater parking lot.

"T, for a second I let myself get pumped about you coming home."

"Then what happened?"

"You started talking for real."

Caleb tells me I have unfinished business. He says if I come home now I'll never know how it might have turned out.

240

I tell him I know exactly how it would have turned out. *Like crap.*

"Well, my friend," he says, "Sometimes it's better to walk through the crap than to walk around it."

"Oh my God, *what?*"

"Imagine you walk to the store and you don't step in any crap. Then, on the way home, you also don't step in any crap. That's a successful shopping trip. But what do you learn from it?"

"I learn that sometimes life actually works the way it's supposed to."

"No, you idiot! You never think about it again and you don't learn anything."

"Kinda like this lecture."

"Listen up, T. What if you're almost to that store and you step in a big ol' steaming pile of dog crap?"

"Is this the best you can do, Caleb?"

"Yes, it is. And you made me lose my place."

"You had me stepping in—"

"Dog crap. Exactly, T. You got a mess on your shoes. And you have to clean it up. But how? Do you use a stick? A wadded-up Kleenex? Your bare finger? No matter how hard you try, you'll still have a poop smear that's gonna stink up that store. But you're too far from home. You can't turn back. You gotta get your granny the medicine."

"What granny? What medicine?"

"The point is, if you open yourself up to the possibility of a crappy shoe, then sometimes you'll get crap on your shoes and you'll stink places up real bad. And when that happens, you know you're living a full life and you got stories to tell."

"I miss you, Caleb."

"I miss you, too. But if you come home now, someday you're going to wonder what would have happened."

I tell him I'll think about it.

But my mind is one hundred percent made up. I'm gonna drive back to the farm, pack my bag, buy my ticket, say my good-byes, and fly home.

I don't want to get to Tío Ed's early. I don't wanna see anyone. So I go into the theater and I watch the new Transformers movie twice. I can't possibly sit through that thing a third time, so I get back in the truck. I'm heading north toward Hatch, but it's still early, so I exit onto Transmountain Highway, just outside of El Paso.

I end up on a Franklin Mountains trail. I hike till it's too hot to move. I hide under a big shade rock and turn off my buzzing phone. And I fall asleep.

A couple hours later, I wake up and climb to the top of the mountain. I watch the sun go down on El Paso, then scramble down the mountain and drive the dark desert freeway back to Hatch.

No one's up when I get there.

I creep into the room.

Manny's sound asleep. No clicking tonight.

I pull my bag out from under the bed. Open the dresser. Throw in clothes. Throw in my notebooks.

I tuck in and close my eyes.

In the morning, I'm on my way home.

The slow click of the bedroom door latching into place. That's what wakes me.

I look over at Manny's empty bed.

He's probably on the porch again.

I check the window.

He's not down there.

I check the bathroom. Sneak to the kitchen. Back up to the room. No Manny.

I wrestle with a pair of pants, but I got 'em going backward, so I yank them off and slip shoes on fast. I bounce down the stairs and out the door, toward the fields.

I spot Manny walking near the storage barn, not far from the road, on the other side of the driveway from the shack.

I don't shout his name. I don't say a word. I just run fast and quiet.

I get to the barn. He's gone.

I look toward the road and catch his silhouette, moving between rows of plants.

I run at him. I'm about half a football field away, and I can see him clearly now, lit up by the stars and moon.

He stops walking. Looks up at the sky.

I don't stop running.

He drops to his knees.

Plants whipping my bare legs.

He looks down at something.

Fumbles with something.

No, Manny!

He lifts a pistol up to his head—*Aw, God, where'd he get that?*

I'm twenty yards away.

Manny looks up at the stars again.

A click as he releases the safety.

Twenty feet away.

I can hear him breathe.

I can't believe he can't hear me.

I lock my jaw.

Clench my fists.

Manny hauls in a last deep breath.

I lower my shoulder.

A howl blasts out of me.

Manny turns. His eyes catch mine.

I explode into my brother. My shoulder cracks his back. My head knocks his head.

My knuckles burn as I punch the gun away.

Manny crumples to the ground.

A clap of thunder as the gun flies into the air.

I slide right over him, into the dirt, over a row of plants.

My ears hiss and burn. I cup my hands to my head to make it stop, but it doesn't stop.

Manny sits up. He takes a feeble swing at me.

I spring to my knees and swing. My fist blasts his jaw.

He shakes it off and comes at me. Misses with another weak swing.

I hit him in the face. I hit him in the gut. In the jaw. I hit him over and over till he's down in the dirt and he's not moving.

I lift him upright by his shirt. Pull his face to mine. "Fight me, Manny! Fight me!"

He's limp. Not moving. But I can't stop yelling. "Fight, Manny! Fight, Manny! Fight!"

I yell it till I got nothing left.

I collapse on top of him.

We lie there in a heap, faces to the earth, desperately heaving, like we're trying to catch the same breath.

"Manny? Manny?"

He doesn't answer me.

I feel his rib cage expand and contract.

I lift him up. My big brother feels so damn light.

I start dragging him back.

Xochitl runs at us, screaming his name, over and over.

Tío Ed is right behind her.

"Is he alive?" She lunges to Manny.

I tell her he missed.

She holds his head in her hands. "You're going to be okay, Manuel. Oh, God, say something, Manny."

Tío Ed helps Xochitl lift him upright. "Ay, mijo."

I hear Luci shout something about an ambulance.

"We love you," Xochitl says. "Do you hear me, Manny?" She gets under an arm and they start dragging him back. "You're going to be okay, Manny. We love you, Manny."

I'm stuck in place, watching them walk away.

I sit in the dirt.

It's cold.

My teeth chatter.

I try but I can't make myself stand.

I bury my head in my arms until I feel a hand on my back.

I look up.

It's Wendy, kneeling in the dirt.

I look right at her.

She looks right at me. Pulls me into her. Pulls my head to her chest and holds me tight.

I hold her right back.

The sound of sirens. We look back toward the house. It's lit up in red lights.

We watch Xochitl and Tío Ed lift Manny onto the porch.

Wendy takes me by the hand. We stand and start walking. Then break into a run.

The EMTs give Manny oxygen. Check his heart. Ask their questions.

Wendy's still got my hand in hers, squeezing as hard as she can.

They move Manny to the ambulance. Xochitl motions my way.

Wendy holds my face in her hands and looks in my eyes. There are no words, but she says everything she possibly can.

I follow Tío Ed to the van. Xochitl pulls me into the front seat. We take off and she reaches out, grips my hand. She's shaking. She's a slobbering mess as she says, "I'm sorry, T, I'm so sorry. You shouldn't have had to—"

I shake my head and squeeze her hand.

"I ruined everything, T."

"No, Xoch, don't—"

"I thought if I could—"

"It's not your fault. You tried, Xoch."

She squeezes my hand back. "You were the one who tried."

She asks me what happened.

I tell her.

She pulls me over. Wraps her arms around me.

I start crying like a baby. "I couldn't stop hitting him, Xoch."

* * *

We sit on a waiting room bench, wondering what you do after your brother tries to kill himself.

Tío Ed walks our way. Sits down beside us. He says they have to keep him in here for seventy-two hours. Dr. Fuentes says he'll sign the release papers after that, but only if he's sure he and Tío Ed have a solid safety plan. Tío Ed thinks that'll mean putting Manny back to work, but with more frequent visits to Dr. Fuentes. More counseling with Dr. Chapman. Tighter protocol regarding meds. He says the group guys will come in waves every day, throughout the day. "I made the calls," he says. "My men are all signed up."

He turns and talks to the reception nurse. Then waves us over.

We're going to Manny's room.

Knots in my stomach. Pains in my chest. A weight in my gut keeps me on the bench.

Xochitl takes me by the hand. Pulls me up. "We're going to tell Manny we love him. And we're gonna tell him to knock it off right now."

"Okay, Xoch."

We walk down the hall. The smell of chemical cleaner. Monitors whistle, beep, and ring in rooms. Machines clunk and whir. Shoes tap on linoleum.

We follow Tío Ed into Manny's room. I look at the first bed. It's some other miserable guy, his face wrapped in bandages.

Manny's by the window. He's sitting up. Tubes for fluids and meds. A swollen jaw and two black eyes. His arms are exposed and there's a couple tattoos I never saw before. One is some army shield. The other one is a fish. And it's right over his heart.

Xochitl ducks under the tangle of tubes and cords. Then she climbs in bed with him.

I did not know you could do that.

She wraps an arm around. Kisses his cheeks. "I love you, Manuel. Don't you ever do that again. I love you. We need you. We want you here forever."

He looks lost on hospital drugs.

"Come to me next time," she says. "Tell me you want to do it. If I think you're a lost cause, I'll put you out of your misery myself. Deal?"

He says it's a deal.

"I'd never do it, Manny."

"Thanks, Xoch."

Tío Ed pulls the curtain between beds. Scoots a chair over. "How you feeling, mijo?"

Manny says he's been better. He asks why his face hurts.

"Teodoro got pissed he had to save his brother's life."

Manny looks my way.

"I'm sorry, Man. But don't do that stuff anymore."

He looks at me like he's begging me to understand. "T, it's not—"

"Huh-uh, Manny. There's nothing you can say that's gonna make it make sense."

He looks down at the bed. Looks like he wants me to go away.

But I'm not going away. I kneel down. Get at bed level. I'm shaking. I got tears blurring everything. "Look at me, Manny."

He doesn't.

"Manny, I know you're messed up. I know you've seen some horrible stuff." I wipe tears. "You know what? Now *I've* seen some horrible stuff. You wanna mess me up, too? You wanna mess

248

up Xochitl and Mami and Papi? Then do your thing and we'll all be messed up forever."

I can't breathe and I can't take the smell. I run out and down the hall and through the waiting room into the restroom. I splash my face with water and let out tears and snot till I got no more.

I sit back on that waiting room bench and bury my face in my hands.

And I try to work out how to undo what I just said to Manny. Then I stop.

Because I don't wanna undo it.

"Hang in there, son."

I look up from the bench. It's an old bald guy. There are four other old guys standing behind him.

"I'm Lou," he says. "I'm buddies with your uncle. So are all these guys."

I shake the group guys' hands.

Lou asks what room Manny's in.

I point and he says, "We're here for Manuel. But we're here for you and your sister, too."

I tell them thanks and they turn to go see Manny.

In a minute Xochitl walks through the waiting room toward the exit.

I follow her.

Outside, she puts a cigarette to her lips. Pulls a lighter out of her pocket.

"Where'd you get that?" I say.

"I saved one in case of emergency. This qualifies."

She flicks the lighter.

I grab the cigarette, and before she can snatch it back, I drop it and stomp.

"What the hell, T?"

"In SeaTac, you said that was your last one ever." I grab the lighter from her hand and stomp that till it's bits of plastic. "You can do this, Xochitl."

"Oh, God, T, it doesn't even matter."

"Maybe not to you."

She looks back toward Manny's room. Looks at me again. "Don't tell Manny I was gonna smoke."

"I won't. I promise."

"I told Mami and Papi I quit, too, so—"

"I won't tell them, either."

"Speaking of Mami and Papi . . ."

Xochitl asked Tío Ed if we could wait to tell them about Manny. She promised him she'd call home soon.

"T," she says, "I don't think it'll help to tell them. Manny will be pissed. And Mami and Papi will freak out. Everything is bad enough. They don't need to know right now."

I tell her if they find out we didn't tell them, they'll never forgive us.

"Up to you, T. You can tell them if you really think we should."

Xochitl heads back inside.

I pull out my phone.

I dial and hear the ring.

Then I press the hang-up cuz I've got no idea how to say it.

The sliding doors open. Tía Luci walks in. She's taking us back to the farm.

MONDAY,
JUNE 29, 2009

Luci gives us long hugs before she goes out again.

Xochitl goes to her room to sleep. I head to the kitchen.

Wendy's there with the cereal box. She looks my way and lifts it up.

I nod.

She pours.

We sit and slurp. Clink spoons on bowls.

Wendy says she's so sorry about Manny.

I nod.

"You were brave," she says.

"Don't, Wendy."

She reaches over and clutches my arm. I can see in her eyes she's about to try to say something hopeful. Then she stops. And that's good.

"You've been up all night," she says. "You should sleep."

"I can't."

Wendy takes her bowl to the sink. She sits down again. "Should we work?"

The way she asks . . . the way she's looking at me . . . The way she looked at me last night . . . when I was the most lost . . .

We might be broken up. But she's here. And I'm here. And if we're working and we keep on working, then maybe my mind can get unstuck from seeing stuff I can't stop seeing. "Yeah, Wendy. If it's okay."

"I want to, Teodoro."

"Me, too, Wendy."

"I'll get our stuff."

"Just work," I say.

"Yes, Teodoro. Just work."

Wendy heads out to get set up. I can't get started till I call home.

Mami picks up.

"I wasn't expecting you this early," she says.

My heart pounds. I swallow a lump in my throat.

"Are you there, Teodoro?"

"Mami, yeah, I'm here. How are you and Papi?"

"Good. I no longer work for Walmart. Papi and I are headed to the Depot in a while. We're both on ten to six."

"Wow, Mami. How is that?"

"I'm going to learn a lot about paint. Your papi likes it."

"Mami?"

"Yes, Teodoro?"

"I miss you guys."

"Are you all right, mijo? You sound—"

"I'm good. I'm fine. Just missing you. Wendy's waiting, so . . . I love you, Mami."

"We love you, too, Teodoro."

I hang up and dial again.

Caleb picks right up.

"Brah from another mah! What is up?"

I tell him I'm going to stay in New Mexico. And I'm gonna step in all the possible crap.

I ask him if he'll check in on Mami and Papi.

They sound good on the phone, but I need to know for sure.

"Of course, T. I'll check in on your folks."

"Thanks. And, Caleb?"

"Yeah, man?"

"I'm gonna call more often."

"You okay?" Caleb says.

"Yeah."

"You sure?"

"No."

"I get it, T. Breakups suck."

"It's Manny. He's in the hospital. I can't talk now, but I'll tell you soon."

"Tell me soon. I'm gonna be worrying."

"I promise. Love you, brother."

"Love you, brother. Take care."

"Oh, and, Caleb?"

"Yeah?"

"Don't tell my parents yet. They don't know."

When I'm distracted, Wendy is patient with me. When I have to take a break, we take a break. It feels messed up doing the same stuff we did before, but it's what I need.

At some point, Wendy's talking logarithmic functions and I

can't keep my lids open any longer. I brush my notebook aside and rest my head on the table. "Five minutes," I say, without even looking up.

"You sure that's it?" she says.

When I wake up, Wendy's head is on the table. Her eyes are closed and she's breathing deep. Her chair is scooted right up next to mine. And her arm is resting on my shoulders.

I have no idea how long we been sleeping like that.

"Five more minutes," I whisper.

It's midafternoon when we finally get up. Wendy says she thought she should let me sleep.

I thank her for that. And I thank her for the sleep hug.

"If there was ever a time to sleep-hug a buddy," she says, "that was it."

We skip the afternoon shack work and put on hats and sunscreen and go out and help Xochitl and Hector in the fields. We weed. Adjust the drip line. Fix it where it's leaking too bad. Wendy and I work hard together.

At some point, Xochitl's working one side of a row and I'm on the other. She tells me she's been calling the hospital throughout the day. Tío Ed and the group guys are coming at Manny in shifts. Always one of them there.

Ed says Manny's mostly sleeping. But when he's not, he's finally talking. *Really talking.*

"That's good," I tell her. "That's real good, Xoch. What about you? You okay?"

"Nothing prepares you, T."

"You think it's all right, him getting out so soon?"

"I talked to Dr. Fuentes and Dr. Chapman. They think they have a solid plan. And Tío Ed is on a mission. He's says he's never lost a group guy. And he's not gonna lose one now."

"That's good, Xoch."

"I'm not giving up on this summer—and whatever comes after. I'm not giving up on our tío. And I'm not giving up on Manny. We can do this. Right?"

"Yeah," I say. "We can do this."

"My God, T, the world would be a different place today if it wasn't for you."

"Don't even say that, Xoch."

"What?"

"I was just there, okay? And I did it. And that's fine. But I can't handle thinking about it, so let's not talk about it. *Ever*. All right?"

"All right."

"Let's just work."

"Yeah, T. You're right. Let's work."

We get back to pulling weeds and checking hose and spotting bugs.

And fighting to stop my brain from thinking about how different the world woulda been.

TUESDAY,
JUNE 30, 2009

In the shack, on the bench, trying to focus on numbers and symbols.

I can't do it. I got images I can't shake. Sounds I can't stop hearing. And tears dripping on the page.

Wendy puts a hand on my back. I know she's telling me to let it all out.

I do that.

And when I'm done, I look up at her, and she's wiping her own tears.

"Enough for today?" she asks.

"Let's keep going," I say.

"I'm worried about you, Teodoro."

"I don't know what would make me feel better than keeping on."

"If that's how you feel." She says it serious, but she's got snot rolling out her nose.

Her eyes get big and she points at *my* nose. "Teodoro, you got a snot stream flowing."

I reach a finger to her face and wipe *her* snot with it. I hold that finger up to her eyes, busting a crazy-ass laugh. "That makes two of us, *Snotty McMocos.*"

"Gross, Teodoro!" She busts out a wild laugh.

"I'm gross?" I say, pointing the moco-covered finger at myself.

"Stop laughing!" she says.

"*You* stop laughing!" I say.

We cannot stop. Wendy grabs a towel and throws it at me.

I wipe my finger off. And I finally get tired and stop laughing.

Wendy stops laughing, too.

I pick up my notebook. Pick up my pencil.

She flips a page in the book. Points at a graph and says, "Look at this. Can you define the slope for me?"

I try to figure it out, but the images and sounds come again. Manny in the field. Manny raising the gun. The explosion. My fist blasting his jaw.

The tears roll again. I shake my head. I fight the pictures. And I work through that graph. I'm real slow. But I figure it out. I wipe tears and snot and I tell Wendy the answer.

"I'm ready to listen when you're ready to talk," she says. "Whatever you need."

"I need to do the next problem."

"All right, Teodoro."

After lunch, I ask Wendy to come upstairs to Luci's office. I sit in the desk chair and boot up the design program.

She says it's cool. And she likes what I've done so far.

I stand and have her take the seat. "Your turn," I say.

I pull up another chair and tutor Wendy on how to use the

program. She picks it up real fast and starts working on the entrances where I'd left off. She asks me questions. I answer them. She has ideas. I tell her what I think. Working together. It's good.

The whole time, we're sitting so close. Arms brushing each other as we point at the screen. Faces close, hands close as we sketch on a notepad and exchange ideas.

I do not feel the need to kiss Wendy.

I don't feel the need to hug her the way I did before.

I just need her.

I just need her here.

THURSDAY, JULY 2, 2009

I wake up when he walks in the room.

But I pretend I'm asleep. I'm too nervous to talk to my brother.

He switches the light on and gets himself ready for bed. When he's all set, he sits on his mattress, facing me.

"Hey, Man." I yawn like he just woke me up.

"Hey, T."

"It's good to see you."

"You, too."

He swallows hard and says, "Thanks for getting in the way."

My God, how am I supposed to respond to that? *No prob, bro. Anytime?*

I don't know what else to say. So I ask him if he really means it.

He says he does and it's not going to happen again.

I let that one hang in the air for a bit. "Really, Man? You sure?"

"Tío Ed and the group guys, especially Charlie and Lou. They just wore me down. They attached themselves to me. Tío Ed almost never left my room. They got me talking. There's stuff I need to do. People I want to see."

"That's good, Manny."

"Mami and Papi. You and Xoch. Frank. I wanna see Elena again. We got really tight in Delano. And Gladys."

"Gladys? Abita's Gladys?"

Manny says they've been texting. She's been rooting for him. He says he let her down with what he did. He says he let us all down.

I tell Manny he scared me.

He says he's sorry.

"I'm still scared, Man."

"Me, too, T. But there's stuff I wanna make right. Stuff I've done that I'm not proud of. If I'm not here, I can't make any of it better."

He starts talking about his future. Going to college. Farming. Getting married someday. Having kids someday.

I tell him it's good to hear him talking.

"I feel a lot better," he says. "But I got a long way to go."

"You're gonna get there, Manny."

"I think so." Then he climbs in bed. "Big workday today. I'm gonna get a couple hours."

"Sleep well, Manny."

He switches off the light. "See you in the morning."

"See you in the morning, Man."

Xochitl flips opens the shade. Sun pours into the room. "Up and at 'em!"

Tío Ed's there, too. He's holding pill bottles and paperwork in his hands. He looks right at me. "First things first. I know that even before you came down here, you've had a rough time sleeping in close proximity to your brother."

"No," I say. "It's fine. I'm fine. What's going on?"

"It's all right, T," Manny says. "We have to talk about this."

What we talk about is everyone involved—including Manny— agreed that he should still have someone sleeping in the room with him. But they're worried about me being traumatized by everything that's happened. In the Captain's Quarters. On the road. And here in Hatch.

So Tío Ed says he'll sleep in Manny's room. Xochitl says, no, she'll sleep in Manny's room. Ed says even the group guys say they'll take turns.

I appreciate that they're worried. I really do. But I want everyone to stop making a big deal about this. I don't want Manny to feel bad. I don't want him to think I'd be relieved to get away from him.

"Tío Ed," I say, "I'm a light sleeper. I know I'll get up if Manny gets up. Xochitl can sleep through anything. Same with old guys. You sleep like logs. So I'm good right here. I'm not switching rooms."

Eventually, they give in and say I can stay with Manny. But the minute things get rough, other arrangements will be made.

Next order of business is drugs.

There will be a daily meds chart—signed and dated by Dr. Fuentes so we know that we're working off the correct, current prescription.

Tío Ed describes the demeaning pill-taking protocol, which I'm going to be a part of.

I hate that we're treating Manny like a baby. "You okay with this, Man?"

"It's fine."

"You sure?"

"T, if I don't do it this way, I have to get admitted. Part of the deal with Doc."

So I do it. I check the list. Check the pill bottle. I watch Manny take one out. Put it on his tongue. Watch him swallow. Then search Manny's mouth and under his tongue for a hidden pill, as he says *AHHH* and makes a big silly show, trying to convince us this whole thing isn't extremely awkward.

The protocol complete, Manny says, "Can we get to work now?"

"Sounds good to me," Xochitl says.

"Let's get to it," Tío Ed says. "The world needs its chile."

FRIDAY,
JULY 3, 2009

We print out our design for the entrance walls of the stand. And we head outside into the sun.

To get the entrances big enough and to make room for windows, Wendy and I have to take out a couple two-by-four studs in the middle and ends of the walls.

We do not know how to do this.

On either side of each of the entrances we'll be stacking windows two by two.

We don't know how to do that, either.

Tía Luci does. And she's here to help. She asks if we need a tutorial on her electric miter saw.

"We'd appreciate that," Wendy says. "I'd like this to remain a nub-free zone."

"Show us how it's done, Tía," I say. "But please watch your fingers."

She shows us how to measure and cut the two-by-fours. Then she teaches us how to reinforce the crossbeams on top of the entrances. That way we can rip out studs without the roof caving in. After that, she shows us how to frame the windows.

I look at Wendy. She looks at me. "We got it."

Luci says to call if we have questions. And she leaves for work.

Wendy and I go real slow. We know that if we do something wrong, we could mess the shack up bad. And we could get hurt.

We check each other's measurements. We swipe a pencil against a square to mark our lines straight. We take turns running that screaming saw and watch sawdust cover the earth and cover our skin. We wear that dust proudly.

We knock out studs for the entrance on one side. We breathe deep sighs of relief, then high-five and whoop when the shack roof does not cave in. Because we reinforced it right.

We frame the windows. And hammer them in.

The way we get it done is not pretty. Wendy and I miss nails when we hammer. I smash my thumb a couple times. We both pound nails in crooked. And take too much time pulling them out again. We even mess up and hammer in boards at an angle instead of square. Whenever it happens, we have to pull them out and do it over.

Neither of us cares that we suck as carpenters. We just do it. We work all day until, finally, as the sun sets, we stand there quiet, looking at a wall with a huge entrance and four windows on each side.

"Hey, Martinez," I say.

"Yeah, Avila?"

"Who ever would have thought?"

"Not me, man."

264

"We should celebrate this, Wendy. Cuz suddenly, we're, like, two people who designed something. Then built it."

"Sparky's?" she says.

"Tío Ed did say they serve the best green chile cheeseburger in New Mexico."

"And that means Sparky's green chile cheeseburger is the best cheeseburger in the whole wide world."

"Are we worthy of one of those?"

"Is that a question people usually ask before they eat a burger?"

"Nope. But we're not people."

"What does that even mean, Teodoro?"

I walk up to the stand, and I hug one of those two-by-four studs that's holding up the roof. I yank on it. I try as hard as I can to pull it out of place.

Wendy sees what I'm doing. She hugs another stud and does the same.

We shake and pull like crazy. And those things do not budge one bit.

"You know what that means, Wendy?"

"I think it means we're worthy, Teodoro."

"Yes. And it means we were professional today."

"I'm starving. Let's go!"

Damn . . . damn . . . damn . . .

Pretty much, that's all we say while we devour the best green chile cheeseburger in the universe. And we say it with our mouths full. And neither of us gives a rip.

After our burgers are gone and we're dipping fries in

milkshakes, I tell Wendy there's another thing I'd like to be honest about.

I tell her the car didn't break down the night of her concert. "I lied about that."

She asks me why I lied.

"Um, I guess I was too nervous."

She asks me why I was so nervous.

And suddenly, I wish I hadn't brought it up. Because the answer is a big crazy conversation you probably shouldn't have with the actual person who you were nervous about seeing. Because the reason you were nervous is you were afraid they might actually like you.

And if they liked you, then they'd want to know you for real.

And if they got to know you for real, they would realize they do not, in fact, like you. And they would stop wanting to be with you.

And that's the reason you lied and you didn't go to the concert.

And you were right—I mean, I was right to be nervous and right to not go. Because, in the end, it turned out exactly like I'd imagined.

I don't say any of that stuff to Wendy.

I just shrug and tell her I don't know why I was so nervous.

"It's okay," she says. "I was nervous, too. And maybe a little scared. And maybe not just a little."

"Yeah," I say, "I just wanted to tell you. Because even though stuff didn't work out, I still want to be honest."

SUNDAY,
JULY 5, 2009

We're home the morning after spending the Fourth with the group guys at a cabin deep in the Organ Mountains. They go up there every year so they can celebrate the holiday as far away from fireworks as they can get. Turns out the popping and whistling sounds are problematic for some vets. Manny would be one of those vets.

When Xochitl and Manny get to work, we sneak into Ed's office. Wendy hands me her thumb drive.

I had told her she had to hear Xochitl's song, and finally, today is our chance.

The laptop is closed this time. The microphone is put away. And the guitar is in its case.

I flip the screen up. There's an e-mail staring me in my face.

I cannot *not* read it.

July 3, 2009

Kristi,

Yeah, I'm sure.

Of course I want to go. But I have to stay down here until I know my brother is all right. I hope you find the right singer and I hope you have a kick-ass tour!

Love and Hugs to all Rays,

X

I don't want Wendy to know that I'm reading Xochitl's e-mail. So I block the screen and scroll down quick.

July 2, 2009

You sure? Anything we can do to talk you into this? We need our X-factor on tour! ☺

-K

I've got to know what came before these mails but reading more of Xochitl's private correspondence will have to wait.

Stealing her private song files, however, cannot wait.

Out in the shack, we download the files onto Wendy's laptop and we listen to that Sally song. Then we listen to all of them. Songs about Manny coming home and more songs from our road trip. They're deep. Slow. Gut-wrenching. Desperate. Beautiful.

There's so much about what's happened that I couldn't describe it to anyone if I tried.

But Xochitl did it in these songs.

Wendy says, "You told me Xochitl was in bands, but I didn't know she had a voice *like that*. And her songs are incredible."

"My sister is the legit real deal."

Wendy says there was a long stretch when Xochitl didn't come into their room until really late. Like after Wendy was already sleeping. The songs explain what she was doing at night and what she had been doing during lunch.

She says that after Manny went to the hospital, Xochitl started going to bed early.

I beg Wendy not to tell Xochitl what we did. If my sister wanted us to know about these songs, she would have told us about them.

Without saying a word, Wendy presses play. And we listen to them all again.

At night, when I know Manny's asleep, I sneak downstairs, back to the office.

The e-mail thread is still there.

I scroll down.

July 2, 2009

Dear Ms. McConnell,

I'm sorry to say there's been a change in plans. I was so humbled that the Ray crew wanted me to open for them and pumped for the opportunity to be on the tour. But now

I've got serious family stuff I have to deal with so I can't make any commitments for a few months, at least. I'm so sorry. Please think of me in the future.

Thanks and keep in touch,
Xochitl Avila

What the hell?
I scroll down.

June 18, 2009

Dear Ms. McConnell,

Count me in! Getting new songs together now. I'll be sending you a demo in a couple weeks. Thank you so much.

Sincerely,
Xochitl Avila

June 18, 2009

Hi Xochitl,

I'm the producer/promoter for Ray Is a Girl's international fall tour. I know Kristi has talked to you about opening for them. Normally, we have another of our own artists open, but the Ray crew is pretty stuck on the idea of you opening. We're looking for a solo singer-songwriter, someone who could sit in with the band on backing vocals for a few songs. If that sounds like something you're into, send me some of your stuff so I can run it by folks here at SubPop.

Just so you know, we'll have a couple weeks of

rehearsal in Seattle in early September. We'll start off with some Midwest/East Coast college shows for a couple months. Then we head to Europe, then back to the East Coast for some shows at bigger venues. We'll work our way west, to LA, SF, and Portland, and finish up in Seattle at the Moore Theatre in spring.

We'll give your demo a listen, and if we agree with the band, I'll send a contract with itinerary and all details.

All the best,
Laura McConnell
SubPop Records

I can't sleep. My mind is stuck on the fact that Xochitl got the word from SubPop right when we got here. And she worked her ass off to make those songs. But she never said anything. She didn't want to get our hopes up? Or was there part of her that knew it might not work out?

Then Manny tried to do it, so she shut the whole thing down and got her mind set on taking care of her brother.

It kills me that when summer ends, I'll be on my way home to start senior year.

And Xochitl?

She'll be hauling chile. Selling the last of the green. Harvesting red in fall. Closing down the farm and the stand for the winter. Driving Manny to see doctors. Looking under Manny's tongue to make sure he's taking his meds. Xochitl will be living in dusty little Hatch, New Mexico, thinking, *Today Ray Is a Girl is in Amsterdam. Today they're in Toronto. Today they're in New York City . . . and I am not.*

FRIDAY,
JULY 10, 2009

I'm cruising through equations—parabolas and ellipses and hyperbolas.

Then, *Boom!* Thunder rattles the shack.

And before I know it, I'm in a ball under the table, trembling, crying again.

Wendy drops to her hands and knees. She gets her face real close to mine. And she tells me it was just thunder.

"I know that, Wendy."

She gives me a hand up. Leads me to the entrance. She pulls the tarp back a crack and we watch the storm roll by.

When rays of sun finally break through, Wendy says, "Let's take a drive."

I get behind the wheel of the Dodge. "Huh-uh," she says. "Scoot over."

Wendy turns right on Valley Drive. She heads into Hatch, then hops onto I-25, the freeway to Las Cruces.

Soon, we're parked in front of Dr. Fuentes's office.

"What are we doing here, Wendy? What's going on with my brother?"

"Ever since Manny . . . Teodoro, sometimes you seem good. And sometimes you seem preoccupied, or lost, or anxious. You've been through a lot. And I want you to feel better."

We're not here for my brother.

"I think going in there could be a good thing, but this is your call. No judgment either way."

I can't move. I can't open the door. I can't walk out of this truck.

Because if I do, I'm admitting something to Wendy.

I get how nuts that is. Because she knows what I've been through. She knows what I've seen. She's seen me cry. A bunch of times. Wendy knows. She knows. She knows. Getting out of this truck and seeing that doctor is not admitting a thing.

But I cannot do it. "I get it," I say. "Thank you. But I'm doing better. I'm fine. I'm good. And we've got a ton of work to do, so . . ."

"Okay," she says. "We'll go back. No worries. It's not my place, Teodoro."

Wendy turns the key and backs the truck out.

And it hits me in the gut, the idea that it's not her place.

"Can you stop the truck?"

She stops.

"It's not your place, Wendy?"

"I don't know." She shakes her head. Laughs like she's confused and exhausted. "Is it, Teodoro?"

"Yes. Yes, it's totally your place."

"Okay. Good to know. What do we do now?"

"I guess you park the truck and I go in there and get my head checked out."

We take a seat inside.

And when I'm called to see Dr. Fuentes, Wendy holds out her arms. She gives me a squeeze and says, "Proud of you, dude."

Doc Fuentes asks me a lot of questions.

I answer him straight up.

He says I've seen a lot of tough stuff, so my anxiety and jumpiness make sense.

He asks about my sleep.

I tell him some nights I sleep pretty well. Some nights, I get stuck on those pictures in my head. But I always get up in the morning ready to work. And even though I'm distracted, I can push through and get stuff done.

I tell him my appetite is fine. I don't want to hurt myself or anyone else. Seeing Manny or being in the same space with him doesn't set me off. It did when we were in the rental. But now I feel better when I can see him.

Dr. Fuentes says he'd like me to try counseling before we go with meds.

I tell him I don't have a problem with meds.

He doesn't, either. He just wants to try counseling first. And as long as things don't get worse in the next couple weeks and I start feeling a little bit better after that, we'll hold off on the drugs. He'll be in contact with me and Dr. Chapman to monitor the situation.

In the truck Wendy asks me how it went.

"Well," I start, "Dr. Fuentes says . . ." I take a deep breath.

"It's all right," she says, patting my back for support. "Whatever it is, you can say it."

"Turns out I have this thing," I say. "And the official diagnosis is . . . oh, what was the terminology he used?"

"Take your time, Teodoro."

"He did all these tests—a whole battery—and he came to the conclusion that I am"—I suck in a deep breath—"*batwack loony!*"

"No, Teodoro!" She covers her mouth.

"Oh, yes. And compounding that situation is, I am *bananas.*"

"I knew it! I knew you were bananas. And . . . ?"

"And several times, he used the term *cray-cray.*"

"You are the cray-crayest, Teodoro Avila."

We laugh for a bit.

And then I take a deep breath. And let it go real slow. "Wendy?"

"Yeah?"

"I need to do this over."

"Do what over?"

"This conversation."

I get out of the truck and close the door. Then I open up and climb back in.

"Hi, Wendy."

"Hey, Teodoro."

"Now you ask me—"

"Got it." She clears her throat. "Hey, buddy. How'd it go in there?"

"Thanks for asking. Um, Dr. Fuentes thinks I got some PTSD-style symptoms from being around my brother. No meds for now. But I'm seeing Dr. Chapman tomorrow. Once a week after that. We're going to try and talk it out."

She smiles at me. "That's really good, Teodoro."

"I think so, too."

Wendy takes the slow, winding way back on Valley Drive.

I spend the whole ride telling her all the stuff that started the day Manny told us he was joining up and going to war. How that changed us. How losing the most important person in my life for all those years changed me. How being afraid I'd never see him again changed me.

I tell her everything that happened after he came home. I tell her why I moved out—why I had to move out—and why I'd do it again. I tell her about the road trip and about what it was like—what it was really like—the night Manny fired that gun, and what it was like seeing him in the hospital.

Wendy pulls into the farm and past the shack. Wendy parks the truck.

"So," I say, "I'm sorry I wasn't up front with you, it's just—"

"You don't have to explain, Teodoro. You've been through a lot."

"You have, too, Wendy." I smile at her and say, "Families, right?"

"Families," she says. "Tell me about it."

I grab the door handle.

Wendy pulls me back and into a hug. And she says she's sorry.

I tell her she doesn't have anything to be sorry about. And I thank her for taking me to see Fuentes today. It wouldn't have happened without her.

"Time to get to it?" I say.

"I'm ready," she says. "You ready?"

"I'm so ready. Let's go!"

FRIDAY,
JULY 31, 2009

Time flies. It's been a couple weeks since I filled up my red folder with stickers. After that, we moved on to physics. The beginning concepts weren't too bad. Then Wendy said I needed trigonometry and the Pythagorean Theorem at my fingertips for physics. I got tripped up on the trig and had a little setback in the ol' academic confidence. So she broke the work down into small bits and took things real slow.

Today, we take a welcome break.

Because tomorrow is the big day.

We're standing in the shack, making a list of all the detail stuff we need to finish up.

And I cannot stop smiling, thinking about the work we've done on this shack these past weeks.

We painted inside and out. We even painted the floor after days of sanding the splinters away till it was smooth.

We hauled two-by-fours from the truck to the shack, Wendy on one end, me on the other. We measured, sawed, and hammered those things to make the frame for the canvas awning. We laid the frame flat on the ground and tacked one side of the canvas down. Then we walked around to the other side. Wendy sat her butt on the ground. She grabbed some of the canvas and pushed her feet against the frame and she pulled and pulled the canvas tight, while I hammered in nails. Wendy's muscles are no longer a joke. Mine, either.

It took a couple days to get the canvas as tight as we wanted. A couple days to hang the finished awning frames on the front and back of the stand. We bolted them to hinges and then we had to figure out how to lift the awning toward the sky at twenty degrees and prop them up with sturdy, secure poles.

We busted Tio Ed's budget when we brought in an electrician.

We hauled in refrigeration. And shelving.

We built a nice counter out of scrap wood, and we sanded and finished it.

We bought an old roaster from a farmer in Deming and hauled it back in the truck. We scrubbed the hell outta that thing.

Wendy made the stand sign, and I never mention it, but I think she's at the very least a pretty darn good artist.

"Hey, Earth to Teodoro!" Wendy's at the counter with a legal pad.

"What, Wendy?"

"We need cash for change. Propane for the roaster. We need tacks for the farm photos. And we need locks for the awnings."

"Sounds like a trip to town."

"Let's go! Let's go!"

SATURDAY,
AUGUST 1, 2009

The group guys show up for our grand opening. Doc Fuentes, too. Folks from Luci's office. Her friend who'll be stocking the salsas. A couple high school kids—relatives of Hector's who've been working the harvest with Manny and Xochitl. They all come out to celebrate.

Wendy's sign is huge. It says LOPEZ FARMS CHILE SHACK. Red letters on a yellow background. Tío Ed loves it. Luci can't stop talking about how bright the stand is inside—she loves the white paint—and she loves how much we opened the space up. She takes a *designers' photo* of me and Wendy standing out front.

Fwoooot! A flame kicks to life as Tío Ed fires up the roaster. He opens the door to the big wire drum and says, "Just one box of chile. Any more and they won't roast even. People will be home peeling bits of skin off chile with tweezers and cursing our name."

Wendy flips the switch and the drum creaks and tumbles slow and steady. There's a hissing sound as hot air forces moisture out of the chile. There's crackling and popping. Sparks float into the sky. The smell of burning chile skin takes over the night. "That's the smell we've been missing," Tío Ed says. "But don't breathe it in or you'll be coughing all night."

Wendy and I roast and box chile till we have enough to send home with everyone. We get a lot of compliments and people are all smiles as they take off. Tío Ed and Luci give us thank-yous and hugs and head back to the house. Manny and Xochitl say they wish Mami and Papi could have been here to see this. "They woulda been proud of you," Xochitl says.

The way she says it hits me hard.

Wendy and I stay back and box fresh chile to sell for our first real day of business tomorrow. We talk through the routine. Make sure we got everything where it belongs. Finally, we drop the awnings and we're standing real close as we lock up. Our eyes meet. We exchange tired smiles and a high five and take a silent walk to the house.

Wendy stops at the door. "Teodoro, there's something I have to say to you."

"Yeah, Wendy?"

She stares at her shoes for a second. Looks up at the sky. Then in my eyes. "It's just that, Teodoro . . . um . . . We did that. *We* did that."

I got so much more, but I just say, "Yup, Wendy, we did that."

One more high five. Then she goes up to her room. And I go to mine.

Can't sleep. I'm thinking about Xochitl. I have to talk to Manny. I wanna know if he thinks he'd be okay down here without her.

But if he doesn't already know about the tour, and if he doesn't feel like he'd be okay without her, I can't tell him about the tour.

If I did tell him, he'd feel rotten that Xochitl's giving up the chance of a lifetime to stay behind with him. And Xochitl would never forgive me.

So I just ask him if he knows how long she's staying down here.

Manny says she's staying past the summer. "I was going to tell her I was doing better and she should get back home and get back in art school. Get singing again."

"She has to get singing again," I say.

"I know," Manny says. "I want to tell her I'm fine. And I have enough support down here. But I'm not out of the woods. Not by a long shot. And there's something different about having Xochitl and you down here with me . . . something I still need. I feel so guilty I'm keeping her here, T."

I tell him not to feel guilty.

He says he wishes it were that easy.

SATURDAY, AUGUST 8, 2009

Just a full week of working the stand together and we've got this thing down.

Wendy flips off the light after another long workday. I hold the awning frame up for her to get outside. She walks past and waits for me to put the locks on.

I give her my arm, *gentleman style.*

"Why, thank you," she says, wrapping her arm in mine.

As we walk, I can't help thinking it's only three weeks till I go home to SeaTac for senior year. And Wendy goes back to Vancouver for senior year. I already know I'm gonna miss everything about this. That chile smell floating off the roaster. Talking to customers. The sound of Coke bottles clinking against each other as I stock the fridge. The satisfaction of snapping the awning into place with Wendy, those end-of-the-night high fives.

I'm not ready for this night to end, so I sit down on the porch and ask her to join me. "I need you to say hi to someone."

"Who?"

"You'll see." I dial and click to speaker.

Caleb picks up. He's talking fast. "Guess where I had dinner last night."

"Where?"

"Your parents have been seeing so much of me, they decided to invite me for dinner. Your mom made these crazy green pepper cheeseburgers."

"Seriously, Caleb?"

"Your parents are doing great and those peppers were amazing and they invited my whole family over next Friday. But there's a problem. They're out of the peppers, so you gotta get some sent up here, stat."

I tell him I'm on it. Then I say, "Caleb Ta'amu, you are on speaker. And I'm sitting here with a nice lady who would like to say hi."

Wendy says, "Hey, Caleb."

Caleb says, "Hi, Barbara."

"*Barbara?*" she says.

"I kid, I kid!" he says. "There are no Barbaras. Or other names of people who are attractive young women. Like Janice, for instance. Or Wanda."

"You sure?" she says.

"I'm pretty sure that there's only one name my boy ever mentions."

She asks him what name that might be.

Caleb asks to verify that he is, indeed, speaking with Wendy Martinez.

"Yes, Caleb."

"He only talks about you, Wendy."

"All right. Enough with the chitchat," Wendy says. "What's the dirt on this guy?"

Caleb doesn't spill any dirt. And pretty soon they're talking about how best to throw a surprise birthday for Caleb's sister and then all kinds of details about setting up a chile stand. That's pretty much it. They just chat. Just two people talking about what's going on.

Wendy hangs up and says, "He's a great guy, Teodoro."

I tell her it's cool to hear them talking.

Wendy starts dialing.

I ask her who she's calling and she says she needs me to know someone.

"Hey, Teodoro," Megan says. "I'm Wendy's piccolo-playing best bud." She says it's great to finally talk even though she's pissed at me for taking Wendy away for the summer.

In this conversation, I learn that Wendy and Megan met in band in seventh grade and ever since then they've been home-work buddies. Wendy's the math and science superwoman and Megan is all about the writing and humanities. She says they're the academic Wonder Twins. She talks about playing team sports at Skyview High with Wendy. She says they're not in it for the competition. More for the conversation. And the costumes. Like superheroes and wild animals because they don't always get a uniform. They see it as their duty to inspire their team while using dramatic absurdity to fluster their opponents. Playing time is not high on their list of athletic priorities.

Wendy tells her we have to go, and Megan says, "One thing, Teodoro. Wendy is extraordinary. So watch your step. Because if you hurt her, I swear I will come after you. And I will mess you up. And I can easily do that because I am a kendo practitioner. Just moved up to fourth dan, Teodoro, so . . . yeah . . ."

"Okay, I do not know what that means, but congrats, Megan! And I promise you, I will be a nice person."

We say our good-byes, and I turn to Wendy. "She's hilarious. And she's got your back."

"I love that girl," she says.

"Wendy, whenever you mentioned practice, I always pictured you blowing into a tuba. I had no idea you were a jock."

She tries to hide a smile and says, "I'm not one of those braggy athletes, Teodoro. I prefer to let my work on the court speak for itself."

I bust out laughing.

Wendy does, too.

When the laughing stops, we're looking out at the farm, over Valley Drive, up those craggy mountains and the biggest, starriest sky I have ever seen.

I bet that someday, when someone says the words *New Mexico*, this will be the image in my mind. This night. This sky. And Wendy.

She turns back and catches me looking at her. Her eyes are, like, shining and she says, "This place is really growing on me, Teodoro."

"Me, too, Wendy."

Late night. I get out of bed and go downstairs to get a snack.

There's a light coming from Ed's office. I sneak down the hall. It has to be Xochitl.

I'm not gonna tell her I know anything. I want to give her a chance to come out with it.

There's no music. I knock. She's surfing the web. I tell her I couldn't sleep. Then I say, "Hey, what're you doing after summer?"

"You know I'm staying here," she says. "I'm not leaving Manny till he's good."

"How will you know when he's good?"

"I don't know, T."

I tell her it sucks I gotta go back. Otherwise, I could stay with Manny.

Xochitl tells me not to worry and she's got things covered down here. "Plus," she says, "you have senior year. And U-Dub. You're working hard and you're going to be a big success."

"Okay," I say, "here's the truth: Sometimes I feel like I'm a really bad actor playing the role of someone who's good enough to succeed. What if I'm not good enough?"

"I think everyone who tries feels that way sometimes."

"Do you? When you think about becoming a big star?"

She laughs.

"You know you think about it," I say. "Your name in lights and all that."

"Yeah, I get scared sometimes. I feel like an impostor sometimes."

"Is that why you quit so many bands?"

"Nah. I quit bands because I was trying to find the right thing."

"I get that," I say. "But maybe the right thing is you, Xochitl."

She scrunches her face and looks at me sideways. "Why do you say that?"

"Because it's true. And because I think you need to hear it."

WEDNESDAY, AUGUST 12, 2009

I wake to Manny standing up on his bed. He's pointing his imaginary rifle at me. Trembling. Muscles tight. He opens his mouth to shout his instructions, but before he can, I slap him in the legs, hard. "Manny, wake up!"

I jump over and grab him so he doesn't fall off the bed. "I got you, Manuel." I say it loud and he comes to. "You're at Tío Ed's. You had a bad dream."

He crawls back into bed. Pulls the covers over his face.

I get back in. Pull my covers up. And figure it's best to act like it never happened.

So I try that for a minute.

But it sucks.

So I get up. Turn on the lights. Nudge Manny in the gut. "Hey, dude."

Manny pulls his blanket back. He looks so damn sad. "I been taking my meds," he says.

"I know you have."

"The counseling is good. Group is good. I love the farm. It's all going great." He grunts and says, "I want this part to be over."

"It's gonna take time," I say. "Just like it did for Tío Ed."

The door cracks open. It's Xochitl. "You guys okay in here?"

"Yeah," I say.

"We're good," Manny says.

"You sure?"

"Yeah," I say. "We're fine, Xoch."

"Okay, guys. Let me know." She closes the door.

Manny says he can't sleep and he could use a walk.

We head out with the crickets and stars. Down the driveway, out to the road.

I can tell he doesn't wanna talk more about what happened because he asks me about Wendy.

I tell Manny he can't tell a soul, but I hope to marry that girl someday.

Manny promises.

"If I ever do, you're my best man."

"What about Caleb?"

"You're my best. Caleb's my next best."

We talk about New Mexico. About him maybe starting school here. And we talk about Mami and Papi. About him being so far from them again.

And because I been curious, I ask him about the ridiculous fish tattoo I saw on his chest at the hospital.

Manny tells me that a couple nights before he left for the army, Papi took him out on the town.

"Like *out*, out? With drinking? You and Papi?"

"Yeah." He laughs at the thought. Then he says, "T, you know my enlisting upset Mami."

"And Papi giving you his blessing upset her even more."

"The truth is, Papi didn't want me to go, either. I think he hated the idea."

"Did he say that?"

"No. He never said anything close to it. But he did tell me a story about when he left home."

Turns out, when Papi decided to leave Santa Ana and come to the US, our Abuelo Julio pleaded with him not to go. He put up a huge dramatic fight. Even told Papi he'd never speak to him again. He made it as hard on Papi as he could. And it changed their relationship forever.

"After that," Manny says, "Papi left anyway. And he made a promise to himself. If he ever had kids, he'd never stand in the way of their dreams. No matter what."

"Are you trying to tell me that you and Papi got tattoos?"

Manny laughs again. "I told you there was drinking."

"Yeah," I say, "No other explanation for a fish tattoo."

"We brainstormed animals that are known for coming home. Our tattoos would be a reminder—or good luck—that I was gonna make it back. We nixed monarch butterflies and all kinds of birds. And we ended up going full-on northwest with the Chinook salmon."

"Salmon come back to make babies and then they die. That's twisted, Manny."

"Like I said, our judgment was impaired."

"It's cool Papi did that."

Yeah," he says. "Look, I don't blame Mami for being upset.

Not one bit. In the end, she was probably right. But Papi supporting me—it meant everything."

We walk along in the dark. And in the sounds of our footsteps, crickets, and coyotes, I think about Papi sending Manny off in style.

And I think about Manny and Xochitl and me.

And I make a plan for my future.

THURSDAY, AUGUST 13, 2009

The stand is closed for the night. We're sitting under the shack awning sipping limeades, talking about the workday. Actually, Wendy's doing the talking. I'm doing the shaking because I'm about to tell her what I've done and what I'm gonna do. And I'm shaking because telling her is a big step toward making this thing real.

"Teodoro, you look like you're gonna be sick."

"Okay, Wendy, here it is. I e-mailed my school counselor. And she did some research for me."

I tell Wendy that Ms. Bradley came up with a plan for fall. I can take a couple classes online. Some at Hatch Valley High School. And I can take some at Doña Ana Community College in Las Cruces. And she can be my advisor for my senior service project and I can still graduate from Puget High on time. I can fly home and walk across that stage next June.

"Wendy," I say, "I'm gonna stay down here with Manny. And Xochitl's going on that tour."

She stares at me for a long time. Then she says, "Wow."

And I say, "Right?"

And she says, "Is this something you think you have to do, or something you *want* to do?"

Oh my God, I want everything. I want to be as close as possible to Wendy this year. I want us to have a chance to get back together. I want those kids and teachers at Puget to see me being great. I want to triumph with Caleb. And the truth is, I'm not sure I can do it without him or Bashir. I want to give myself the best chance to get into U-Dub. And I want to move back in with Mami and Papi.

But I want Xochitl to have her shot. I need her to have her shot.

And I can't leave Manny. I need to be with him. I want to be with him.

So I tell Wendy, "I need to do this. And I want to do this."

"I see," she says.

Then she hands me her glass, stands up, and walks.

I think she's going back to the house, but she just takes a lap around the shack.

And by the time she makes it back to me, she's got a huge smile on her face.

She grabs the limeade out of my hand. Chugs it. Gives me the glass back. Then she socks me in the arm.

"Jesus, Wendy."

She shrugs her shoulders, her eyes bright—she's smiling that smile.

"What, Wendy?"

"Teodoro," she says. "You surprise me."

I ask her if that's a good thing.

"Yup," she says. "It is a very good thing."

Then she asks me if I think Ms. Bradley really has it all figured out.

We scoot our chairs close. I tell Wendy Ms. Bradley wouldn't let me do this if she thought it might not work.

"We still on for U-Dub?"

"Definitely! I just have to get accepted."

"You'll get accepted," she says.

"What if I don't?"

"You will have given it a heckuva shot, Teodoro. And there are plenty of great schools out there. You'll get into one and you'll work hard and show those U-Dub admissions jerks just how wrong they were. Then you'll get into grad school somewhere and you'll work hard there and become a great architect."

"All right, then. I'm gonna do this, Wendy. But please don't say anything till I figure out how to tell Xochitl. If she gets wind of this, she'll shut it right down."

"Why?"

"Because my sister is stubborn and she has to be in charge. I gotta be sneaky about this. Would you like to get sneaky with me, Wendy? I might just need your skills."

"I got mad sneaky skills, Teodoro."

We stop talking and look out at that view. Sitting so close without words.

I start thinking about where we've been and how far we've come.

And I'm thinking this feels like a moment.

But I'm not sure if it is. So I keep looking up at the sky. And I inch my hand slowly into the space between our chairs.

My hand dangles there for a while, all by itself.

Then she sees it. But she doesn't want me to see that she sees it. So, real quick, she looks away from my hand and back up at the sky.

I keep looking up there, too. I don't want her to know that I know she rejected my hand.

I start to retract it, real slow.

But just as I do, I feel it—her fingers touching mine. Palms. Wrists. Hands exploring hands like for the first time. And we keep on exploring till Wendy's fingers slide between my fingers and we squeeze tight.

I turn to her. She turns to me. Our eyes meet and—*oh man*—there's another same-time breath, then we both look away. I don't know why but we do.

Then I turn back to her.

And she turns back to me.

"Hi, Wendy Martinez."

"Hi, Teodoro Avila."

That's it. We sit like that till it's real late. Just two warm hands squeezing. Just us under that ocean of starry sky.

And that's enough.

FRIDAY,
AUGUST 14, 2009

When everyone is out for the morning, we sneak into Tío Ed's office and back into Xochitl's e-mail account.

We copy the necessary addresses. Then we take off for the shack. Wendy helps me create a new e-mail account for Xochitl. We message SubPop Laura and Kristi from Ray Is a Girl—as Xochitl—from the new account. We tell them, *My old e-mail account was compromised, so . . .* and we tell them, *My plans have changed and I can go on tour!* And we attach six song files to the mail.

We cross our fingers and hope they don't already have another singer lined up.

Then we do our tutoring and we sell our chile.

And we wait.

Kristi responds first. Then a couple more Ray's bandmates. They say SubPop's been pitching them one opening act after another. And they keep on fouling them off waiting for Xochitl to change her mind. Somehow they knew she'd make it. And as far as they're concerned, she's on the tour.

It's gonna happen!

But before we can break the news, we get mail back from Sub-Pop. Laura McConnell loves the songs. But people at the label want video of Xochitl doing her solo stuff in front of an audience.

"We can make it happen," Wendy says.

"We need an audience," I say, "a good video camera, and a high-quality mic. We need a stage."

It's obvious to both of us. Sparky's is the only game in town. They have shows going all the time. The have all the sound equipment. And everyone in Southern New Mexico knows exactly where it is.

So we shut down the stand, grab Manny, and hop in the Dodge.

And we explain everything.

Manny is down for the whole deal.

Later that night, I call home. Papi picks up and puts me on speaker.

"I have cool news to tell you guys," I say. "But first, um, I'm sorry it took so long for me to tell you this thing, and if you never forgive me, I totally understand. Mami, Papi . . . Manny tried to take his own life. And it was weeks ago."

There's silence on the other end.

I ask them if they're okay.

Mami says she's okay.

"Papi?"

He says he's all right.

I tell them that Tío Ed has got Manny stable. I tell them how we do Manny's meds and tell them about the group and about how hard Manny's been working. How much better he's doing. How he's gonna stay down here for a while—maybe a long time.

That's when Papi says, "Mijo, your brother told us a few days after. He told us everything. We talk every day. We talk to Ed, too. We know."

I ask them to please forgive Xochitl and me for not telling them right away.

"Oh, mijo," Papi says. "Forgive us for not being there. Forgive *us*."

They say they know what I did that night. Mami starts crying. "We wanted to talk to you about it. We did. But we were waiting for you to bring it up, because . . . The weeks went by and you never said anything. We should have asked. I'm sorry, mijo. Are you doing okay?"

"I'm better, Mami. I'm seeing a counselor."

"We know, mijo," she says.

"It's good, mijo," Papi says.

Then I tell them the rest of the news. I tell them about Xochitl's songs. And about her SubPop opportunity of a lifetime. About how Wendy and I went behind Xochitl's back. I tell them how, on the way to talk to Sparky's booking agent, Manny came up with the idea of selling the night as a fund-raiser for the Wounded Warrior Project. I tell them how amazing Manny was talking the Sparky's lady into the whole thing.

I tell them me and Manny were so afraid Xochitl would say no because she wants to be here for Manny. So Manny decided not to tell Xochitl she's the main act. *She'll know when I announce her.* That's what Manny said. *No way she can say no.*

Mami says, "That's a good plan, Teodoro. Cuz if she knew what you did . . ."

Finally, I tell them Manny and I saved up from working down here and we just bought two plane tickets—Sea-Tac to El Paso. "And we're not telling Xochitl you're gonna be at Sparky's."

There's a celebration on the other end of the line.

But things get quiet again when I tell them I want so bad to be back home with them, but Manny still needs someone to stay with him after the summer. And I'm going to be that guy. "I can't wait to see you two!" I say, trying to break the silence. "Mami?"

"Oh, I cannot wait to see you," she says.

"Me, too, mijo," Papi says.

MONDAY, AUGUST 24, 2009

I'm standing with Wendy and my sister in a tiny room, looking out at the Sparky's stage.

We watch the men of Cactus Wine set out instruments and get tuned up.

When Manny told the group guys about the show, they mentioned Charlie's bluegrass band. So Manny asked if they'd open for Xochitl.

But when Manny told Xochitl about the event, he lied and said Cactus Wine was the headliner and he asked her to open for them. Xochitl agreed to play, like, Janis Joplin and Johnny Cash—a couple songs to get the crowd warmed up.

She's got her guitar strapped on. Cracking jokes. Hopping around. Trying to keep everyone loose.

I am the opposite of loose. Because who knows how Xochitl's gonna react to what's about to happen? And I got huge stuff I need to tell Wendy before she goes. And Mami and Papi's flight got delayed. And Lou's grandson—Lou promises he's a video "expert."

But is he really? If he doesn't get Xochitl on camera with good sound, we're screwed.

One positive is we're not going to owe Sparky's any money. The place is packed. The group guys were our marketing team. They loved the idea of a fund-raiser for vets, so they got the word out to the community. The VFW. The VA. The newspapers. Wherever they could find vets. So the crowd is full of men and women in military baseball caps and jackets telling everyone what branch, unit, and war they fought in. There are a couple of vets in wheelchairs. And one dude with a missing arm. *Wounded Warriors.* And they brought their families. Kids. Grandmas and grandpas. They all came out to show their support.

The Sparky's stage manager gives us the sign.

Wendy nods to me.

This is it.

I look over to Manny standing at the stage doorway. He volunteered to emcee this thing. It's his moment. Time to get onstage. Time to walk through that door.

But he's frozen. Desperate breathing. Trembling. Looking gone.

"You're on, Man," I say.

No response.

Xochitl throws me a look. She's thinking the same thing I am. It's Florence Frank's front door all over again. We're outside the church door in Delano all over again. Outside Elena's front door. He can't walk through.

Xochitl scoots up to Manny's side. Takes his arm in her hands.

I grab his other arm. Feel his shakes. Those frantic breaths.

"Manny?" Xochitl says.

He doesn't look up. "Yeah, Xoch?"

"We're walking through this door together. We're going up there with you."

He looks at her blank.

"We're not going to leave you alone," she says.

"I need you to leave me alone," he says.

Xochitl tells him he doesn't have to emcee. She'll do it.

Manny starts laughing. I can't tell if it's funny laughing or crazy laughing. "I'm nervous," he says.

"I know you are," she says.

And he says, "Nervous as hell. So I'm going to take five more breaths. Then I'm gonna shake myself onto that stage. And I'm gonna talk to the people. But I need you to step back and give me space."

We step back.

We count Manny's deep breaths.

After the fifth, he turns to us and shoots a wink.

And he walks through that door.

Alone.

There are some hoots. Some claps.

Manny wrestles the mic from the stand. He holds it out to the crowd and lets them see it shaking. Then he says, "That's not so much because I'm nervous about talking to you. It's because I'm always nervous. And sometimes I'm so nervous I can't function."

He has to stop and take another deep breath.

Someone shouts, "You got this!" Claps and hoots of support.

Manny nods his head in thanks. "There's a lot of action over there. You have a job to do. Buddies to protect. People counting on you. You have to be relentlessly alert. Your mind gets locked into survival mode. Because it has to."

Manny pulls the mic away. Clears his throat.

"Then you come home. And that kind of vigilance is no longer required. Life is about doing the mundane, everyday things normal people do to get by. But men and women who come back like me—with a brain that's been knocked around too much, a brain that can't stop being at war . . . we have a hard time."

Manny talks to families now. He tells them there are men and women in this room who are alive because of them. Manny looks offstage at me and Xochitl, then points at us. We point back at him. And he asks the vets in the house to give it up for their families. They do. They clap for a long time and it's real emotional.

Manny says families can't do it alone. He talks about the good people at the VA struggling to give care under tough circumstances. He talks about the support groups and he thanks Tío Ed and the guys. And he talks about the Wounded Warrior Project and organizations like it. "We need a big village to make it. And that's what this night is about."

Manny freaking nails it. Xochitl flashes me a huge smile of relief.

"Now," he says, "I think we all came here to eat some famous green chile cheeseburgers and barbecue and listen to some amazing music."

Huge applause this time.

Xochitl leans toward the stage, about to walk on.

I block her way and say, "Change of plans."

Then I get in Wendy's ear and whisper, "You're up, Martinez."

Manny sets up a chair and grabs a tuba I hid behind the stage.

I grab the music stand and the sheet music for "Andante and Allegro"—Megan told me the name of Wendy's solo piece and I rented the tuba from a music shop in Las Cruces.

"Now," Manny says, "it's my pleasure to introduce tonight's opening act—all the way from Washington State—Vancouver's premier high school tuba soloist, Wendy Martinez!"

The audience politely applauds Wendy.

She gets in my face and says, "You are dead." Then she walks onstage.

After a too-long period of mouthpiece licking, silent air blowing, music stand fiddling, and tuba adjusting . . . the *bloomp-bloomp*s start.

And I think it's good?

Good or not, with red balloon cheeks and eyebrows scrunched—the way she's hugging that tuba and bouncing those buttons with her fingers, cheek-puffing her heart out—Wendy is one hundred percent foxy.

Xochitl laughs and gives me a thumbs-up. She whispers in my ear, "Nice move, T. Very sneaky."

"There's more where that came from, Xoch."

Wendy finishes up. The crowd gives her a polite round. She walks right at me.

And she punches me hard in the shoulder.

Then she hugs me and gives me a kiss on the cheek. "I am furious with you, Teodoro Avila . . . but that's maybe the sweetest thing anyone's ever done for me."

I tell her I been waiting a long time to hear her play.

Manny takes the mic again. "Thank you, Wendy Martinez! That was a low blow, if I ever heard one. Right, folks?"

He waits for a laugh.

Doesn't get one.

"All right, everybody, put your hands together for . . . Cactus Wine!"

Charlie and his guys walk on from the other side of the stage.

Xochitl turns to me. "What the hell is going on?"

Manny races off the stage, right at her. He closes the side door fast but quiet. "There have been some changes, Xochitl. I heard these guys rehearse and it turns out Cactus Wine is the absolute worst. You have till the end of this song to get yourself ready, because you are now the headliner."

"What the hell, Manny?"

"Truth?" he says.

"Now!" she says.

Manny points at me. "Your agent promised SubPop we'd send them video of your road-trip songs. So there's a camera rolling out there. They need to see you play those songs before they let you go on tour."

Xochitl busts out a stream of s- and f-bombs, and there is a good chance this night is going down in flames.

Manny says, "You're going on tour and T's going to stay and be my wingman."

Xochitl's face is fire red and there's a vein pulsing hard on her forehead. "That wasn't your decision to make, Manny."

"You're wrong. I need someone sleeping in my room at night and it can't be you because you snore like a freight train. So you are out and T is in."

Xochitl looks at me. "You're dropping out?"

"Nah. Turns out they have schools down here. So it's all good."

Manny grips her by the shoulders and says, "I love you. I love every single thing you've done for me. Now I need you to do me one more. Get out there and sing your songs and blow some people away before they turn hostile and run me out of town because of *that*. . . ." He says it pointing out at the stage, at Cactus Wine.

You'll never know, dear, how much I love you,

Please don't take my sunshine away.

There are a couple isolated claps. A squeal of feedback. And silence. It's like folks are trying to figure out how a classical tuba solo and an out-of-tune rendition of "You Are My Sunshine"—completed after two restarts—fit into this special night of music.

Manny rushes onto the stage and Xochitl charges at me, poking her finger into my chest. "You snuck into my e-mail!"

"Yes, I did." I hand over her journal. "This, too. You might need it for lyrics and stuff."

"That's private, T!"

"It shouldn't be. It's awesome, Xoch!"

"You lied to me. You lied to a bunch of people. Why didn't you just tell me what was going on? Why didn't you just tell me the truth?"

"Why didn't I just tell you the truth?"

"YES, T!"

"Well, Xochitl Avila, I did not tell you the truth because, if I had"—I take a big breath and let it out—"you never would have come."

And, *my God*, those are some satisfying words.

"Thank you, Cactus Wine!" Manny shouts, smiling huge and clapping hard. "Ladies and gentlemen, that heartbreaking performance is more proof of the dire need for ongoing PTSD research. And the need for improved care that our vets so truly deserve."

A slurping sound as some kid sucks up the last of his Sparky's milkshake.

"Moving on! Let's welcome our headliner, an up-and-comer who will soon be singing her heart out on stages all over this great nation and around the world. Give it up for Xochitl Avila!"

Manny walks off to unenthusiastic applause.

Xochitl heads on.

Manny stops her. "You got this, Xoch."

Xochitl approaches the mic. Looks out at the crowd. She lifts the guitar and pulls the strap over her head. She lays it down in the middle of the stage and bolts right at Manny and squeezes the hell out of him. Then she rockets offstage and she squeezes me and plants a big kiss on my cheek. She does the same thing to Wendy.

Then she leaps back onstage. Slips her guitar back on. Sets her journal on a music stand off to her side. She strums a couple chords. Does some fine-tuning. Thanks the crowd.

Then she looks right at the video camera and says, "I'll be seeing you all real soon."

She smiles when she says it, but this is the first time I've seen my sister look like this onstage. Xochitl looks scared.

I get close to Wendy. She takes my hand. We watch as Xochitl's eyes drop down to her guitar strings. To her fingers. No strumming. She sings to her guitar real quiet.

I dreamed I was acting on a stage

The cast were all people I knew

I was terrified, I didn't know my lines

In a play that was the story of you

Xochitl looks offstage. Her eyes find Manny.

I turned to run—Thank God you were there

I said, What the hell do I do?

You just froze, looking scared as me

Said you'd forgotten the story of you

Xochitl lets the echo of her voice die and the words sink in.

Then she starts strumming hard and fast, her eyes locked on the strings.

People scoot their butts to the edge of their seats, leaning in to get closer, like they want to get inside the song with Xochitl.

And when she knows she's got every one of them . . .

She lifts her eyes.

Inhales the crowd.

And her voice is a bomb.

So I took your hand and away we ran

We ran, drove a car, hopped a bus

Hoping maybe if we just retrace our steps

We could rewrite the story of us

The place erupts as Xochitl tells our story.

And this . . .

This is her night.

But because she's Xochitl Maria Avila, everyone in this place feels like it's *their* night.

They came to Sparky's. They gave their money to a good cause. They tasted the best burgers in the world. They were treated to an odd tuba solo and had their ears assaulted by the worst band to ever walk across a small-town stage. And all that will be part of this memory they'll keep forever. The memory of the night they saw Xochitl Avila, a future star with a voice that plunges into your guts and mixes 'em up like a blender, a voice that's a hand wrapping its fingers around your pulsing heart. And tonight she's doing it with songs she wrote.

There's the "Brother of Mine" song, one about Manny's shaky toast the day he came home. She sings the Sally song. One about Manny and Elena holding each other. One about Manny telling his desert story—the one from the ditch in California.

It's all so damn personal. But Manny's not hiding. His head is up. His chest is puffed. He's looking proud as hell. Cuz he knows these songs aren't just ours. Xochitl wrote songs that belong to every person in this room.

I look at Xochitl and she's still singing and strumming, but now she's jumping and pointing over the audience all the way to the door.

We crane our necks and we can tell someone's dancing.

It's Mami and Papi, holding each other, moving to the sounds of their daughter's voice.

They notice Xochitl noticing them. They blow kisses. Xochitl blows them back.

Wendy and I just stand and watch.

Xochitl launches into "Con los años que me quedan," Mami and Papi's song they danced to when we were little.

Con los años que me quedan

Yo viviré por darte amor.

With the years that I have left, I will live to give you love.

Wendy rests her head on my shoulder as we watch Mami and Papi dance again.

At one point, he nods to her.

She nods back.

They freeze on the same beat.

And Papi freakin' dips her.

She looks up, into his eyes, smiling so big she can't hold back a laugh.

I squeeze Wendy's fingers tighter. She pulls me close till we're face-to-face. I wrap my free hand around her back. Wendy rests her hand on my shoulder . . . and we move to the slow beat.

She looks into my eyes. I look into hers. She lifts her head so her cheek touches mine. I feel her breath on my ear as she says, "I am going to kiss you now."

She does.

We do.

And it's different than it ever was. I don't know how, exactly.

Nope. That's not true. I do know.

Wendy takes her hand off my shoulder.

And reaches into my pocket.

How'd she know?

She pulls out a battered little box. She gives it to me. And she holds out her hand.

I'm a trembling mess as I pull the bracelet out and slip it over her wrist.

As we kiss, my mind flashes to that first night in Florence.

I really thought that's what it was supposed to feel like. But that wasn't it at all.

This is it. This is what it feels like to love Wendy Martinez.

So I say the words.

And she says them back.

Then she hands me another little box. I open it. It's a string of flat, connected turquoise squares. Wendy puts it on my wrist. She rests her head on my shoulder and we dance all the way through the night till the final verse of Xochitl's last sad, slow, quiet song.

Everyone asks

How's he doin'?

All I think is

wish I knew

I just say "He's doing

the best that he can"

Then they ask "And

how are you?"

I say, "I'm fine"

But I wish I knew

I tell myself I'm doing

the best that I can

I watch his face

Listen to his voice

The way he says, "I'm fine"

I know, I know

the best that I can

ain't enough, no

The best that I can

ain't enough

TUESDAY, AUGUST 25, 2009

Wendy and I put Mami and Papi to work selling chile in the stand.

Papi loves how we fixed it up.

I show them our designs, and Wendy and I tell them all about building the thing together.

And I tell them about my big dream.

Mami and Papi look so proud.

Like they know I've changed since the last time they saw me.

They've changed, too.

Manny's changed, and Mami says she can't believe how much.

Mami and Papi spend a ton of time with him. Manny teaches them everything he's learned about farming chile. He shows Mami the NMSU catalogue. She loves that and she tells him the big news that she's starting up at Highline CC in the fall. Papi gives Mami a huge smile when she says that, and the two of them seem as happy as I ever remember them. Happy for Manny. Thrilled for Xochitl. Happy about this choice I'm making. Happy about me and Wendy.

But so sad about leaving.

Believe me, I'm a wreck about being left.

TUESDAY,
SEPTEMBER 1, 2009

After a week together as a whole family, it's time.

There is not one dry eye as we say good-bye to Mami, Papi, and Xochitl. Xochitl is going home for a couple weeks to rehearse with Ray Is a Girl before the tour, so she's taking the same flight. Even though she'll only be there a short time, Manny and I are relieved that we're not sending Mami and Papi back to the empty rental alone.

I hug them good-bye till Thanksgiving—Ed and Luci invited them down.

I hug my sister and tell her, "Keep in touch. I'm going to need to hear from you every day. Like maybe a couple times."

She laughs at that.

"Promise?" I say.

"Promise," she says.

"Thanks for everything, Xoch." But there's no way I can make that sound as big as I mean it.

She just squeezes me hard and looks at me right in the eyes and says everything she needs to say.

Back at the farm, Wendy's packed for her flight. She takes off early tomorrow for senior year in Vancouver.

I ask her if she'll join me on a date.

Tío Ed and Luci work the stand.

Wendy and I head into Hatch. This time it's the Pepper Pot.

It's a converted house with a very lived-in vibe. And they serve some of the tastiest food around. The lady asks if we're ready. We tell her we'd like Cokes, green chile stew, and enchiladas.

"Red or green?" she says.

I go with the green chile.

"Red or green?" Wendy says. "I cannot decide. So make mine *Christmas*." She says it like she's a real New Mexican.

The lady walks away and Wendy says, "Teodoro, I've been waiting so long for the chance to say that. And now I have to leave here and go home to a place where Christmas has nothing to do with chile. It's just Santa and Baby Jesus and that just isn't enough anymore."

We hold hands across that little table. And we smile at each other till our food comes. We devour the feast and Wendy says she's so jealous that I get this food whenever I want.

I scoot my chair right next to Wendy. I take out my phone. Boot up the camera. We make sure we both have mouths full. I reach my arm way out. *One, two, three . . .*

"Damn!" we say. Then I click the shot.

Wendy checks it. "Delete that now."

"You look radiant in this photo. I will never delete it."

We get quiet again.

I tell Wendy I love her again.

She tells me she loves me.

We go over our long-distance plan. Texts. Phone calls. Old-fashioned pen-and-paper letters and postcards.

I'll go home for Christmas.

Maybe she can make it down for spring break.

Pretty soon the words stop.

We pay for our food.

And we walk.

We hold hands up and down the main street, and Wendy says, "Good-bye, street where Wild West gunslingers once roamed."

We walk inside Sparky's and check out the empty stage. "Good-bye, place of magical musical memories," she says.

We hop in the truck. We drive to the dump. Wendy says, "Good-bye, dump."

We meander down Valley Drive. Into Las Cruces and back. Wendy says good-bye to the Organ Mountains, good-bye to the Chihuahuan Desert, good-bye to pecan orchards, cotton fields, hundreds of acres of chile, and good-bye to the Rio Grande.

We head back to the farm and work our last night together. We kiss as Wendy retrains me on money and inventory counts—her old jobs. Then we sit under the stars, under that ocean of sky, holding hands, kissing, and talking. Kissing and remembering. Kissing and making promises until night turns into morning and Wendy says, "Good-bye to the place where I fell in love."

WEDNESDAY, SEPTEMBER 2, 2009

She's gone. I'm working the stand alone. It is weird. It is sad. It is lonely.

There are no customers and I have a couple calls I need to make. So I pull out my phone.

First off is Bashir.

It's great to hear that dude's voice. He seems happy to hear from me. They moved him up to a host position at 13 Coins. He's in his last semester at Highline Community. He catches me up on stuff about his family.

I tell Bashir about life in New Mexico. And that I won't be seeing him in the fall.

He loves it that I'm helping out my brother.

"Bashir, I called to tell you that you saved me. I was drowning and I needed a tutor—a good one. And you helped me get over a major hump and helped me believe I could do it. I just wanted to say thanks. And I miss you, man."

Bashir says he had a great time tutoring. And he wishes me all the luck.

The next one is hard.

It's been a couple days—okay, a few days—since Caleb sent me the *When are you coming home?* texts and voice mails.

First off, I tell him I love him. And I thank him for everything.

"You sound like you're not coming home." That is not a happy sentence. "What the hell, T? You get married? You're just a kid!"

"I didn't get married, Caleb. I have to stay down here this year."

I tell him about Xochitl. About how we sent her off to the tour. About how Manny needs me. I thank Caleb for being an amazing friend. And I thank him for believing we could succeed from the very beginning. "If I get into college, if I graduate, if I become an architect someday, I've got you to thank."

We make plans for Christmas. Plans to talk on a regular basis. Academic check-ins. Caleb says I'm still part of the AVID gang and he's going to see if Ms. Hays will let me Skype in for Socratic Seminar and tutorial sometimes.

I tell him that would be cool.

And I tell him to thank his parents. For everything.

Then Caleb says, "We were going nowhere fast. *Together.* Then we decided to be better. And life pulled us apart. Maybe for a long time."

"Just a year, Caleb."

"I don't know where I'm going to college," he says. "Might not be here."

"What?"

"I don't know, T. Maybe I need something new. We'll see."

"Yeah, Caleb. We'll see. Wherever it is, you're still my brother."

"You're still my brother."

"Talk tomorrow?"

"Yeah. Let's talk tomorrow."

I pocket my phone. And I feel a tap on my shoulder.

"Hey, T."

It's Manny. He's sporting a brand-new baseball glove. He's got one for me, too.

"Where'd you get these?"

"I went shopping."

We step outside and Manny throws me the ball.

It *SNAPS!* as it hits my glove. I throw the ball back.

SNAP! Manny pulls the ball from his glove and points to the sky. He throws me a pop-up. "You sure about all this, T?"

"About staying in New Mexico?" I catch it and pop one back. "Yeah, I'm sure. But I'm gonna need some help with physics."

"*Physics?* What is that?"

"It's a thing you're gonna teach me because you aced it in high school."

"Oh. And when exactly is this going to happen?"

"Tomorrow. Seven a.m. In the chile stand. And every other day."

"I'll do my best, T. But I might be a little rusty. And a little asleep."

"That's okay. I might cry. Because I miss somebody."

"Damn, T. I feel so guilty."

He's not joking. I can see it on his face.

"This is a guilt-free zone," I say. "Got that, mister? All you have to do is teach me physics. And wipe my tears. And throw me that ball."

Manny throws me the ball.

I catch it and throw it back.

Manny catches. Manny throws.

I catch.

I thought I stayed here so Xochitl could chase her dream.

I throw.

Manny catches. Manny throws.

And I thought I stayed to help my brother.

I catch.

But maybe I stayed in New Mexico for *this*.

I throw.

Manny catches. Manny throws.

Me and my brother, making up for too much lost time.

I catch. I throw.

Manny catches. Manny throws. . . .

WED SEP 2 8:38 P.M.

T: Make it home ok?

Wendy: Yeah. I miss you bad, Teodoro.

T: I miss you worse.

T: Wendy, will you go to prom

           with me next spring?

Wendy: Wait. I'll go ask my mom. ☺

T: HA! Tell her I still have her twenty

           bucks! No way she can say no.

Wendy: Huh?

T: Nothing. Will you go to prom

           with me?

Wendy: In New Mexico?

T: I was thinking of Puget. But we could do prom down here too.

Wendy: And Skyview High. Gotta do the 'Couve!

T: That's a lot of proms, Wendy.

Wendy: It's not that many proms. While we're at it, I think we should go for the all-time proms record.

T: How many?

Wendy: 47 proms. Set by a couple from Louielexnoxingtonsville, Kentucky, if I'm not mistaken. 1985, I believe it was.

T: It's awesome knowing you will forever have information like that at the ready.

Wendy: Aw, you always say just the right thing, Avila.

T: Let's make this happen, Martinez. It's gonna take a lot of planning. A lot of airfare. A lot of understanding high schools.

Wendy: A lot of deodorant and gallons of mouthwash.

Wendy: But I think we can do it.

T: Wendy? Will you go to 48 proms with me?

Wendy: Oh my God, Teodoro, I thought you'd never ask.

T: I love you.

Wendy: I love, *love* you.

T: Oh, hell. This is serious now.

Wendy: Yes it is.

T: Good. I love, *love* you, too, Wendy Martinez.

PTSD Resources

Manny Avila came back from war suffering symptoms related to post-traumatic stress disorder (PTSD), depression, and traumatic brain injury (TBI). The statistics of veterans suffering from PTSD are difficult to determine for many reasons. But according to a 2014 RAND Study, twenty percent of Iraq and Afghanistan War veterans suffer from PTSD and depression. Those statistics climb when TBI is included. If you are worried about a family member who is suffering from PTSD, TBI, or general depression issues, including suicide, know that there are people and organizations who want to help and who are ready to help. Here are some resources:

Veterans Crisis Line: 1-800-273-8255 #1

stopsoldiersuicide.org

www.ptsd.va.gov/public/index.asp

woundedwarriorproject.org

Like Teodoro, if you have been in close prolonged contact with a vet suffering the effects of trauma caused by war, and you're concerned about your own mental health, talk to people. Reach out. Here are some resources:

www.ptsd.va.gov/public/family/index.asp

veteransfamiliesunited.org

familyofavet.com/secondary_ptsd.html

giveanhour.org

mentalhealth.gov

A Note on the Department of Veterans Affairs and the Veterans Health Administration

Xochitl explains to T that Manny became frustrated and refused to go back to the VA after hearing the policy regarding VA coverage of PTSD treatment.

Before 2010, veterans were required to provide documented evidence of a "stressor related to hostile military activity" in order access full coverage for PTSD treatment. In 2010, the requirement for documented evidence regarding a military stressor was dropped. This action streamlined the PTSD claims process at the VA and reduced the time and frustration traditionally involved when veterans applied for disability compensation for PTSD and access for mental healthcare.

Manny had his issues at the VA, and Tío Ed later states, "Manny ain't stepping foot in no VA." Although its efficiency is regularly questioned, the VA is the primary source of health care for millions of American veterans, and its importance in their lives cannot be overstated. The VA is a crucial and indispensable resource, and it is up to all Americans to ensure that VA healthcare professionals and administrators have all the resources and support they need to treat veteran health issues in the manner veterans deserve.

Acknowledgments

I am so grateful to the many the folks who joined me on various legs of this long publishing road trip.

Thanks to those who generously volunteered their time and minds to read drafts, provide answers to research questions, and give indispensable feedback and loving encouragement: Christopher Baker, Nena Boling-Smith, John Brockhaus, Erin Courage, Vincent Delaney, Donte Felder, Andrea Flores, Dr. Ernest Flores, Maria Flores, Emma Flores-Scott, Andy May, Doug Kasischke, Jessica McClinton-Lopez, Dickie Ogaz, Bruce Patt, Wendy Rasmussen, Heidi Raykeil, Meg Richman, Charlie Scott, Maria Scott, Eric Smith, Angie Stark, Cristian Uriostegui, Aldo Velasco, and Dorothy Velasco. Thank you all.

Thanks to Joy Allison and her students at Tiger Mountain Community High School, and Jeff Kass and his students at Pioneer High School.

Thanks to the members of my Ann Arbor "Newbery" book club and critique group for the much-needed comradeship.

Thanks to Jessica Anderson at Christy Ottaviano Books/ Henry Holt for all of her work in support of *American Road Trip*, and to Starr Baer and Katie Klimowicz at Macmillan for the production editing and design work that helped bring readers this story in such a beautiful package.

Thanks to my agent, Steven Chudney, for understanding and supporting this project from the outset, and for years of persistence in helping to advance this book through all of its stages.

Thanks to my editor, Christy Ottaviano, for seeing the potential in Teodoro's story through the mire of early, epic drafts and pendulum-swinging rewrites. Thanks for keeping the vision of what this book could be throughout the process and for managing all of my post-deadline requests. Thanks for guiding this road trip home.

Thanks to my boys, Carlos and Diego, for joining me in my office for early-morning group writes and for all the hugs and cheerleading.

Thanks to my wife, Emma, for her never-ending love, for her belief in my storytelling life, and for helping me to keep my feet as near to the ground as possible. Without her, there is no way I'm typing these words that can only come when a book is finished.

And finally, thanks to the Scott, Hernandez, and Flores families for their undying support and for being a constant inspiration as I worked to write the story of a family that perseveres.